I0565131

When Ericka Woke Up

a novel

Ev Outlaw

Chocolate Chick-Lit Books
Archer Lodge, NC

Contents

For my mom, my biggest fan, who I know is bragging on me just as hard in heaven as she did on earth.

Part I
Spring, 2009

Not having dreams mean
Nothing to look forward to
And a dull night's sleep

—A haiku

Chapter 1

Like a Super Hero's Cape

I had just put the first annual Pap smear appointment scheduled after lunch into exam room two when a shrill urgent beep chimed out noisily through Dr. Curtis' pager. She took it out of her pocket and looked at it. She grimaced at the beeper and went over to the phone at her hallway workstation.

"This is Dr. Curtis . . ."

While she was on the phone, I stepped back into the lab to check the pregnancy test that was percolating on the counter. It was negative. Crystal, the young college student waiting to get her Pap smear in the exam room would probably fall off the table from relief. She had confided earlier that she had caught her boyfriend cheating on her in his fraternity house and she wanted a complete STD work up and pregnancy test along with her yearly Pap. *At least she doesn't have a baby to worry about in all this mess*, I thought, shaking my head. I hadn't heard Dr. Curtis ring the doorbell signaling for me to join her as her chaperone for the rest of the patient's exam, so I went ahead and dipped Crystal's urine sample to check for traces of blood and protein.

As I approached the workstation to document the results in her chart, the doctor was already on her way out of the exam room with samples in her hand.

"What's your hurry, sister?" I joked.

She gave a half smile, visibly distracted.

"Sorry. It would have taken too much time to wait on you to come in. I gotta get out of here like right now," she said. She wrote furiously while she talked.

"Dr. Shaw is going to finish up the rest of my annuals for the afternoon, but I need you to call my other patients and reschedule them. Tell the two follow-ups that they can come first thing in the morning, or they can come about three for-ty-five. I should be out of surgery by then."

"No problem, boss," I said. "Are we having a baby, today? I don't remember anyone being due this week."

She sighed deeply.

"There's not anyone. Sonia is in distress, again."

"Oh, no," I moaned.

Sonia was kind of the sweetheart of our practice. She had been through so much trying to have a baby. She had already gone through two miscarriages and had a stillborn. For some reason, as each pregnancy progressed, she would develop pre-eclampsia, a condition in pregnant women that causes their blood pressure to climb dangerously high, putting both mother and child at risk.

But through it all, she managed to still be in great spirits. She was always cheerful and positive. We loved it when she came into the office because she always brought sunshine, no matter how rough a day we happened to have. She would bring cookies and other goodies for us all the time. She was like a part of our extended family.

I had never met her husband. Apparently, he worked out of town during the week, so she would always come in for her appointments by herself. But I assumed that they were close because she talked about him all the time, and she showed no evidence of being unhappy with their arrangement. She told us that he was making preparations to start his own business that he planned to have up and running by the time the baby came, so he could spend more time at home. I had never met him, but she affectionately called him 'Bay,' short for 'Baby' so much that even the girls in the office referred to him in conversation like that, too.

She was so close, this time. She was almost at the end of her twenty-eighth week. I said a quick, silent prayer that she would be able to hold on long enough to bring this baby safely into the world.

"Okay, I'll take care of everything for you. Tell her that we're thinking about her."

"I will. I'll call you all later to give you an update."

She rushed out of the office, her lab coat blowing behind her like a super hero's cape. As I watched Dr. Curtis leave, I hoped that her super powers would be enough to save Sonia's baby.

Chapter 2

Wild Nights of Fantasy Passion

I had apparently dozed off in a fitful sleep waiting for Maurice to show up. It was almost two o'clock but still no signs of him having been to my house. The heat was unbearable. I had to peel the soaking wet sheets from my body to get out of bed. Why in the world was it so hot in here? I staggered into the bathroom and splashed cold water on my face to try and cool off. Now, I was just hot and wet.

I made a face at myself in the mirror and wandered into the living room to see what temperature the thermostat was set on. Somebody must have accidentally turned the heat on by mistake. But that couldn't be right. Maurice wasn't in the house enough to be messing around with the thermostat, and I didn't even think Tomika realized what it was for.

I could see a dim light around the corner as I started down the hall towards the living room. That's strange. Tomika and I like complete darkness when we go to sleep, so we never leave lights on in the house at night. Maurice is the one who's afraid of the dark. He always comes in at some God for-saken hour turning on lights, talking about how he can't see. If he ever spent any real time here, he wouldn't have to worry *about bumping into things in the dark. He would instinctively know how to maneuver around them like we do.*

He must have fallen asleep in the living room watching television or something. But he wasn't on the couch. And he wasn't in the bathroom. I just left there. Maybe he left and just forgot to turn the light off.

As I approached the kitchen to get a drink of water, I saw that the light was coming through my open refrigerator door. I know he didn't leave my refrigerator open. As I made my way over close to it, I froze in my tracks noticing a figure bent over, rummaging in my fridge. What the hell? He was so engrossed in its contents that he didn't seem to notice that I had come in. I backed away from the kitchen's entrance slowly, hoping to make a clean break to my room and retrieve the aluminum baseball bat that I kept under my bed. As I did an about face, he spoke.

"Where are you going? I thought you were going to join me for a midnight snack."

I froze in a silent panic.

He spoke again.

"You got any whipped cream?"

What was he planning to do, eat me?

I found my voice and demanded, "How the hell did you get in my house?"

The man turned from whatever had his attention in my refrigerator and looked at me. I could barely make out his face in the dim light emanating from the fridge, but there was something strangely familiar about him.

"I told you. I am wherever you will me to be, my love."

My mouth dropped.

"Desmond?"

He smiled.

"You know that surprised act is getting a bit old."

He casually rose to a standing position, opened my freezer, and scooped some ice cubes into a bowl he was holding.

"Desmond, what are you doing here?" I asked again, staring at him in disbelief.

"Relax, baby. I came to cool you off."

He took me by the hand and led me into my bedroom.

Too dumbfounded to say anything else, I watched him as he set the bowl of ice on my nightstand. He slowly and playfully peeled off my pajamas, scooped me off my feet, and laid me gently on the bed.

"Oh, I couldn't find the whipped cream, but this will work," he said, nonchalantly holding up a bottle of chocolate syrup.

"Desmond!" I gasped. But there was nothing else for me to say. I was speechless.

He sat down on the bed next to where I lay, leaned over and whispered in my ear.

"Are you ready?"

I nodded dumbly.

"Are you comfortable?"

"Yes," I whispered back.

"Good," he said, satisfied. "I just want you to lay back and enjoy the ride."

Desmond took a chunk of ice from the bowl on the nightstand and put it in his mouth. Then he moved down to the foot of the bed. He lifted my legs over his shoulders and lowered himself down on his stomach between my thighs. I could feel his icy breath tickling my insides before his lips even made contact.

"Ohhhh, Desmond," I moaned . . .

I jolted straight up in bed, panting. My pajamas and sheets were covered with wet, sticky remnants of a dream that I never wanted to wake up from. It was a dream with a recurrent theme, becoming more and more real with every forty winks that I took. I had been having these wild nights of fantasy passion ever since I reacquainted myself with Desmond Wright a year ago.

It started as a harmless-platonic-haven't seen my old friend in a while-let's keep in touch kind of thing. All I did was stop by my old job to visit people that I hadn't seen in a while. Well, I really did want to see Desmond in particular, but I swear it was completely innocent. Aside from the fact that I had always had a secret obsession with Desmond, I considered him to be enough of a friend to want to keep in contact with after I left my job with Global Technology. So, I stand by my decision to pay him a visit after not having seen him in a couple of years, even if my motives weren't necessarily pure.

I met Desmond about five years earlier while working a temporary job at Global Technology, one of the major corporations in the Research Triangle Park area. I had previously separated from the army after four years of active duty service, where I served as a hospital medic at Fort Ord in California. I had trouble finding a job once I returned home to North Carolina that would accommodate my skills without the civilian credentials. The civilian work force was not very accepting of military training methods and most places refused to hire even the most qualified candidates without formal schooling. So, I secured a position driving a forklift in one of Global Technology's warehouses while I put myself through school. There, Desmond also worked as an up and coming young professional.

The first time I laid eyes on him every ounce of religion I ever had oozed right into my panties, along with the excitement that welled up me as I shook his hand. He was the most beautiful man I had ever seen. He was about five-foot-ten with a medium build and slightly bowed legs. His mocha chocolate complexion was flawless, and I was sure that he could read my mind with those piercing, dark brown eyes. His bright, sincere smile turned up only at the left corner, giving him the look of a young boy up to no good. And the waves in his hair made me seasick.

He wore an oatmeal-colored sweater that clung to his frame nicely. It was a crew neck sweater with two buttons at the neck with no collar. And those brown steel-toe boots made me wonder if it was true what they said about men with big feet.

But it wasn't his handsome face, that well chiseled body, or those huge feet that captivated me attention. It was his hands. His nails were uncharacteristically clean for a warehouse worker and wrinkles around his knuckles gave his hands an inviting look, like slightly worn leather. I could tell by looking at those hands that he was no stranger to hard work, but they felt smooth like a new baseball glove. His strong grip oozed confidence. And I could just feel them caressing my body. I couldn't help but notice how that simple gold band on his left finger made the rest of his hand that much more attractive.

People gravitated to Desmond. The staff always went to him when they had issues even though he wasn't supervisor. He was always willing to help and always had a kind word for everyone. He had a way of making you feel seen and appreciated. So, the guys on the job respected him. And the women shameless fell all over him.

Somehow, he took a shine to me and would frequent my work area just to chitchat whenever we had down time. He was always intrigued by my outside interests. We had a lot in common like our love for motorcycles, our love for the beach, and jazz music. Our close association didn't sit well with the rest of the female staff, who felt like I was getting too much of Desmond's attention. I was regularly interrogated.

"I noticed that Desmond picked you to go with him to the new warehouse this week. Are you sure that's the only place y'all went?" Pam, one of my co-workers asked me one day.

They always tried to make light of their accusations, but

I knew they were hoping I would confirm their suspicions to justify their hating on the close contact I had with him.

"Girl, we went to his house and had a long lunch," I would tease with a smirk. Nosy heifers.

I finally found a job in my field at an obstetrics practice and left the jealous women of Global Technologies, along with my friendship with Desmond. But the energy between us was unmatched and Desmond expressed his desire to keep in touch after leaving the job. I gladly gave him my number and agreed to meet for lunch or something whenever time allowed.

We talked on the phone quite a bit at first. But after a few months I guess we both got busy, and the calls became less and less frequent. Then, I moved to another part of the city, changed to an unlisted number, and became engrossed in other things and other men. I still thought about him from time to time, but when I finally tried to contact him at work, his extension and his beeper number had both been assigned to someone else within the company. I hadn't spoken with him in a couple of years until recently.

I won't pretend like it was by sheer accident or fate that I ran into Desmond again after all this time. My boyfriend Maurice had been missing in action so much lately that instead of absence making the heart grow fonder, it made my mind wander. So, one evening after work about eight or nine months ago, after having been stood up the night before for the hundredth time, I decided to pay the old Global Technology crew a visit. Okay, so I really had no interest in seeing anyone else. My sole motive for driving thirteen and a half miles in the opposite direction of home was to see if there might be a chance that Desmond still worked there. I figured that a little harmless ego stroke from another man was just what I needed to boost my morale. It wasn't like we were going to cuddle or anything. It was just harmless conversation. And Maurice was always too busy for conversation.

Desmond, indeed, still on the job, was now in charge of the second shift crew with a lot more time to talk on the phone these days, and he seemed to be just as starved for soothing small talk as I did. Since that day, we conversed almost every night around right around ten o'clock and then he haunted my dreams for the rest of the evening. I rolled over and turned on the lamp on my bedside table to wake myself up. I felt like I had actually had a man in my bed the night before. These dreams had become more vivid and intense in nature, each one leaving me breathless and horny. It was like being trapped in a porno movie. Fortunately for me, Maurice was out of town. These wet dreams made me feel like I was cheating, and I was beginning to feel a little guilty about reopening this little can of worms, even though Desmond and I were doing nothing more than talking on the phone. And the last thing I needed was to have an orgasm in my sleep and breathe Desmond's name in the process.

I went into the bathroom and turned on the water for a shower. I briefly entertained the notion of turning on the cold tap in order to snap myself out of the horny state I was in, but quickly dismissed it. Hell, it hadn't gotten quite that bad, yet. I chuckled under my breath and went into the other room to wake up my daughter, Tomika.

Tomika lay on her stomach spread eagle in the middle of the bed, like the coyote after the landing at the bottom of a cliff. Her mouth hung open, but she had her thumb stuck in it just the same. She looked so peaceful lying there that I hated to wake her. I stood there for a minute and watched her. She was the spitting image of me when I was a child, but she looked just like her father when she was asleep. It was always amazing to me how a child could look exactly like both parents at the same time. Too bad Lance wasn't interested in what she looked like. We hadn't heard from him since she was two years old.

I turned on the light and called to her.

"Time to get up, baby," I said to her, as gently as I could. Neither of us are morning people so we always treaded lightly in each other's territory in the mornings. When it comes to stank attitudes, I gave birth to myself. As sweet as she was as a child, she could really test my gangster, if provoked. So, I quickly left the room so I would not have to see that first eye roll or hear that first mumble under her breath.

Chapter 3

Is There Any More Room for Me in Those Jeans?

After a stressful work week, I was really looking forward to meeting my girls at TGI Friday's on Wake Forest Road. They transformed the ordinary chain restaurant into an adult night spot and checked ID after 10pm on weekends. It's like being at club with no dance floor, complete with one of our local celebrity deejays, Kool Sheed. We were regulars and had commandeered our own section in the upper level with a great view of the bar and the front door. And we also always requested the same waiter, Ronnie, a cute little white guy that we adopted as our own personal manservant.

We had a ball on these occasional girls' nights out but not without its share of drama. Once the drinks started to flow at a steady pace, one person usually ended up getting double-teamed by the rest of the group and the insults would start to fly. The person on the receiving end usually ended up mad until someone at the table bought another drink to smooth things over. Then we'd all go back to having a good time again; just like blood sisters.

My on again, off again relationship with Maurice caused me to be mostly on the receiving end. They thought that I was being a door mat. Renee was harder on me than the rest. She's the youngest, but the only married person in our group. So, she thinks she knows more than the rest of us about relationships. She also has three kids, set of twins, a boy and a girl, Lindsey and Sydney who are the same age as Tomika, and the baby girl, Terri, who is four. She leads Tomika and Sydney's Girl Scout troop, and she lives to play cook, housekeeper, and chauffeur to her family. You'd think she had enough to do besides try to play mom to us, too.

But outside of that old soul is a pretty, thick chocolate girl with round cheeks, full lips and a strong Creole accent, that she brought when she moved here from New Orleans some years ago. And it comes out thick when she's on her soapbox, which is most of the time, with her opinionated ass. We keep her around because she also has a fun-loving, Mardi Gras spirit. She loves to laugh and have a good time, and she's also a great cook. And she's always full of moral support and is good for a last-minute babysitter or a meal if you don't feel like cooking.

The night started out cool enough. And I thought I had gotten of being the center of discussion. Renee, however, couldn't resist putting her two cents in my business.

"So, did Maurice come over last night, Ericka?" She glanced up from her drink.

"No, Renee. He didn't make it over last night."

"Have you talked to him today?" she wanted to know.

I sighed, deeply. This heifer thought she was slick. "No, I haven't talked to him, either. We've both been working."

She shook her head. "Well, when was the last time you spoke to him?"

I could feel the devil creeping up my back. "I talked to him on Tuesday." That was all the fuel she needed.

"You hear that, y'all? She ain't even heard from this boy since Tuesday. Here it is Friday. Natalie, when is the last time you talked to Tarik?"

Natalie shifted uncomfortably in her seat. "I talked to him before we left. He said he might meet us out here."

Renee turned back to me. "Doesn't it bother you that Tarik is so attentive to Natalie, but Maurice doesn't even have the decency to pick up the phone just to make sure you're not dead? That boy don't care nothing about you. When are you going to stop letting him play you?"

Now, old Lucifer was standing on top of my head, massaging my scalp.

Natalie spoke up. "Leave it alone, Renee. It's not your business. And besides, Tarik said that Maurice would probably come out here with him."

I could see the frown lines forming under the ringlets that softly fell around Natalie's golden brown face. Her soft, brown eyes had clouded over, and her usual wide grin full of the whitest teeth I'd ever seen were no longer visible as the conversation took a turn for the worse.

Natalie and I have known each other the longest. We had been friends since high school. I think she felt obligated to defend Maurice because she was instrumental in him and me originally hooking up. She dated his best friend, Tarik. She had the eldest of all of our children in the circle, a son, Savion, who was thirteen. She had him our last year of high school. She was a free-spirited fashion plate, and she was the one who originally started this girl's night out thing. I wondered if she regretted it tonight.

"Damn, Renee. You always got to be getting drunk and talking shit. It's embarrassing."

The next person to speak was Toy.

"Yeah, Renee. Why you always got something to say about Maurice? Everybody can't have a henpecked man like Terrell. I came here tonight because I needed to relax and have a good time. I didn't come here to hear this mess, again."

Renee was heated, then.

"Oh, shut the hell up, Toy! You can't talk about me or

my man until you go out and find you a man, a woman, or whatever the hell your preference is."

Toy's eyes got big.

"Oh, bitch, I know you didn't! You better be glad we're in this restaurant, or I would get up and pimp slap you."

Toy and I went to school together but didn't become friends until we ended up at the same base in the army. In fact, I can't really say I remembered her at all from school. She's not even in the yearbook. Apparently, she stayed to herself, mostly, purposely making herself invisible. She won't say why, just that she was an awkward teenager. But I'm not sure how she managed to stay under the radar. She may have been forgettable in high school. But at almost six-foot-tall, slim, and gorgeous, she is definitely a head turner, now. That is, she would be, if she didn't look like such a stud. I have been a known tomboy all of my life, but Toy makes me look like a girly girl. Thank God for natural beauty because she has never been compelled to do anything to alter her appearance for the sake of attracting a man. You will absolutely never see her in a skirt. And I seriously doubt that she owns a pair of heels. She's got a gorgeous head of luxurious hair, though. It's all hers and she does go get it done sometimes. But mostly, it's pulled back in a ponytail.

She plays basketball with a group of guys every day after work at the gym, and yet with access to all types of men that most women only dream about, she's never had a date that we know of. She never talks about men unless it's one of ours, and she doesn't seem too concerned about having one. She's never been married and even though she insists that she does entertain male company, none of us has yet to hear her mention any man's name, much less see her with one.

Renee insists that Toy is either gay or bisexual. Maybe I'm just naïve or in denial, but she would actually have to produce a man or a woman at some point in order to be considered anything. Natalie seems to think that she just hates men. I'm not sure what to think. I do know that she's very attractive for a woman and could easily have her pick and choose of any man or woman, but for whatever reason, she has chosen to remain single. Toy's sexuality has been a major issue of debate between the sisters both behind her back and in her face, believe it or not. But what we say never seems to offend her. I don't believe she cares one way or the other.

Ronnie, our waiter came back to our table.

"You ladies need refills on your drinks?"

I nodded toward Renee. "This trick right here don't need nothing else, Ronnie. She's had enough."

He and the rest of the table laughed.

"Yeah, I got your 'trick,'" Renee mumbled under her breath.

After he left, Toy spoke again. "Seriously though, Ericka. It does look like Maurice is taking you for granted. He's never around, even when we all hang out as a group. Tarik even shows his ugly face once in a while."

Natalie raised her eyebrows at Toy. She continued.

"And when he does come over, it's late at night and most decent folk have gone to bed. What's that about? Hell, you don't even talk to him every day. The man is more like an acquaintance than a boyfriend. Are you really cool with that?"

No, I wasn't cool with it. But I also wasn't cool with having to talk about it when I was supposed to be having some much needed down time.

"Yeah, Ericka," Natalie chimed in. "I love Maurice like my brother. But we all know that he could do a lot better by you. He doesn't take you anywhere. He doesn't even act like you guys are together unless he thinks somebody else is looking at you. It's like he's not even a boyfriend. He's just a booty call."

She was right. And I was getting tired of trying to justify this faux-relationship to everybody.

"Y'all looking at it from the outside. You don't see how he is when it's just us. Things ain't been perfect, but they're better than they were even six months ago. And we've been through too much for me to just give up on him now."

Renee jumped back into the conversation.

"So what? You gonna wait for him and Cassandra to have another baby? He didn't even have the decency to tell you that he had somebody pregnant. And you took his sorry ass back."

"Renee, I'm not taking any more of your shit tonight, okay? First of all, we weren't even together when that baby was conceived. And second, if he didn't care about me, why is he still spending all of his money at my house? Reese pays bills at my house like Terrell pays bills at yours. You know how men like Reese are. They're too macho to romance you, so they give you all of their money to show you that they want to take care of you."

"Now, she got a point, there," Natalie agreed. "A dude that hustles love money more than he loves his own mama. So, he must really love Ericka if he thinks enough of her to share."

Toy said, "This is exactly why the only man in my life is Pookie."

Pookie was her cat.

"The crap y'all have to go through with these men is ridiculous."

Renee looked at Toy.

"Heifer, that ain't why. You just don't want no man," Renee said to her with a smirk.

"Just so you know, Renee," Toy fired back. "I may not be interested in no man, but trust and believe that Toy gets what she wants, when she wants it, from whomever she wants it from, okay?"

Everyone's jaw dropped on the table. And just what, exactly, did that mean?

Before anyone could comment, Tarik came up behind Natalie's chair. He leaned over and gave her a peck on the lips.

"What's up, ladies? Y'all didn't invite us to the hen party," he grinned.

We all mumbled greetings, still looking in Toy's direction. She ignored us.

"Who's 'us'?" she asked.

"Reece is down at the bar," Tarik said.

I looked down at the bar and saw Maurice talking to some other guys. I smiled. He had on a Carolina blue Akademiks tee shirt with a baseball cap to match. My baby could really coordinate.

Tarik joked around with us for a few more minutes and then returned to Maurice and the other guys at the bar. A few more minutes went by, but Maurice still hadn't come to our table, or even acknowledged my presence in the restaurant. I nervously began to fidget with my napkin.

Toy, sensing my uneasiness, said, "Ericka, he won't even come to the table and say 'hello'. You've got to admit that there's something strange about your relationship."

Renee, never to be left out, backed her up. "Why don't you just go down there and speak to him?"

"Nah, I'm not doing that," I said, shaking my head.

"Why not? He's supposed to be your man, right? And you can't even go down there and say nothing to him?"

She shook her head like she pitied me.

"I don't need to go down there sweatin' him just to impress y'all, okay? Damn, why can't you all just leave it alone? I swear!"

I rose from the table.

"I'm going to the bathroom," I said, leaving the table. "I don't have to justify my relationship to none of y'all. I'm thirty fucking years old and I haven't lived at home in quite a long time, okay?"

"Bitch, you thirty-five," Renee sneaked dissed.

I glared at her hard enough to bore a hole through her soul, and then stomped away from the table without bothering to reply.

I couldn't get to the bathroom without passing Maurice, so I did my best to pretend that I didn't notice him as I passed the group he was talking to. A couple of his boys spoke to me, but Maurice had his back turned on the phone and either didn't see me or purposely didn't say anything to me.

I didn't actually have to go to the bathroom. I just needed to remove myself from the middle of the conversation. I knew my girls meant well, but I didn't come here for a lecture. I came to have a good time and relax. I dealt with Maurice's foolishness on a daily basis, and the one time I had to get away from it, my own girls brought it to me.

I checked my hair, put on some more lip-gloss and headed back to my seat.

I felt a gentle tug on my hair as I passed Maurice's group again. I turned around to see him grinning at me.

"What? You gon' pass by me and not speak?"

I couldn't help but smile.

"You were busy talking when I walked by the first time."

He leaned over and whispered, "Is there any more room for me in those jeans?"

A broad smile came over my face.

"A gracious plenty," I replied, seductively.

He nodded, approvingly.

"All right. Go on back up there with your girls. I'll deal with you later."

When I got back to my table, I found Toy cursing out Renee for asking her whether or not she was attracted to any women that were in the restaurant.

Ronnie came back again, this time with a tray full of drinks.

Natalie looked at him, puzzled.

"We didn't order these," she said.

"Yeah, where these drinks come from?" Toy asked.

"Compliments of the gentleman in the light blue tee shirt at the bar," he said.

I looked down at Maurice, who was still talking with Tarik and the rest of his friends. He wasn't paying our table any attention.

I smiled, triumphantly.

"What you got to say, now, Renee?" Toy asked, spitefully.

"Humph!" Renee grunted, as she took a sip of her free drink.

At the end of the night, Natalie and I decided to crash at my house. Toy wanted to come with us, but Maurice and Tarik would be following us to the house soon after we got there. She was still pissed off at Renee, so she declined Renee's offer to sleep her drinks off in one of her kids' rooms and drove herself home.

I could hear the answering machine beeping before I opened the door. I set my purse on my bed and pressed play while I fished a silk scarf out of my dresser drawer to put on my head.

Beep.

"Hey missy, this is D. I had a free moment, so I just wanted to call and holla at you for a few. You and your girls must still be out having a good time. Give me a call when you're free. Later."

Natalie came out of the bathroom with a shocked look on her face.

"No wonder you're not trippin' about Maurice."

"It's not even like that," I said.

She probed me for information, but I heard Reese's key turning in the door. I told her that I would tell her later, then hurriedly erased the message from the machine.

Chapter 4

Extended Dance Party USA Routine

The rest of the evening went off without a hitch. Maurice and Tarik met us back at my house right on schedule. It was late, but we still had plenty of energy, so we ended up playing dominoes at the kitchen table and eating the rest of a cheese-cake I had left over from a recipe I tried earlier in the week. The cake must have given us a sugar rush because we got all pumped up listening to the old school hip-hop that was playing on the stereo. We began to reminisce about parties we went to and old dances we used to do back in the day. Pretty soon we had turned my small living room into a dance floor and started jamming like we were at the club.

We went on like that for a couple of hours until the jams gave way to the quiet storm radio program. That put us all in a mellow, romantic mood. Natalie and Tarik said hasty good-byes before hurrying off into the night where they could be free to romance each other or freak each other for the remainder of the evening; whichever was the case.

Once we were alone, Maurice and I went outside into the night air to cool off after our extended Dance Party USA routine. We took our favorite place on the front porch of my duplex in the two-seat glider in front of my front window. I lifted my legs up and placed them in his lap. He then took my left foot and began to gently massage it with his strong hands. All that dancing mixed with those drinks we had at Friday's made me a little giddy, so I took a deep breath to suppress my urge to giggle at the tickling sensation Maurice was bringing to my tired foot.

"You have fun, tonight?" he asked me, looking out towards the stars.

"It was cool. The night started out a little shaky, but things turned out okay," I answered, watching the intensity on his face as he gazed at the moon like a trained astronomer.

He turned his attention away from the moon and studied my face for a moment. He was well aware that the focal point of most of my friends' discussions was him. But even so, he never did anything to try to appease them, or me, for that matter.

"What them cluck heads talking about, now?" he asked, pretending to be exasperated.

I rolled my eyes at him.

"Don't do that," I said. "That's not cool."

He laughed.

"It's not cool for y'all to be sitting up there at the bar tearing me down, either, but you do it anyway."

He chuckled to himself and returned his gaze to whatever had his attention in the sky.

I wish I could be that self-centered. Maurice absolutely did not give a damn what people said or thought. He did exactly what he wanted, when he wanted, and how he wanted. And he was never ruffled about anything that anyone ever had to say about it. In most instances, that would be a pretty decent quality to have, but in our case, it was the nail that sealed the coffin on any chance that I could ever have at improving our relationship. Not only did he not seem to care about what my friends said, he wasn't all that interested in what constructive criticism I had either. And the most puzzling part of all was that he was always so nice about it. He was not cocky or arrogant; he was actually a sweetheart. But with him, it was just what it was.

"I don't tear you down," I said, plaintively. "In fact, I spend most of my breath defending you."

"Well, I don't understand. Just what is the problem that everybody got with me, now?"

For the first time in the conversation, I had his full attention. It was on, now. I shifted to a more comfortable position on the settee and propped my arm over the back. I looked at him carefully, in deep thought. I knew that this discussion would require me to use the 'six-second rule,' which simply says that I wait six seconds before I let anything come out of my mouth. That usually lowers the chance of me saying something stupid or hurting someone's feelings.

"You should be more worried about the problems that I have with you," I said, finally.

Maurice sighed heavily.

"What problems you got? Dang, I thought I was doing better. I just can't win with you."

"Maurice, be for real. Would you have come to Friday's tonight if Tarik hadn't asked you to come? You didn't come out there to meet me. You didn't even know I was gonna be there because I haven't even talked to you in almost a week. You were following your entourage, like normal."

"E. Middle, I knew you was gonna be there. Tarik told me. That's why I came. I sent you and your girls some free drinks. I even sent one for that damned Renee, and I can't stand her. I can't even get no points for that?"

He shook his head.

I tried again.

"Look, I don't want to make it seem like my friends are gassing my head up or nothing, Reese. But you have to admit that this is not a normal relationship. Yeah, we hung out together and had a good time. I'll give you that. And I'll even give you an extra ten points for sending those drinks to the table. You're a smooth pimp for doing that, okay? But you have to admit that we don't do things that normal people do in a relationship. You won't take me anywhere. We don't even see each other regularly. Hell, you don't even call me once a week!"

Maurice was very laid-back by nature, and he hated confrontation. He sat there with his head bowed and pretended to listen to what I saying. But the truth was, he had most likely memorized this argument and could probably recite it in his sleep. He was just too polite to stop me and tell me he didn't want to hear it, anymore. And we both knew that things would remain the same, even after I presented my strong, passionate point. I took advantage of his silence and kept going.

"Reese, it's been six years. How long do I have to keep sitting around here waiting on the relationship to go the way I want it to go for a change?"

"I'm saying, Ericka. What is it that you want? I'm up here thinking that I'm doing what I'm supposed to be doing. Now, you sitting here telling me that I ain't doing nothing. I'm confused."

He was always confused. His confusion was what pissed me off the most. Whenever I tried to explain to him what I wanted out of the relationship, this above average intelligent man would suddenly become an idiot. I may have switched up a little on my approach every now and then, but the argument was always the same. And each time, he always claimed that he didn't get it. I tried, yet again.

"Okay, Reese. Here's the deal. Whenever I go anywhere, I'm always by myself, unless I have Tomika with me. You never go anywhere with me. It makes me feel like you trying to hide me. I feel neglected. What's wrong? Are you ashamed of me or something, or are you trying to hide me from somebody?"

"No, girl. You trippin'. As much as they see you at the shop, all the boys know you my woman. How am I gonna be ashamed when everybody already knows the deal between us? And don't you think if I had some other chick, she would have walked up on you by now?"

"I'm not talking about your boys. And that doesn't matter, anyway, because I don't hang out anywhere that those thugs from the shop are at. And as far as another chick is concerned, you ain't bold enough to give her the okay to hang around that shop, because you know I will bust both of y'all in the head. I'm just saying in general. When's the last time you came and picked me up and took me somewhere?"

As he sat there thinking, I thought I saw a puff of smoke rise from the top of his head. He must have blown a fuse trying to strain his brain for an answer that we both knew was not there. He couldn't even come up with a good lie.

"I'll do you one even better. When's the last time you came over and had dinner with us? Hell, when is the last time you came over here at a decent enough hour to even still be hungry? Most of the time when I see you, it's close to eleven or twelve o'clock. By then, I'm too tired to enjoy your company."

Maurice spoke up.

"The reason I get here so late is because I be out all day hustling. I'm trying to get this money. You think I be out there B.S.'ing with them niggas at the shop. But they come to me. They might be in there shooting dice or playing cards, or whatever, but while I'm in there, I'm working. And when you be seeing me all late, I may be just coming back in town from Charlotte or somewhere just so I can satisfy a customer. And a whole lot of times, I don't even feel like coming by here. I just want to go to the crib and get in my own bed and fall out. But, if I don't come by here, you'll lose it and be threatening to bust the windows out of my shop and stuff."

He chuckled at the little funny he made at the end. I had

to laugh in spite of myself, while I pictured myself heaving a brick through the plate glass window at Hot Wheelz with a horrified Maurice standing by, watching helplessly.

I hated it when he did stuff like that. No matter how mad or how serious I tried to be with him, it was absolutely impossible to stay that way.

"I never told you that. I told you that I was gonna let the air out of all your tires," I said, trying to stifle my giggle.

"See? Why women always gotta be so violent?"

The conversation kind of went south for a minute, after that. He had almost managed to weasel his way out of the discussion, again. I stopped laughing, abruptly.

"I'm not joking, Reese. This is serious, now."

He tried to wipe the smile from his face.

"Okay, baby. I'm sorry. What else?"

"I'm saying, Reese. I wanna hang out and do stuff like Nat and Tarik. I wanna go out on dates, like to the movies and stuff."

"You don't even like the movies, E. And besides, you don't need to be trying to have what you see somebody else with. You don't know what they went through to get it. I don't know what Nat is filling your head with, but Tarik is in my face at the shop more than he is hers, so y'all 'bout in the same boat. She just don't be getting mad all the time like you do."

"Well, maybe, but there's still a big difference between our relationship and theirs."

He looked puzzled.

"What?"

"Tarik cares enough about Natalie that he actually sets aside time for her. Even if she only gets to see him once a week for two hours, she knows that's her time and nobody else's. He doesn't answer his phone or make plans during that time. For those couple of hours, it's all about her, even if they're not doing anything special. You know what I'm saying? Even

I know not to call her on Thursday nights after eight because they always watch Smack Down together. Think about it. Y'all are tight friends, but do you and him ever do anything together on Thursday nights?"

He scratched his head.

"I don't know. I never thought about it."

"Yeah, right. You do know. Because you were just complaining a couple of weeks ago about how Tarik wouldn't even answer his phone when wrestling came on. Y'all dummies think he's over there ignoring your calls because he don't wanna get interrupted in the middle of wrestling? He just don't want his quality time interrupted with his woman."

Maurice seemed to be in deep thought. I continued.

"Ya'll so wrapped up in trying to get paid and trying to stay in relationship with each other that your girlfriends can't even get in where they fit in. You've been missing the whole point of these talks we always have."

"Well, what is the point?" Maurice asked, sincerely.

I rolled my eyes in the dark.

"Reese, I don't require that you spend every second of every day in my face. All I want is for the time that we spend together to be my time. Even when you do come see me, your damn phone rings a hundred times the first fifteen minutes you're here."

As if on cue, his cell phone rang. He looked at it, pushed a button and turned his attention back to me.

"Don't you need to answer that?" I asked.

"Naw, go ahead. I can call him back later. That wasn't nobody but Will. He don't want nothing."

"See? That's what I'm talking about. What if every time you came by here, my phone was blowing up and I stopped you fifty times in mid-sentence to talk to somebody else?"

"Well, first off, I wouldn't trip because I would hope that it would be an emergency at this time of night if I'm at your house," he said, indignantly.

"That's my point," I said. "You own a tire and rim shop. Ain't nobody buying no damn tires and rims after midnight."

"So what? You think that females are calling me on my phone?" he asked, defensively.

This whole conversation was getting tiresome. He just didn't get it. He never did. Personally, I thought he acted this ignorant on purpose.

"I don't care who you talk to, Maurice! All I'm saying is this. I know your free time is very limited because of the business. But when you do have free time, for the most part, it's spent with your boys. That leaves no time for me. I don't fit in anywhere. And I'm tired of sitting here by myself all the time. I don't like the fact that I'm turning into a nag like Renee. I know we both have our own lives, but what's the use of having a man in your life that you don't ever get to see? I get tired of having to beg you to spend some time with me, to look in my face sometimes, or just to pay me some attention! Either you want to be with me, or you don't. I can't keep going on like this. I'm getting tired of the same old."

"So, you telling me that you want to go be with somebody else?"

His voice was a mixture of fear and surprise.

"No, Maurice. I'm not saying that I want to be with somebody else. I just want the man I got to pay me some attention sometimes. That's all. Why is that so hard for you? If you can't do it, just say so because where one won't, another one will."

His head snapped back at that last sentence and his eyes got big. I kept talking, unfazed.

"Look, I'm just keeping it real. When I'm out by myself, guys approach me all the time. But, I'm loyal to a fault. If some of these men knew how much time I really spent by myself, I would have a date every freaking night if I wanted one. But I wouldn't do anything scandalous like that because I love you and I respect you as a man. And plus, that wouldn't be cool if one of your boys saw me out kicking it with some other dude. But it's time for you to step your game up, son. Because I'm tired of trying to justify in my own mind that things are fine the way they are. Because they're not."

He sat there, still and silent. I couldn't tell if he was really thinking about what I said, or if he was just being quiet in hopes that I would hurry up and finish bitching so he could move on with his life.

I asked, "You don't have anything to say to that?"

Without looking up, he said, "Yeah. I mean, you saying that you want me to make some time for you. I got you. I hear what you saying."

It amazed me how we managed to have this exact same conversation every couple of months and neither of us ever seemed to deviate from the script.

"Okay, so what are you going to do about it, Maurice?"

"I'ma just have to start spending more time with you."

"When, Reese?"

"Well, dang, E. Middle. I'm here, right? And you wasted most of the night fussing. That's why I don't take you nowhere. You like to fight, too much," he said, grinning. "So what? Do you wanna go ahead on and box right now and get it over with, or do you want to have some quality time with your man?"

His beautiful smile shone brighter than the moonlight. And that wonderfully unusual scar that branded him from the top of his forehead to his chin made his face beautifully unique. His face seemed to take on a whole different look in the night shadows. True, Maurice may have had his faults, but to me, he was still perfect.

I smiled at him and tickled his ribs with my toes. There was no way I was going to spoil the rest of my quality time. There was no telling when I would get any more any time soon.

Chapter 5

Being So Bad Tonight!

The chivalrous stunt that Maurice pulled at Friday's got the girls off my back for that moment, but things pretty much went back to the way they had always been after that. I hadn't even seen Maurice since that night. I had spoken to him a few times and made attempts to get him to come by the house to have dinner or watch a movie, but he blew me off.

Apparently, the boys at the shop had developed gambling fever and whenever money was falling, Maurice had to be right there to catch it. He allowed the guys to shoot dice in the back of the shop in the evenings, sometimes into the wee hours of the morning. Every now and then they would play cards, but they primarily preferred a spirited dice game. I wasn't too crazy about the late night gambling that went on at Hot Wheelz after hours, but Maurice insisted that he couldn't count on a weekly paycheck like me and other people who had regular jobs. So, he did what he had to do to feed his family when business was slow. He included me and Tomika as part of the family to make it sound good. But I suspected he did it to have an excuse not to make time for me.

The guys that hung out at the shop used it as a refuge from their wives and girlfriends, as well. His regulars were always there no matter what time of the day or night it was. This one guy they call 'Pop,' I would swear had a bed in the back of the shop had I not actually been back there to see for myself. What's worse is that he has a wife and four or five kids. Whenever I saw him, I always wondered whether or not he caught hell from his wife for being gone all the time, or whether or not she got tired of not ever having a break from all those damn kids. And I wondered what it was exactly that has kept them married, since they are obviously leading separate lives. It seemed that they only got together once a year to make a baby. Then I wondered why and the hell I allowed myself to be basically in the same boat as she is, since I didn't see Maurice any more than Pop's wife saw him.

What I really had a hard time understanding is why Maurice and all the rest of the hoods that hang out at his shop even had the desire to have women in their lives at all. It's like having a girlfriend was just their way to let everybody know that they could get one if they wanted one. Or they have to have women to show each other and everyone else that they weren't gay. But the way they stay up under each other all the time without their women around, who's falling for that?

I hated feeling like I was sweating this dude. And my insecurities were fed by the fact that he had secretly had a child by someone else while we were 'just kicking it.' The excuse that time was that I didn't seem concerned with being serious, so he didn't think I wanted a relationship with him. But when we first got together, Maurice made it clear that he just wanted to be friends. I saw other people as I assumed he did. Eventually, we started hanging out more and more to the point where I naively thought neither of us had time to be around anyone else. I felt so stupid and heartbroken, I broke things off once I found out about the baby. But about a year later, he came crawling back, promising things would be different. I took him back like a fool and now, I saw him even less than I did when we were just friends.

I know I should've been gone. But we've been together since my daughter was two-years old. And being a single parent doesn't allow you the freedom of a frequent or spontaneous dating life. I'm too busy working or playing Mommy to entertain a bunch of men. And as horrible of a boyfriend he is to me, he's a great male figure to Tomika. She loves him. And he takes care of her financially, as though she was his. I'd feel a little guilty taking that from her since we haven't seen her biological since shortly after she was born.

What's crazy is, I think Maurice uses my desire to be a good mom against me, too. I can't jump at the drop of a dime and go when and wherever I please because I have Tomika. He won't actually say it to me directly because he would never intentionally hurt my feelings. But he figured out a long time ago that he can't call me and ask me to meet him anywhere after work. Nor can I take impromptu trips like he's used to doing. So, he doesn't ask. And I also can't pop up on him in the street when he's out all times of the night doing who knows what. While I sit at home waiting on him to show up, he has the appearance of having a dutiful woman who lets him be a man. And he obviously prefers it that way.

But I don't and I'm lonely. And bored. I rationalized that since he wouldn't let me walk away, he must've really loved me. In reality, I had broken up with him so many times that he'd grown confident in the fact that I wasn't really going anywhere. If I'd tell him to stop calling me, he'd just wait about a week until things calmed down a bit, then call and act like nothing happened. He knows I'd take him back and wallow in all the guilty attention he lavished on me, hoping that that time the change in him would be permanent.

Desmond's phone calls are a harmless distraction while I wait. Tomika's in bed by the time he called, and Maurice is nowhere around. He fills the hollow feeling of emptiness that takes over at night. He hangs on to my every word. He flirts and I feel sexy and not like an afterthought. If he wasn't married, I would probably have already given him some right under Maurice's nose as payback.

As I lay in bed contemplating my situation, the phone rang. Desmond was his normal cheery, sexy sounding self.

"So, what have you been up to these days?" I asked trying to play catch up. I hadn't spoken to him in a couple of days.

"Working on my golf game."

"I didn't know you played golf."

He chuckled.

"I do lots of things. I'm multitalented."

"I see," I said.

"So, tell me something. When are you free?"

"I'm never free," I responded. "But I'm reasonable."

He laughed.

"I had to ask."

"Yep. Walked right into it. But seriously, I'm usually free after five during the week and all day on the weekends."

"Well," he said, slowly, "that wasn't exactly my definition of 'free.'"

I was puzzled.

"Oh. Well, do you mean free as in time of day, day of the week, or free as in not busy?"

"No, I mean free, as in do whatever you want to do when you want to do it, free."

I didn't know what he was getting at, but I played along.

"Oh. Well, in that case, never. But under the circumstances, I think it can be temporarily arranged."

"Okay. Think about it and call me. And maybe I can pay you a surprise visit and bring something with me when I come."

Desmond was a master ego stroker.

"Oh, really?" I said, curiously. "Something like what?"

"Sometimes, knowing takes all the fun out of the surprise," Desmond said, devilishly.

I could picture an impish grin spread across that handsome, chocolate face of his.

"True, but all the fun is in the anticipation," I retorted in my own mischievous voice.

"You might have a point on that one. And while I'm there, I can show you my golf swing."

I smiled.

"That must be one hell of a swing."

"Oh, yeah. I can really drive that ball hard off the tee . . ."

"Careful . . ." I said, stopping him in mid-sentence. Desmond was in rare form tonight. I wondered what had gotten into him.

"Yeah, I know. Thanks."

He paused, giving us both time to regain our composure. Then, he sighed.

"Anyway. Can you handle those two tasks I gave you?"

"Yep. I'll let you know when I'm free, and I'll be thinking about what it is that you're going to bring me."

"You got it."

"No problem, mon," I said, trying to sound Jamaican. "I'm not hard to get along with. I'm very easy."

"That's all right with me, missy. You just continue to be as easy as you want to be with me."

I gasped.

"You are being so bad tonight!"

"I know. I'm not sure what's gotten into me."

I laughed at his poor innocent routine.

I could hear a muffled knock on his end of the phone.

"I think you'd better go take care of that person waiting outside your door so you can compose yourself, mister."

He laughed along with me.

"I think you're right."

"Have a good night."

"You, too."

There was nothing in the world that I hated more than speech making. But I had already promised Dr. Curtis that I would give a presentation at the next conference. I tried not to think about it. It snuck up on me so fast that I barely had time to sweat over it. And tonight, as I stood at the podium in front of all these people, I wished that I had never even heard the word 'presentation.'

I was a nervous wreck. My palms were all clammy and my legs felt like jelly as I rested my hands on the podium in an attempt to hold my balance. I wanted to run to the bathroom and throw up. I stood there with my head bowed, pretending to consult my notes before I began while I tried to muster up some hidden strength to open my mouth to say something.

I thought about what one of my co-workers said after finding out that I had been drafted to make this month's presentation.

"Try picturing the audience in their underwear as you talk. I heard that's supposed to calm you down and take your mind off being nervous," she had said.

I wasn't so sure, but I was willing to try just about anything to get me through this speech. The sooner I got it over with, the better.

Here goes nothing, I thought, mentally shrugging my shoulders.

I took a deep breath and slowly lifted my head with lips parted to address the group. A gasp escaped from somewhere deep inside me as my eyes focused on my listeners.

My co-workers trick really worked. Picturing the crowd in their underwear really did take my mind off having to speak in public. In fact, my mind was not on the task at hand, at all. My audience consisted but of a sole member. It was Desmond sitting front row, dead center watching patiently for my mouth to move.

I stood motionless, not sure what to do. I guess I could

tear up my notes from my original speech. Before I could decide my next plan of action, Desmond stood. To my sheer horror and delight, I discovered that he was not wearing underwear. He was wearing his birthday suit.

Chapter 6

Your Undivided Attention

Exactly three weeks, two days, seventeen hours, and forty-two minutes following the post-Friday's gathering at my house, I decided to break down and call Maurice. There was nothing unusual about that, seeing as how I did most of the calling anyway. But this time, I had been bound and determined not to be the first one to call. Solange, the receptionist in the office where I worked asked me to call him for her to see if he could get her a good price on some new tires for her car.

"I was wondering why you hadn't called me," Maurice said, cheerfully.

I took the receiver from my ear and looked at it. This dude must be Superman because he had nerves of steel. I decided to pretend to be as unbothered as him.

"I've been busy," I replied, casually.

"Busy doing what?" he wanted to know.

I had to will my face to come out of the frown that had quickly spread across it like an out-of-control wildfire.

"I just had things to do," I responded, coolly.

"Oh," said Maurice, dismissively. "What size tire did you say your girl needed?"

Grateful for the distraction, I fiddled around for the piece of paper that I had written Solange's tire size on.

"Sixteen's. She said she wanted some just like the ones that were on the car when she bought it. Some Goodyear's."

"All right," he said. "Tell her that I can get them for her for about eighty-five dollars apiece or she can get the whole set for three hundred. If she gets the whole set, the price includes the charge to put them on and everything."

He must have been in a good mood today.

"That's all? Why you being so nice today?" I asked.

"Consider it my good deed for today. And besides, if I give your girl a discount, then she'll tell her girls and her man. Then on and on until I've got fifty new customers. I'm making a long-term investment, plus scoring some points with my woman."

Yeah, whatever.

"Oh, since when do you feel like you need to score points with me?"

He laughed.

"I can't never rack up enough points to keep you off my case, girl. I'm just trying to make enough hush money to put you in an X-5 and a house in North Raleigh."

It was just like him, trying to buy my silence. But little did he know there wasn't enough money in the US treasury department to buy a zipper for my mouth.

"In that case, you better charge her full price for them tires," I said, dryly.

He laughed again.

"All right, then. Big Daddy gotta go get this paper, now. But, I'ma try to get over there about six tonight, okay?"

He said it so casually, no one else would have ever thought that I hadn't seen him in almost a month.

"Okay, Reese. But can you make sure you call first before you come, please?" I asked, sweetly.

I smiled, sinisterly to myself. I knew that was a loaded question.

He paused.

"Why all of a sudden you want me to call you before I come? You got somebody else coming over tonight, or something?" he asked, warily.

I got so tired of playing this game, but I loved it when he felt his ego was in jeopardy.

"No, honey," I answered, innocently, "I might want you to stop by the store for me on your way in for some ice cream, or something. I've been craving sweets, lately."

He tried unsuccessfully to hide the relief in his voice.

"Oh, okay. That ain't no problem. I'll give you a call when I'm on the way."

"Okay, baby," I replied, with smug satisfaction. "Enjoy the rest of your day."

I had long since grown tired of these sporadic visits from Maurice, but since he apparently wanted to spend some time with me for whatever reason this day, I decided to prepare a special meal in honor of having my man home with me for a change. He was never at my house during dinner, and I could count on one hand how many times he had actually eaten my cooking in the last six years. Since he opted to eat with us that night, I decided to remind him that his girlfriend was capable of feeding her man. I prepared a feast of barbecue chicken, turnip greens, macaroni and cheese, which was Tomika's favorite, and potato salad.

Maurice was unusually punctual, and he stood in the kitchen and talked to me while I finished up with dinner. Tomika was in her room playing with her dolls and for a moment, all was right with the world.

Once I was done making iced tea, I asked Reese to go wash up for dinner and get Tomika so she could do the same. He left the kitchen, and I prepared to take the food to the dining room table. Just as I was taking the hot pan of chicken from the oven, the phone rang. I had stuff piled up on just about every inch of counter space in my small kitchen and was trying to clear an open space on one of the counters so I could set the chicken down.

"Maurice, can you answer the phone for me, please?" I yelled at him.

After another half of a ring, it stopped. I waited to hear Maurice yell back for me to get the phone, but after a couple of minutes, the only thing I could hear was the television playing.

That's strange, I thought while I stirred a pot on the stove. Maurice and I didn't live together, and he was rarely here during evening hours, so I knew whoever was on the phone couldn't have been calling for him. And besides, he had a cell phone and a Nextel two-way. All his friends and business associates knew how to reach him on one of those or they paged him. I looked up from the pot to call him again, but then finally decided that it was Natalie or Toy talking his ear off, or it was a wrong number.

Tomika came dragging into the kitchen with a Barbie doll head that was dangling from a comb that was hopelessly tangled in its head.

"Is it time to eat yet, Miss Lady?" she asked, properly.

"Almost," I answered. "Is Maurice still on the phone back there?"

"I dunno. You want me to go see?"

"Yes, please ma'am. Can you tell him to hurry up? It's almost time for din-din."

"Okay," she bubbled and bounded out of the room.

Moments later, she returned to the kitchen, minus the doll head.

"Did you tell him what I said?" I asked.

"Yes, he said he will be in here in a minute," she reported.

"Thank you. What's he doing back there, anyway?"

"Umm, looking at something on your dresser, I think."

He was worse than Tomika about snooping around in my stuff. I never could figure out what was so fascinating about the things on my dresser, but Maurice could never leave my room without moving stuff around on my dresser, first.

I shook my head and smiled.

"You and Maurice ramble more than anybody else I know."

She adamantly denied the charge but couldn't resist laughing at the truth in my statement.

"Not me. I don't ramble."

"Yeah, right," I teased. "Have you washed your hands?"

"Oops!" she exclaimed, having forgotten, and rushed into the bathroom.

"Reese, are you ready to eat, baby?" I called into the bedroom.

"Yeah, babe, I'm coming!" he called back.

"What are you doing in there, Rambling Ron? Your partner in crime, Rambling Rose told me that you were in there on my dresser, again," I said, when he appeared from the back of the house.

He chuckled.

"Dang, she ratted me out, huh? She's supposed to cover for me when I do that."

He laughed and gave me a peck on the lips.

You must not be paying her enough," I said. "Don't change the subject. What were you doing in there? And who was that on the phone?"

"Oh, some cat named Desmond. He said for you to call him when you got a chance."

"Oh, okay," I said, trying to appear nonchalant.

I didn't even think about the possibility of it being him on the phone. It wasn't even seven o'clock. It was normally a lot later when he called, but it never really mattered because Maurice was almost never here. He didn't even know

Desmond existed until now. But he didn't appear to be fazed about the call.

"Who is Desmond?" he wanted to know.

"And old friend from Global Technology. He calls every now and then to talk."

"Mm hmm. Is this somebody that you used to kick it with?"

Maurice refused to outwardly express any displeasure about the notion of my entertaining other men because he knew I would use it against him. But I could tell that he was a little concerned about Desmond. When we were just "friends," Maurice would get upset about other guys calling the house. And I would always ask him if he were jealous enough to give in. That usually shut him up. This was the first time that he was aware of another man calling the house since we actually got together. I guess he had taken for granted that I had cut everyone off after we became an official couple.

"No, silly. He's just a close friend. And anyway, that's a married man. He can't do nothing for me," I lied.

"So? That don't mean nothing."

"Well, the only person I'm interested in right now is you. How about that?"

I wrapped my arms around him and gave him a big kiss.

"You sure you're not waiting on that dude to divorce his wife?" he asked, trying not to let on that he was indirectly probing me for information.

I rolled my eyes at him.

"Naw, man. I'm waiting on you to divorce your crew."

A broad smile involuntarily invaded his lips.

"Oh, here we go with that, again."

He threw up his hands and sighed.

"I don't know why you always trippin' about me and the boys. I mean, it ain't like I'm out there with other women. You always know where to find me. I'm either at the shop, home, or here. And if you need me, all you got to do is call."

I turned to face him.

"But where are you the majority of the time? It sure ain't here with me, and you only use that apartment to have somewhere to keep an extra bed when you don't feel like being bothered with me."

"But where am I right now" he asked, desperate to change the direction of the conversation.

"That's not the point."

"Well, what is the point, E. Middle?"

"I'm not supposed to have to fight with other people for quality time with my man!"

"Woman, please. You don't never fight with nobody else, but me."

Before I could come back, his Nextel two-way beeped.

"Saved by the bell, punk," I mumbled.

I recruited Tomika to finish setting the table while I finished what I was doing in the kitchen. I could hear Tarik's voice coming from the two-way.

"Where you at, Big Dawg?" he spoke.

Maurice answered back, "I'm on Poole Road getting ready to box."

Tarik laughed. "Oh no! Don't hurt him over there, E."

"Tarik, what do you want? You're interrupting my dinner!" I yelled from the kitchen sink.

"Oh, my bad, baby. I didn't want nothing, no way. Just wanted to see if Reese wanted to hang out later on with the boys."

I looked at Maurice, expectantly.

"Man, didn't I tell you that I was in here about to box with this woman? You tryin' to get me hurt up in here," he joked with his friend.

"So, is that a no-go, my brotha?"

"A definite no-go, bruh. I'm chillin' with the fam tonight," he answered. He came up behind me and nuzzled me on the neck. I couldn't help but smile. We had never been referred to out loud as 'the fam' before. "Ten-four, good buddy," said Tarik, trying to sound like a trucker. 'T-man out."

"Peace."

"You know, you can be good when you want to be," I said to him.

"I'm good all the time. That's why you love me."

He walked up behind Tomika and pulled her ponytail.

"You ready to eat, Baby Girl?"

She giggled, inching away from him with her shoulders hunched up toward her neck.

As we sat down to eat dinner, Maurice's phone rang again.

"Hello?" he asked, trying to spoon turnip greens into his plate and hold the phone to his ear at the same time.

I glanced warily in his direction but pretended to be unaffected by the unwelcome intrusion upon our "family" dinner.

He frowned and covered the mouthpiece of the phone.

"'Scuse me for a sec, E. I gotta take this one. Go ahead and start without me. I won't be long."

Without looking at him, I continued to pour tea into our glasses and fuss over the table to distract myself from the anxiety that was building up in my insides. Tomika and I sat down and bowed our heads simultaneously to say a silent grace. She sensed the tension, as well, and looked up from her plate every few seconds toward the bedroom door where Maurice had retreated to take his phone call. My stomach was doing flip-flops and suddenly I wasn't hungry, anymore.

There always seemed to be someone around undermining every attempt that I made to be happy with Maurice. The shop closed at seven, so there shouldn't have been but so much business being conducted this late. I wondered if his phone rang like this when he was by himself, or when he was with his loyal subjects that appeared not to be able to do anything without 'King Maurice.'

The call was not long-winded like I thought it would be and in a matter of minutes Maurice had returned to the table his usual jovial and famished self. He sat down at the table, bowed his head for a lightning quick blessing of his food, and dove into his plate almost face first.

"Boy, can't nobody cook like E. Middle."

I looked up from my plate, blushing.

"Baby Girl, I'ma have to start going with you to Tae Kwon Do class if your mama keeps feeding us this good."

"Well, you can go with me to class, Uncle Reese, but you will have to be in the white belt class with the other people that just started," Tomika said, matter-of-factly.

"Why can't I be in the class with you, Baby Girl?" Maurice asked.

"Because I just passed my test last week and I'm an orange belt, now," Tomika boasted.

"An orange belt?" Maurice asked. "And what does an orange belt mean?"

Tomika put down her fork. "It means I got skills!"

Maurice and I laughed together. Tomika had been taking martial arts training for the last few months and was really doing well. Her confidence was through the roof, and I was pleased that she was so sure of herself these days. At almost five feet tall and not quite nine-years-old, Tomika was exceptionally tall for her age. Before starting Tae Kwon Do, she wasn't really interested in sports or anything else if it didn't involve Nickelodeon television.

Maurice turned to me.

"You didn't tell me that Baby Girl earned a belt. That's hot!"

"I probably just hadn't gotten around to it. It's so late when you get here most of the time that I'm half asleep when you come in."

Tomika interrupted.

"Uncle Reese, I got a trophy, too!"

"You did?"

"Uh-huh. I was in a tournament, and I won a match."

"You go, girl!" Maurice encouraged. "Can I sit your trophy up in my shop for a little while so everybody can see that my baby girl won her first match?"

He was as proud of her as I was.

"Yeah, and . . ."

I interrupted.

"Slow your roll, Tee Tee. Mommy doesn't want that trophy to leave this house. Understand?"

"Yes, ma'am," Tomika pouted.

"Tell you what," I offered. "Instead of taking the trophy, why don't we . . ."

Before I could finish my thought, the phone rang again.

"Damn! Oops. Sorry, Tee Tee. Wait a minute, baby. Hello? Yeah, wassup . . . Naw, man. I'm chillin', tonight . . . for real? Naw, that's all right. Peace."

He turned back to me.

"Now, what were you saying, Ma?"

I rolled my eyes down into my plate. Those thugs that hung out at the shop never seemed to have anywhere else to go unless they could be accompanied by Maurice. It burned me up that I always had to compete with them for his attention.

"Nothing," I said through clenched teeth. "I was just saying that instead of taking the trophy to the shop, take the certificate and hang it up, instead. It's the same thing. Them Negroes can read, can't they?"

He laughed.

"Most of them can."

I relaxed a little. Maurice was so easy-going that it was contagious. I smiled at him as he and Tomika continued to chat about her match. Things would be so much better if he would only try a little harder.

His phone rang again.

Tomika got up from the table and carried her plate to the sink.

"Mommy, can I go play with Haley and Shalimar, now?"

"Did you get enough to eat?"

"Yes, ma'am."

"Well, you tell Miss Tina to send you home at seven forty-five and call me before you leave."

"Okay."

When I returned to the table after making sure Tomika got to the neighbors' house safely, Maurice was still on the phone.

"A'ight, I'll holla."

I was through pretending that I was still hungry by this time and got up to clear my plate from the table. Maurice came up behind me and squeezed my elbow.

"You finished eating, already? Now I got to eat by myself."

I rolled my eyes at him.

"You don't need my company. Just take your plate and the phone in the bedroom and finish eating in there."

"See? You trippin'. All those calls were important, or I wouldn't have taken them. And one of them was an opportunity for me to make some money, but I turned it down to be with you. And for what? For you to spend it with your mouth tore up, as usual. Damn, Ericka! You always complaining about me not spending no time with you, but when I'm here, all you do is complain. I'm doing the best I can. What else do you want?"

"You know what? I don't want a damn thing from you, okay? I didn't think your undivided attention every now and then would be too much to ask, but apparently, I was wrong. My bad."

I set the dishes in the sink and continued to clean the kitchen. I was mad enough to throw stuff, but since everything in the house was mine, I stayed calm. No use breaking up my own dishes because I'm mad with someone else. He was just like a little kid. He didn't understand anything, and I was tired of trying to explain it to him. Tomika was my child, and I had taken on another one by involving myself with Maurice. My expectations for a nice evening at home with my man had been shattered. Oh, well. At least my kitchen would be clean.

Maurice sighed deeply and started toward the door, but stopped short as the phone rang yet again. He walked back to where I stood in the kitchen, the phone still ringing in his hand.

"You know what, Ericka. I apologize. Part of this is my fault for not doing this a long time ago."

He switched off the phone in mid-ring and handed it to me.

"Tonight, this belongs to you, and you belong to me."

Chapter 7

There It Is

"If you could have anything in the world for your birthday this year, what would you ask for?"

Until now, Desmond and I had only hinted about taking our relationship past the safe boundaries of the telephone. I proceeded with caution.

"Who am I asking for it?"

"Anybody."

I needed clarity. "Even you?"

"Especially me," was his sly response.

This married man was really starting to grow on me, and I was honestly starting not to care. We slipped further into an informal level of comfort that was borderline inappropriate. Our attraction was creating a magnetic energy that drew us dangerously closer together. So much so, we took care to keep our distance from each other in person. But more and more, I was becoming aware that lately, we weren't even really trying anymore. I began, slowly.

"May I be real with you?"

"I've grown to expect nothing less from you at this point."

He anticipated what was coming next.

Carefully, I started again.

"Well . . . if you really want to know the truth, what I'd really like for my birthday is to be with you."

Silence.

I tried to explain.

"What I mean is, well, um . . . Look, Desmond. Let's stop frontin' like all we're doing is enjoying the fruits of our intellect in stimulating conversation."

He tried to sound surprised, but I detected a hint of amusement in his voice.

"Well, isn't that what we've been doing?'

He was enjoying this, but I had placed myself in a vulnerable position as the aggressor. That made me the guilty one. Whatever happened at this point was on me. Before it had just been a game. Now, shit was suddenly becoming very real. I tried to pivot.

"Yeah, but you know what I mean."

He tried to suppress his amusement.

"I'm sorry if I'm putting you on the spot, and yeah, I know what you mean. I'm just curious to hear where you are in all this."

We were both aware of the electricity between us. I felt the energy when we worked together. I knew exactly what I was doing when I reconnected with all those months ago. Right or wrong, he wanted me. And I craved that feeling of being wanted. But I had crossed the line from flirting and there was no going back. And he had no intention of letting me off the hook. Not only that, but he was going to let me start the affair. I had never had an affair before and the very thought of being the other woman made me feel grimy. But the connection was so strong between us. I was lonely. So, Maurice deserved it. And besides. I just needed to get it out of my system. Nobody had to know. I shushed the pragmatic voice in my head. Here goes nothing.

"Well, here goes nothing. Desmond, I think you know that I have always been attracted to you, ever since the first day we met on the job. I even have dreams about us at night after we talk on the phone. Really nasty dreams . . ."

Hmmm, that's interesting. Go on."

That's interesting? He was milking this shit for all it was worth. There was no turning back now. I continued.

"Well, I know I shouldn't feel this way. You got a wife. But I've always wondered what it would be like to have you as my man for just one night. And since you asked, for my birthday that's what I want. I want to have you for just one night. I want to pretend that you belong to me."

No response. He seemed to be in deep thought. I waited in uncomfortable silence.

After what seemed to be an eternity, Desmond inhaled sharply and began.

"When had you planned to speak up?"

Huh?

"I didn't. Unless you brought it up, first."

He seemed to be taunting me.

"Why?"

"I wasn't gonna volunteer to be a homewrecker. And I wasn't trying to be out here looking crazy, if this energy I was feeling between us turned out to be my imagination. And besides, aren't men usually the aggressor?"

He chuckled. "You've been watching too much *Lifetime*."

I was starting to feel silly. What was I really doing?

"You know what? Just forget it."

Desmond was apologetic.

"Come on, Ericka. I'm just having a little fun. Truth is, I'm just putting it all on you because I'm nervous, too. You scare me."

"Scare you?" I had been lying across my bed, and suddenly sat up at his last comment. "How?"

"I can't explain it, really. I know with all the flirting and stuff we do, you probably think it's just my nature to be a cheating asshole because I'm married."

Now, I was confused.

"Well, aren't you?"

His voice was suddenly strained like he was uncomfortable.

"No! I've never cheated on my wife. I never get out of pocket with women."

"Yeah, right," I interjected, sarcastically. *But flattery will get you most places you want to go . . .*

He skimmed right by my comment, not breaking his train of thought.

"I've never been willing to risk our friendship by saying something you might consider disrespectful. I mean, you have always been careful not to step too out of line when we talk. And amazingly enough, you've always had the utmost respect for my marriage. In some ways, even more so than I have at times, I'm sorry to say. But I didn't want you to think less of me for not having as much respect for it as you did. And I also didn't want to disrespect you, either. But the truth is I've been attracted to you since we met at work. And there are other ways to be attracted to someone besides sexually. And you grab me in so many ways, I can't stop thinking about you and I've developed a craving for our friendship."

A craving?

"I stay on the other end of this phone because I'm kind of afraid that the craving will manifest itself into something that I may never be able to or want to control. I guess you might say that I'm afraid of you, Ericka."

I was feeling his pain. He scared the hell out of me, too. I steered clear of the subject of Mrs. Wright, not out of respect for her, but fear for me. An affair with a married man, especially one as fine and charming as Desmond, could only lead to trouble. I wasn't crazy about the idea of becoming a scorned psycho. But I wasn't all that crazy about being with a man who didn't even realize I was alive unless another man noticed me first. So married, attentive man, it was.

"So, we gonna keep being scared on the phone or are we gonna go on and get it out our system?" I asked boldly.

"I think we are perfectly capable of behaving like adults," he said, hesitantly.

"Absolutely," I exclaimed, a little too enthusiastically. That's just what I was hoping for. I began rubbing my mitts together with anticipation.

You ain't shit, I scolded myself.

None the wiser, Desmond asked, "What day is your birthday on, again?"

"June 1st; that's on a Friday."

"Cool. We still have some time. We'll continue this conversation before then. Is that okay with you?"

"Fine with me. I need to lie down, anyway. It's almost twelve o'clock."

"I understand. Same time, tomorrow?"

"Yep. I'll charge up the cordless."

He laughed.

"You're too much."

Smiling to myself, I responded, "I know. Be careful going home, rest peacefully. Speak to you tomorrow."

"I will, you, too, and looking forward to it."

So, Pandora's Box had been opened, and all I could do now was to wait for the mayhem to ensue.

I could sum it all up with a quote from my favorite Genuwine song. "There it is."

It was almost midnight when the call was made over the loudspeaker to begin boarding my flight. The airport still bustled with people making their respective connections, but oddly enough there was still hardly anyone waiting to board the huge commercial airline that would take me home. The attendant explained that it was not unusual to have an almost empty flight this time of evening. After all, it was the middle of the night. She gave me a reassuring smile as I boarded the plane and chose a window seat in the rear. Other than the lights that lined the runway outside, there was only dark-ness as far as the eye could see. I settled back into my seat and closed my eyes, listening to the roar of the engines as we taxied down the runway for takeoff. The hum of the motor was comforting, and I began to doze off at once. The gentle touch of a hand on my shoulder interrupted my thoughts. I opened my eyes to see the handsome pilot standing in the aisle next to me. Though his hat covered most of his face, I could tell from his strong jaw line that he was a beautiful man. He had smooth, chocolate skin, and a smile that lit up the cabin. And the sound of his smooth, velvety voice lit a fire under my skirt.

"Excuse me, miss, but I understand that you are traveling alone on this flight."

"Yes, I am," I answered, slightly startled and confused.

"Well, I've come to guarantee that your flight is the most pleasurable and memorable flight you've ever had."

I smiled at him. "Well, thank you. I'm very flattered, but shouldn't you be flying the plane?"

He leaned over and stuck his hand between my legs. "I guess I should, but if I do that, then what is the co-pilot sup-posed to do?"

I squirmed in my seat in anticipation. Here I was being groped by a strange man that claimed to be the pilot of an airplane that I was flying in. But incredibly, I was aroused instead of alarmed. I grabbed his necktie and pulled his face closer to mine. As he fell toward me, his hat came off. To my amazement, the pilot turned out to be Desmond and he had come to induct me into the mile-high club.

Our welcoming tongues danced to the beat of the song that was playing in our heads. We began to explore one another right there in the back of the plane. The temperature in the cabin seemed to rise as fast as the intensity and the urgency of our lust. Our clothes seemed to melt off in the heat of the moment as I straddled his seated frame.

Desmond entered my flesh with a forceful thrust and my body reciprocated with all the yearning and fire that had been pent up inside both of us for so long. I oohed and ahhed in ecstasy, not caring if the other passengers on the plane overheard my moans.

I rode him, long and hard, faster and faster until my screams became impossible for me to suppress . . .

Chapter 8

Yours for Tonight

I decided not to take the day off for my birthday. Maurice and I had originally planned to go to Myrtle Beach, but he was unexpectedly called away on business. Tomika went with my parents to Philadelphia for a family reunion, and I didn't want to go to the beach by myself. Besides, I could use that vacation time for something better once Maurice came back.

He sent me a dozen roses and some ballons to my office. And my co-workers chipped in and bought me a bottle of Carolina Red wine from Duplin and a gift certificate for a manicure and pedicure at this new day spa in town that I had been talking about going to. Dr. Curtis even took me to Sullivan's Steak House for a long lunch. The day turned out pretty well, considering I still had no plans for the rest of the evening.

I spent the rest of my day trying unsuccessfully to keep my mind on reconciling some past due accounts, and at the same time figure out how I would spend the rest of my birthday. I thought about treating myself to dinner at Zydeco, a hot restaurant and lounge spot in downtown City Market owned by former pro football player, Antoine Harris. It was a laid-back spot for the metropolitan thirty-plus crowd that everybody went to get away from the young college scene that all but dominated Raleigh's nightlife. The music is great, and Mama Harris' wings are good enough to make you think about slapping your own mama. And besides that, the Jus Once Band and Show, my favorite local go-go band, was going to be there. I called Renee to see if she wanted to go with me. Besides liking the spot, she said the name Zydeco and the food made her think of her home in New Orleans.

"What's up, birthday girl" she greeted me in her usual cheery fashion.

"Nothing much. You busy?"

"I guess I should be, but I'm not," she laughed. "What time are you and Reese leaving for the beach?"

"Change of plans. Maurice has to go out of town on business," I answered dryly.

"Girl, what happened? I thought you were having sex on the beach for your birthday."

"I was, but somebody's rims got lost somewhere down in Florida, so he had to go out of town and find them or get some more. He left before the sun came up this morning."

She was livid.

"Maurice is losing cool points with me at a rapid pace, Ericka. That's the third time in a month. I mean, damn, it is your birthday. How he gone make up for that shit?"

"I don't know, man. I'm trying to be understanding because he is working. Now if he was canceling on me to go to bike week, or something trifling like that, then we might have some problems. And besides, who am I to stand in the way of a man that actually wants to work?"

She was unwavering.

"Yeah, but still . . ."

"Renee, shut up. You are giving me a headache. There's nothing I can do about it now. He's gone. And that's not why I called you, anyway."

Sometimes she got on my nerves. She's always got something to tell you about you and your man, yet ain't nothing ever right between her and her own man.

"Well, what do you want, heifer? Boy, you are starting to get evil in your old age."

Sometimes, I could just strangle her Creole ass. I took a deep breath.

"I would check myself, if I were you, chicken. None of these flowers and balloons on my desk came from you. And we been on the phone almost ten minutes and you barely said 'Happy Birthday.' Damn."

She laughed.

"Well, my bad, 'Queen B.' Happy Birthday. What is it that you called me for? And I baked you a cake, so recognize that, heifer."

"Aww, thank you, boo. I called to ask you if you wanted to go with me to Zydeco tonight to see Jus Once. I made the reservations for 7:30."

"That will be cool. Terrell can watch the kids since his boring ass don't never want to do nothing else."

"Why don't you ask him if he wants to come? Can't your mom or your sister keep the kids?"

She replied, "You know he's not trying to go nowhere with me, you, Toy, and Nat."

"They're not going. They both made plans after I told them I was going out of town with Reese. So, it's just me, right now."

"Cool. Then I'll ask Jason to come with us, so you won't have to be a third wheel," Renee added, mischievously.

It was no secret that Renee hated Maurice and had been trying to get her brother, Jason and I together for years. About a year and a half older than she, Jason was a successful contractor who was also an amateur motorcycle racer. Besides being twenty-six and a little young for my tastes, he was the exact opposite of his chocolate sister with fair skin, curly hair, and freckles. But he was a really nice guy, and I secretly thought that he was one sexy, red man. Well, it wasn't really a secret because Big Mouth told him that I thought he was handsome. But it turned out that the feeling was mutual, so now we just flirt and make goo goo eyes at each other. Since we're both seeing someone, we don't go any further. Renee was displeased with the choices that Jason and I made, but she still held out hope that we would dump our respective mates and turn to each other.

"You can ask him, if you want to." I tried to sound nonchalant.

She giggled, "See, you ain't shit."

"Oh, go to hell. Just have yourself and whoever else wants to take part in the birthday festivities at my house at 7:00 sharp. My birthday did not start on CP time, and neither will my party. You got that?"

"Yeah, whatever. Anyway. I'll see you at seven. I'll call you on your cell once you leave the office."

"Cool. I'll holla later."

The day could not have gone any slower. I was tired just from staring out the window, until Dr. Curtis finally came in and told me to go on and enjoy my birthday. I gathered my purse and the balloons and flowers that Maurice sent and headed out to the back parking lot where my car was parked. Most of the other employees had already left for the weekend.

As I approached my vehicle, an unusual sight stopped me dead in my tracks. Someone had left some balloons tied to my car. I looked around the parking lot, waiting on someone to jump out and yell 'Surprise!' but there were only a few other cars in the parking lot.

Strange, I thought to myself as I untied the card from the balloon string. I put all the balloons in the back of the truck and weighed them down as best I could so they wouldn't block my view while I drove home.

I climbed into the driver's seat and stared at the large envelope with my name neatly printed on it. On the front of the card, there was a beautiful picture of a handsome black couple on some exotic beach watching the sunset as they held each other. It reminded me of how I was supposed to be spending my birthday. I sighed wistfully to myself, and as I opened the card, a piece of plastic fell into my lap. It was a hotel room entry card. My heart began to pound as I read the inside of the birthday greeting.

Happy Birthday and Congratulations. I'm happy to inform you that your birthday wish has been granted. Your presence is requested at the beautiful Marriott Hotel on the Virginia Beach oceanfront. There you will spend a magical evening with the man of your dreams. Your instructions are to drive directly to the hotel, stopping only for gas. Everything you need has already been provided and is waiting for you in your suite. Drive safely and see you soon. Yours for tonight, Desmond.

I couldn't believe this was happening. Desmond and I had not continued the birthday wish conversation as agreed, and I had all but forgotten about it. In fact, I hadn't even talked to him since I called him that Monday night after finding out that Maurice had canceled our plans. Desmond had told me that he had a class to attend out of town for his job, and he wasn't scheduled to come back until Tuesday. So, that was it. When I told him that Maurice was not taking me to the beach for my birthday after all, he must have made the plans then. This was just too much. I had to call Renee.

The phone rang, just as I was about to dial. It was her calling me.

"Girl, guess what?" I was dying to tell her.

I told her about my little surprise.

"Oh, my God! That is about the most romantic thing that I've ever heard. Are you on your way, now?"

"Not yet, I barely got in the car. I'm leaving now, though. Are you cool with me breaking our plans like that?"

She sucked her teeth. "Girl, please. Far be it from me to

stand in the way of somebody getting some birthday booty. And in a high-class place like that, too? I'd be mad if you didn't go."

I laughed. For a married woman, Renee was the most scandalous female I knew.

"You mean, you don't have a problem with my traipsing off to have an affair with a married man?"

"Girl, no. As long as it ain't my married man."

"Oh, please. Don't nobody want Terrell's ass, but you."

As much as those two argued, they loved each other to death. It was sickening.

She laughed. "Anyway. I heard that Marriott was expensive. Damned if you didn't hit the jackpot on this one. I knew you were an undercover Ivanna Trump ho. You need to teach me them coochie tricks, so I can get Terrell to come out of his pockets and buy us a house."

"What coochie tricks, fool? I haven't been with Desmond."

"For real? I could have sworn that you already slept with him" For some reason, Renee thought that I was an undercover freak, or something. She thought I had slept with everybody, including her brother.

"Nope, not yet. But call me next week to schedule an appointment for your first lesson," I joked.

"You so crazy, "she replied. "You better put it on him, too, girl. Make Mama proud."

"I'll see what I can do. So, are you still going to Zydeco?"

"Yeah. Terrell still hasn't made up his mind about whether or not he's going. But Jason definitely wants to go, so it may just be me and my brother."

"Almost makes me want to change my mind and go with y'all," I mused.

"You better try to stay where you are, 'cuz Jason wouldn't take you to no Marriott in Virginia Beach, even if he had the money. Trust and believe, you are much better off, even if the man is married."

"Oh, well, didn't hurt to try, I guess."

"Call me and let me know you made it safe. I can't wait to hear all about your weekend."

"Okay."

"Holla at you, later. Be careful."

"I will. And y'all have a good time, tonight, too."

I laid my head back on the seat and closed my eyes. This was almost completely overwhelming. It was kind of like getting to the good part of a Terry McMillan novel. Desmond had actually booked us a suite at an exclusive hotel at the beach. And the note said that everything I needed would already be at the room. Did that mean I had clothes, too? It had to, because I was instructed not to go home and pack a bag. This was definitely soap opera material. I wasn't sure that I was ready for all the drama that was sure to come with it, though. No matter how good everything seemed to be, he was still married, and things were bound to take a turn for the worse.

Why was I sitting here having this tug-of war with this moral dilemma like I didn't create it? I was the one who made the bold proclamation that I wanted him for my birthday like I was making an indecent proposal. I could have lied and said that I wanted an mp3 player or something. Instead, here I was sitting in my car afraid to start it up and drive, like a disobedient kid stalling to avoid a punishment.

If I were being honest with myself, I really didn't have any qualms about going. We always knew that at some point it would all come down to this. My problem was that I knew I was dead wrong for wanting to be with another woman's husband, and yet, I was still willing to go through with carrying on with an affair. I mean, what the devil was wrong with me? Was I that thirsty? He was someone else's soul mate, and entering into an affair with him was enough to put the chances of finding my own soul mate in jeopardy. He wasn't going to leave his wife to be with me, no matter what problems they were having, and getting involved lowered my chances of ever being married. Not to mention, if Maurice found out that I had been seeing someone else, he would never speak to me again.

You mean, like how you found out Maurice had a whole baby when y'all were on a break?

After over an hour of being in deep thought, I realized that I was almost in Suffolk, about sixty miles away. I had about another hour to drive before I reached my final destination. It was too late to turn around, or at least, that was my way of justifying not doing a U-turn right there in the middle of the road. But even after listening to the voice of reason in my head, I had decided that I wanted to go and be with Desmond more than I wanted to do the right thing. I continued on.

As a distraction, I decided to call him at the hotel. He sounded so relaxed. "What cha know good, Birthday Girl?"

"I know that I'm a little less than an hour away from you, right now," I said, as casually as I could muster.

"Glad to hear it," was his response. "You kind of had me worried for a minute. I thought you were calling to tell me that you decided not to come."

"After all the trouble you went through putting everything together, I wouldn't dream of standing you up," I lied.

"I would have understood. After all, it was short notice. I imagine that you probably made other plans after Maurice canceled on you," he said.

"Well, I did, actually, but Renee didn't have a problem with me switching up on her after she found out that her birthday present had been so easily topped," I laughed. "And besides, it's nice to have regained a little bit of the spontaneity of my youth."

"I'm surprised she didn't try to come with you," Desmond teased.

"She didn't, but I don't think she would have turned me down if I had suggested it to her."

Changing the subject, Desmond said, "You must have been speeding. You got here almost 45 minutes ahead of schedule driving in afternoon traffic. It's not even six o'clock."

"No more than usual," I responded. "I left work early."

He had already talked me the rest of the way to the hotel, so I ended the conversation abruptly.

"I'm at the valet. See you shortly."

Chapter 9

Honey, I'm Home!

I was nervous with anticipation and feeling some residual guilt about not turning around and going back home. I shook it off as I started toward the hotel entrance. The lobby was a cheery hub of activity, teeming with weary travelers ready to start a weekend of fun and relaxation. Still others headed out of the hotel, possibly on their way out for an evening on the town. I smiled at an older couple who looked as though they were dressed for dinner. They both waved a friendly greeting. I could feel my blood pressure drop ten degrees. It was going to be a great birthday, after all.

Are you checking in, ma'am?" the desk clerk asked cheerily.

"Yes, Ericka Middleton." Although I wasn't really sure whose name the room was in.

"Yes, ma'am," answered the desk clerk. "Ah, yes, Ms. Middleton. We've been expecting you. Take the elevator to the top floor and take a left. You have your key already, correct?"

I nodded, feeling a little like Liz Taylor, but more like Lil' Kim.

"Your traveling companion has taken care of everything." She sounded a little too chipper for me, like she knew my dirty little secret.

"Good. You'll also need to use your key in the elevator to get to your floor. Let us know if you need anything at all. Happy hour is from five till 7. Here's your drink tickets." She handed me three. "Do you need any assistance carrying your bags?"

I was impressed. Now I felt like Beyonce' coming to meet Jay-Z.

"No, thank you." I patted my purse that hung on my shoulder. "I'm traveling light, this time."

"Very good, then, Ms. Middleton. Let us know if there is anything at all that we can do to make your stay more pleasant. Oh, by the way, Happy Birthday." She gave me a sly wink.

Wow. How did she know? "Thank you . . . thanks you very much."

Sensing my confusion, she explained. "We have been helping Mr. Wright prepare for your birthday almost all day. It's all very romantic. Have you two been seeing each other a long time?"

"Um . . . well, actually, this is my first birthday with him officially." If she only knew.

"Well, I think that's great. You're very lucky."

I smiled at her. "I think so," was all I could think of, in response.

"Well, you have an awesome evening night ahead of you. I hope you two have a great time. Oh, and be sure to act surprised." She grinned widely back at me.

"I will, and thanks for the heads up."

When I got to the room, I took a deep breath to gain my composure and inserted the hotel card in the door. I didn't see Desmond at first, so I called out, "Honey, I'm home!" Then he appeared from the other room in a fitted white tee and a pair of grey sweatpants. I was not ready. I stood in the door, frozen in complete awe.

He walked over and took my hand, gently tugging me across the threshold into the suite. He embraced me and kissed me delicately on the forehead, at which I shuddered. I had never been that close to him intimately. And his lips had never actually made contact anywhere on me before.

"Happy Birthday, Good-looking. Glad you made it safely. Twenty-five looks good on you." He joked.

"Thanks," I quipped. "It looks a little better each time."

I looked around the room. This place was almost the size of my apartment. Everything was absolutely gorgeous. The color scheme was soft neutral, coastal colors. The décor, contemporary beach house, without the cheesy lighthouse paintings and decorations. I had never been in a hotel this fancy. I was overwhelmed.

"This is a beautiful room," I whispered, suddenly nervous again.

Desmond walked up behind me and put his hand on my shoulder. "Glad you like it. Now, let me show me where you'll be sleeping."

He then led me to the bedroom, and on the bed were several outfits that he'd apparently picked out for me for the trip. There was a skimpy two-piece bikini with a snakeskin print and a long, black sarong to cover the bottom. A white tennis skirt with a yellow halter-top, with a strap that went around the neck; a pair of jean Capri pants with a matching camp shirt and red halter shell; and some new platform sandals that I'd not been able to find anywhere; and a deep mauve, silk lounge outfit with a pair of drawstring pants, a tank, and robe. The man had taste in clothes, too.

I picked up the pajamas and began to absently stroke them across my cheek.

"Have you been stalking me?" I asked with faux indignation.

A broad smile came over his face. "Me? Nah, I'm just a good listener." Desmond stood there, quite pleased with himself. And with good reason.

"I'll say you are. Everything is perfect!" Before I could stop myself, I had tossed the pajamas back onto to the bed and flung my arms around Desmond. As I went in for a kiss, I froze. *What the hell was I doing? You just got here and you're already throwing yourself on the man!* I released him and took a step back.

"This is all amazing, Des. But what are we doing here? This isn't right. I shouldn't be here." I looked down at the floor.

Desmond took a step toward me and lifted my chin so that our eyes met. "Ericka don't leave. You're making more out of this than it has to be. We are two friends hanging out for your birthday. It doesn't have to be anything more than that. I promise."

"You promise?" I pouted.

He held up two fingers. "Scouts honor. In fact, I have my own room."

I could help but be a little crestfallen. "You got two rooms?"

"Don't sound so disappointed," he chuckled. "We talk a lot of trash on the phone, but I don't want you to think that my sole reason for bringing you here was to get you in bed. There's plenty of cheaper hotels in Raleigh, if that's all I wanted to do. But you've been a great friend to me over the last few months. Things have been really rough for me, and just having you to talk to has been so helpful. Consider this my way of saying 'thank you.'"

His mood shifted slightly. He became serious, like something else had his attention far away. I wondered if it had anything to do with his marriage. I had so many questions. But now, just didn't seem to be the right time. It never seemed to be the right time. The thought of asking seemed so intrusive.

And anyway, would knowing his marriage was on the rocks make me feel any better about any of this? I knew the answer without finishing the thought. So, I changed the subject.

"Is it time for dinner? It smells so good in here; my stomach has started a protest." I rubbed my rumbling stomach.

"As soon as you get comfortable. Why don't you go freshen up, while I finish up in the kitchen."

"Okay," I replied, excited that my inner fat kid was about to be appeased. "By the way, do I smell crab legs?"

"Yep."

"I don't know if you know this or not, but the best way to a woman's heart is also through her stomach," I said, heading down the steps.

"I know," he called behind him. "I'm way ahead of you."

I showered and lotioned my body with my Bath and Body Works Apple Martini scented lotion, which was my favorite scent. Afterwards, I slid into the new loungewear that Desmond bought. I loved the way silk felt against my skin. I sprayed a hint of body spray behind each ear for the full effect and headed downstairs for dinner.

We had dinner outside on the balcony overlooking the ocean. The food was wonderful, and the view was spectacular. We started out with a salad followed by a yummy she-crab soup. I could have eaten that by itself, had I not known that the seafood boil was to follow as the main course. The meal would not have been complete without a bottle of the finest wine, and Desmond did not disappoint. To go with our meal, we had a chilled bottle of the hood's finest, Andre' champagne. He remembered my fond recollection of my first legal drink, in which I drank nearly a whole bottle by myself. Actually, I only recall the first two sips and even that second sip is a little fuzzy. For dessert, we had peach cobbler with a thick homemade crust and vanilla ice cream.

"Oh, my God, Desmond! Everything is delicious." I gave him a side eye. "You did all this by yourself?"

He gave me a sly grin. "You might say I was the 'project manager.'"

Once we were both stuffed to the point of popping, I suggested that we take a walk on the beach to digest some of the food we had eaten. I went into the bathroom to brush my teeth, while he went to change his clothes. Then, we headed out into the moonlight.

We walked along together in comfortable silence. The sky was dark with only the moonlight shimmering onto the sand, like velvet black light art from the seventies, making a thought pop into my head.

"You know what would have set this night off for real? I asked, absently.

"What's that?" Desmond said, continuing to look off into the ocean.

"A blunt."

His deep laugh pierced the peacefulness of the night.

I looked over at him as our pace slowed, confused as to what was so funny about what I said.

"I learn something new about you every day."

I smiled. "I can't tell you everything all at once. It's too much for you to handle."

"Yeah, you are too much." He continued to laugh but stopped walking and began digging in his pockets. He came out with a lighter and a pretty decent sized blunt.

My eyes grew wide. "You smoke, too?"

"Why is that so hard to believe?"

"I don't know. You just seem like a square to me. Even though we're friends rather than coworkers now, you're still 'Work Desmond' to me, I guess."

Desmond shook his head, clearly amused that I thought of him as a square. He handed me the blunt and I put it to my lips. We looked around for a couple of seconds to make sure no one was around, before he leaned over me and lit the blunt, carefully shielding the lighter's flame from the wind. I inhaled eagerly and began to cough. Then I handed it back to Desmond.

"You okay?"

I nodded, as he took one smooth drag and looked up at the sky, savoring smoke as it entered his lungs. He hit it once more and handed it back to me.

I took another hit and closed my eyes. Desmond Wright was officially the G.O.A.T. He took a beach towel that he brought from the room and spread it across the sand. We both sat down, and I reached for the lighter to reignite our joint.

"So, what do you think about your birthday weekend, so far?" he asked, handing over the lighter.

I gave a slight chuckle. "Shiddd. Best birthday ever." I lit the blunt again, and took another deep drag, and then watched the smoke escape my lips and float out toward the horizon.

"Good to hear," he said. "You know, I've always wondered what it would be like to just hang out and spend time with you. I'm so drawn to your energy."

"So, what is your initial first impression?"

"As cool as I thought it would be. And more so, now that I know you smoke, too."

"Oh? Your wife doesn't smoke?" I didn't mean to ask. It just kind of slipped out. But if Desmond was annoyed by the question, he never let on.

"Nah. She stopped when she decided she wanted to get serious about starting a family."

"Oh." They didn't have kids to my knowledge. Maybe she was pregnant. I shook the thought loose from my mind. *We're just two friends hanging out for my birthday, I thought.* I changed the subject.

"You know, since I was a kid, moving to the beach was always a dream of mine." I thought aloud. "Money was tight then and we could never stay more than a day or two.

But I never thought it was enough time. So, I would always promise myself, 'When I get grown, I'm gonna move here so I don't ever have to leave.'"

We sat quietly for a few minutes, savoring our highs. Then Desmond spoke out of the blue.

"So, when you leaving?"

"Huh? Leaving here? Sunday." The weed had fully kicked in, and my thoughts had started to play in my head like movie clips. It had become a little hard to keep up.

He started to laugh again. Yeah, we were good and high now.

"No, not leave here. When are you leaving to come back here? You said you wanted to move."

"Ohhh," I sang. "That was just me as a kid dreaming. It was a childish thought, really. I can't afford to move to no beach. And besides, black people don't like a whole lot of water."

He shrugged. "We do and we're black."

That's different."

"How?"

"I don't know." I started to shiver, and Desmond put his arm around my waist and pulled me close to him. We continued to stare out into the dark ocean night in silence but now I was focused on his notion that I should entertain the idea of moving to the beach.

"I guess as an adult, I never thought about it as a possibility. That's for white people with money. I've never known any black people who live at the beach."

"So, you don't think you can live here because you don't know any other black people who do?" he asked, thoughtfully.

I wasn't sure how to answer, so I stayed silent to avoid further embarrassing myself. My entire thought process sounded so silly once brought to my attention. Desmond spoke again.

"You know what I've noticed about you? You are really smart. You know how to do so many things. But you make most of your decisions based on the happiness of other people. Don't get me wrong. I get it. Tomika is your baby. You have a responsibility to her. But we've talked about your desire to make a change for a while. But so far, it's just hopes and dreams. Have you ever considered that you put so much time into your relationship with Maurice out of fear?"

I wanted to be offended, but why get mad at someone for telling the truth? But I had to disagree with him about the fear part.

"What would I have to be fearful about?"

"The unknown is enough to scare anybody," was his simple response.

"Does it scare you?"

He turned to me and nodded.

"Well, what do you to fight the fear?"

He paused briefly. "Close my eyes and do it, anyway."

I thought about his answer as we took a couple of more pulls from the blunt and got up to head back towards the hotel.

Once back at our suite, Desmond retrieved the rest of the Andre from the refrigerator and spooned up some more cobbler.

"You want me to fix you some more of this?" he asked when I appeared.

"I don't want another bowl by myself," I responded, "but can I have some of yours?"

He patted the cushion on the couch beside where he was sitting. I sank into the deep cushions, and opened wide, as Desmond shoveled a spoonful of cobbler toward my mouth.

The mood was set. The only light burning in the room besides the candles was the light from the television that was muted, while "Scandalous" by Prince ironically played softly on the stereo. The candles placed strategically around the room seemed to sway to the beat of the music. And there we sat, cuddled together on the couch, staring out of the window, watching the waves crash against the surf. It was the perfect ending to a perfect birthday.

During the course of my birthday celebration, I had put all the apprehension about being with Desmond in the back of my mind. Though it had turned out to meet and exceed any expectations I had, it was still much different than I had expected. It was truly a romantic evening, yet as the evening progressed, romance had not been transformed into regret. As I lay back on the couch being fed peach cobbler by Desmond, I did not feel cheap and slutty like I thought I would, sharing the company of a married man.

We did eventually go upstairs to bed and have loud, back-breaking, spine-tingling sex. I would not go home, feeling guilty at having fulfilled my dream. Instead, we sat, engaging in light, friendly conversation, as we usually did on the phone; nothing more and nothing less.

After a couple more glasses of Andre', we began to nod out on each other with our feet propped up on the coffee table, and our heads touching as we both succumbed to the sandman. The music had stopped playing, and the silence in the room caused me to wake. I yawned, and kissed Desmond on the top of his head. "I think it's way past our bedtime," I said, stretching.

"Yep. I had actually got comfortable here on the sofa with you, though," he yawned. "And now I don't want to sleep by myself."

"You don't have to," I told him, shrugging.

I stood, opening my arms and motioning to him like I was going to try and pick him up. He laughed, stood up, and scooped me up like a sack of flour, and carried me to his bed since all my stuff still littered mine. I squealed in mock protest.

"So, how was your evening?" he asked.

"Perfect. I haven't had a birthday this good since I got those Public Enemy concert tickets when I turned fifteen."

"Wow. I must be the bomb to be compared with Chuck D," he said.

I replied, "Yeah, I would say that y'all are running pretty much neck in neck."

Shortly thereafter, I fell into a dreamless sleep, Desmond lying on his back, holding me in the safety of his arms.

Chapter 10

Sin on Some Level

The entrance of the sun, peeking out from the horizon, disturbed my sleep. I reached out for Desmond, but he wasn't there. I didn't hear the shower running or the television. *That's funny*, I thought to myself. Maybe he went out for a morning run or downstairs to the lobby for something. I lay there for a while; just to rehash the previous evening's events, while they were fresh in my mind.

It had been the best time that I've had in a long time. Desmond took the time to prepare my favorite foods, take me to my favorite place in the world, and make sure that everything was to my satisfaction. He picked out clothes that I adored; he booked the type of hotel suite that I had always dreamed of staying in. He provided the means for me to enjoy my birthday in a way that I would never been able to afford on my own. No expense was spared. Only my likes, wants, and needs were taken into consideration for this trip, and better still, I would go home with a clean conscience, because no intercourse had entered into the equation.

Other than the affectionate hugs and pecks on the lips, there had been no seduction. There had been no long awaited, bed breaking, judgment clouding sex. I had not involved myself intimately with a married man. I had not alienated his poor wife's affection by sleeping with her husband. I had not placed myself in the 'payback zone,' as my mother calls it. I had not cheated on my boyfriend. I was going home with a clean conscience. I could finally exhale completely. Or could I?

If I had not done any of those things, then what was it exactly that I had done? I mean, it wasn't really cheating unless you had sex with the other person. And of that, I was innocent. But I still spent the night with a man who was married to someone else. We had slept in the same bed as a husband and wife would, we just had not consummated the relationship. Didn't that still classify as a sin on some level? Without thinking, I knew it did, but since I had not committed the ultimate disrespect to his marriage by screwing this woman's husband, I decided not to agonize over it, anymore. I had a beautiful birthday with nice gifts and a perfect gentleman to spend it with. Why ruin it?

Speaking of the perfect gentleman, I had become so lost in my thoughts, I didn't notice that Desmond still had not emerged, nor did I hear him come in or leave. Miffed, I rolled out of bed and went to investigate. He was not in the living room or the bathroom. Maybe he went down to the beach for a swim, I thought, as I approached the kitchen. There was a folded piece of paper propped up on the vase of fresh flowers on the kitchen table with my name on it. I opened and read:

Dear Ericka,

I had to go take care of some urgent business at work that couldn't wait until I got back. You were sleeping so peacefully, I didn't want to wake you with bad news, so I let you sleep. Thanks again for a wonderful evening. It was your birthday, but I received the wonderful gift of your company. My goal was to plan an evening that would allow us both to go home with pleasant memories and no regrets. I hope that your wish was granted to your complete satisfaction, and that I was

satisfactory in showing you a good time and making you feel special. The suite belongs to you until checkout time tomorrow. Enjoy yourself. I promise to call you later. Thanks again for a lovely evening, and I'm sorry to have left so abruptly.
—*Desmond*

I looked down at my watch. It was about a quarter till eight. I stretched and yawned loudly. *"Well, I guess it's just me and you."* I said to myself. I went into the bathroom and washed my face and patted my hair. According to the girl at the desk, room service was due to bring up breakfast at nine and I didn't want to scare them away.

I dragged myself out of the bathroom and back to bed. I was going to enjoy this suite as much as I could before I left. I lay back down on the bed and looked out the window. It was a picturesque scene. The light of the sun sparkled like diamonds against the ocean waves. There were boats already on the horizon, and little kids with sand buckets and shovels were already milling around the beach looking for seashells and building sandcastles.

I missed Desmond, but I had to admit that it was probably better that he did leave while I was asleep.

I heard a knock at the door.

"Room service!" was the call from outside.

Chapter 11

Queen for a Day

The room was kind of empty after Desmond left, and I contemplated checking out later that day, but I decided against it. There was nothing special waiting for me at home. Tomika wouldn't be home for another week or so, and Maurice wasn't due back until Monday.

I had retrieved the messages from my answering machine. I received several birthday wishes from family and friends, along with a few annoyed calls from Renee. I had not called her when I got to Virginia Beach like I promised, and she was concerned about my safety, or so she said. I thought that she was more nosey than anything else and decided not to call her until I got home the next day. Maurice had called a couple of times expressing his remorse for missing my birthday. I opted not to call him back, either.

Room service brought up a breakfast fit for a queen. And since Desmond had crowned me 'queen for a day', I happily feasted on the delicious platter of bacon, scrambled eggs, French toast, grits, and hash browns. I washed it down with a cold glass of orange juice and fell into a deep, satisfied sleep for another hour or so. I was awakened by a knock at the door from room service, wanting to clean the room.

I called out to her to give me ten more minutes and went into the bathroom to dress and do my hair. I put on the tennis skirt outfit that Desmond bought, with my bathing suit underneath in case I got the urge to go in the water while I was out. I pinned the top part of my hair up in a neat bun and curled the remaining hair in the back into a flip and allowed it to fall neatly to my shoulders. I gave myself a once over in the mirror, grabbed my keys and purse, and headed out into the crisp, morning air.

I had no clue where I was going. I hadn't really spent a lot of time at this particular beach in the past, so I wasn't sure about the happenings, if any, in the area. I started out in the back of the hotel and strolled aimlessly down the beach. It was a gorgeous day, and even though I was alone, I didn't feel the usual twinge of loneliness that I felt when I was all by myself. Today, I was totally at peace with the concept of singularity, and I even felt a slight spring in my step as I walked along with absolutely nothing on my mind. It was a free feeling that I never remembered feeling before. It was strangely liberating. I tilted my head back and let the ocean breeze kiss my face. I never wanted to leave.

I thought about the conversation that Desmond and I had the night before about my dream of living close to the beach. *What exactly was I afraid of?* I didn't have a degree yet, but I had plenty of marketable skills in the medical field that would allow me to land a job anywhere. The cost of living here was not much different from home, which was already high rent district without the luxury of a neighborhood body of water. Tomika would love being able to be within walking distance from the beach. She loved the water as much as I did. And it was only a little over three hours from home, so I could come back as often as I liked. It was something that I always wanted to do, so why couldn't I just move?

I strained my brain to come up with an excuse. Well, the only thing I could come up with was the news report I had seen on television the previous week about the National Weather Center's prediction of a very active hurricane season for the next ten years. But mostly everyone that lived on the eastern seaboard experienced a hurricane every now and then, and I was no exception. Hurricane Fran almost blew Raleigh off the map in 1996, and the floods of Hurricane Floyd almost washed us away a couple of years after that. But Virginia Beach rarely received direct hits from storms.

The only other reason I could think of for not moving was that I did not want to leave Maurice. Deep down, I really loved him and hoped that someday we would make a life together. But hell, I couldn't even get him to pass up hanging out with those thugs at the shop to go with me to the movies, much less follow me to live at the beach. As much as I worked at our relationship, I couldn't deny the fact that Maurice didn't seem as interested in holding up his end as I would have liked. And as much as I tried to make excuses for his lack of attentiveness to me, I was more apprehensive about us than I was happy, most of the time. He was partly responsible for me being where I was on my birthday, in the situation I was in, at that very moment.

Those two reasons aside, I had really been feeling the urge to move in favor of my situation. I was struggling to make ends meet in a dead-end job, living in a city with an extremely high cost of living. And there was really nothing to do in Raleigh that didn't require money or a partner, neither of which I really had access to. Most of my girlfriends were married, getting married or playing house, so I never really had anyone to hang out with anymore. I had been in this rut for a long time but hadn't really had a clue how to dig my way out.

I began to make plans I continued down the boardwalk. There were plenty of schools in the area I could attend should I decide to go back. Tomika and I could both make new friends and become official beach bums. Maybe I would even open my own beachfront hotel or buy some condos to rent.

The possibilities were endless. Maurice could decide whether or not he wanted to visit. I was becoming tired of playing the game by his rules and I still was not completely satisfied with our arrangement. I would never be able to control his actions. But I could control my own. I decided to pick up a local newspaper before I left and search the Internet for a job and place to live the moment I returned home.

Taking control of my destiny felt good, so I returned to the hotel and jumped in my car to take a ride. As I rode along, I looked around at the place that I had decided to make my home. People riding around on scooters and golf carts, children carrying pails and shovels. No one seemed to have a care in the world. I pictured myself sitting outside on my deck reading a book. I couldn't wait.

I continued to ride along until I got to the city of Norfolk. The downtown area directly faced the riverfront with modern neighboring condos, shops, restaurants and hotels. I got out and strolled along the riverfront watching people shop at a Farmers' Market as a man strummed an upbeat folk song on his guitar. People lined the river's edge to board the Spirit of Norfolk for an afternoon cruise. The toot-toot of the trolley horn reminded me of an old Mr. Rogers episode. Yeah, this spot would be perfect for Tomika and me. After a full day of exploring every square inch of Norfolk's downtown scene, including the zoo, a few consignment shops, and a bakery with cupcakes to die for, I rode through some of the neighborhoods. Just as I had decided to head across the bridge in Hampton, I stumbled on the cutest neighborhood right on the bay called Ocean View, home the world's longest fishing pier. The area was just like any other, with a grocery store and small shops, banks, restaurants. Even a liquor store. The only difference was when you came out of the store and looked across the parking lot, there was the Chesapeake Bay right in front of you. I had never been in a real beach town before. Every beach I'd ever gone to was surrounded by tall hotels and was crowded with people. Here, regular people were going about their day as if there was no water in sight. *How do people do this?* I thought. I vowed to figure it out.

I circled the area, writing down the numbers of realty companies in front of apartments. I had lunch at this black-owned spot called My Mama's Kitchen. The food really tasted like someone's mom was really back there, although it was run by two guys around my age. I took in the scenery, particularly the sexy red guy behind the counter with the freckles and muscles. I inhaled that shrimp po' boy like I hadn't eaten in days and took some wings to go for later. Then, I made a mental note to try another place further up the road called Shipwreck Sally's and headed back to Virginia Beach. Once back at the hotel, I lugged my bags of souvenirs up to my room and set them on the floor outside the door while I fiddled around in my purse for my room key. I could hear the television playing before I entered the room. I didn't think I had left it on when I left. I peered around the door looking for signs of an intruder. To my surprise, Desmond lay on the couch, snoring lightly.

I stood in the door for a moment, watching the rise and fall of his chest as he slept contentedly. I smiled to myself, pleased he had come back. He had apparently been asleep for a long time because he didn't stir when I came in, nor as I made noise rattling all my bags as I set them down. He looked so peaceful lying there, like he was right where he was supposed to be. Except he wasn't. Not with me, anyway. I walked over to the sofa and eased down beside him. He woke up and inched his body close enough to me to lay his head in my lap. My body shuddered involuntarily as he wrapped his arms around my waist.

"What are you doing back here?" I asked, lightly stroking his hair. "I thought you had a pressing emergency."

He closed his eyes and smiled. "Actually, my business was in the area. Got finished earlier than expected, so I came back. Why? You wanted the place to yourself?"

I laughed. "Not at all. In fact, I'm glad you're back. I enjoyed myself today. But it was nice to come back and find you here."

"Cool. What did you end up doing?" he wanted to know.

Desmond listened attentively while I ran down my adventures of the day. He smiled when I announced to him that I had decided to seriously look into relocation.

"I may have some leads on a job for you," he said, thoughtfully.

"That would be amazing! You know someone that works in the medical field?"

"It's not medical. But I still think you might be great at it."

I wasn't sure about that. I'd done other jobs, but I wasn't that confident about stepping outside my comfort zone. And I told him as much.

"Now, you know the only other place I've ever worked besides a hospital or doctor's office, is driving a forklift at a warehouse with you."

Desmond left his comfy position in my lap and stood up to head into the kitchen.

"Exactly. I've worked with you before so that's how I know you'd be perfect for the position."

I turned my body toward his direction from the sofa.

"Is it driving another forklift?"

"No," he answered, grabbing a bottle of water from the fridge. But he didn't offer any other information.

I shook my head. "You got enough confidence in me for the both of us. I wish I was as sure that I could pull some of this stuff off as you think I am."

He looked me and shrugged. "Do it, anyway."

It was still kind of early, so Desmond and I went back out to explore together. We drove across the Hampton Roads Bridge Tunnel over to Fort Monroe and walked along the water there. The tiny former military base is surrounded by a moat and connected to Hampton by a bridge. It was a quaint little space with housing, a restaurant and bar on the water, and even a lighthouse. We left there and went into downtown Hampton, having dinner at Mango Mangeaux, another popular black-owned spot. The cuisine was New Orleans style, and its claim to fame was the owners being on the show, Shark Tank. I had the Salmon Lafayette and Desmond had the Bayou Steak and potatoes. I made a mental note to bring the girls here for a mango martini. After dinner, we crossed the street to get a couple of hunks of cakes from Scratch Bakery. After all, it was my birthday, and no birthday is complete without cake. And they did not disappoint. That red velvet melted on the tip of your tongue.

Back at the hotel, music was playing so we ordered a couple of drinks from the bar and danced before heading out the rear exit to the beach to smoke the rest of the blunt left over from the night before. Then we came back and danced until the music stopped, finally going upstairs to bed around three a.m. Luckily, we had a late check out, since I awoke to a slight hangover. Unlike the previous morning, I woke up to find Desmond propped up on his elbow, watching me intently. When I opened my eyes, he smiled and planted a kiss on me that made me drunk all over again.

"So, did your birthday weekend meet your expectations?" he asked, pulling me closer.

I squirmed with nervous anticipation.

"And then some. Thanks for everything. It was amazing.

We lay in bed and cuddled for about an hour until we both got hungry. We got out bed, dressed, and went downstairs to have breakfast in the hotel restaurant. From there, we headed back to the beach, where we lollygagged for the rest of the morning. Later that afternoon we said our good-byes, held a deep kiss for way too long, and reluctantly returned to whatever reality awaited us at home.

Chapter 12

Ghetto Heaven

I sweat all the way to Virginia Beach dreading the moment that we both gave in to the desires of our flesh to roll around in the bed screaming and moaning in the throes of passion. Yet, after all that time we spent together, we were able to control our hormones and avoid the inevitable. And to tell the truth, it really wasn't that difficult. It was almost like best friends spending the weekend together out of town. Accept we shared a bed, and we kissed a couple of times. Other than that, he had been nothing short of the perfect gentleman.

I exhaled; a great weight having been lifted off my shoulders. I thought that I would be well on my way to hell, by now, after having betrayed my boyfriend and sleeping with someone else's husband. But we both woke up respecting one another in the morning, and I was free and clear of all wrongdoing. Right? I mean, I had not actually done the deed, but could I actually call myself innocent? I thought about Maurice down in Florida feeling bad for missing my birthday, while I shared a room and a bed with another dude without a second thought about him. Even if Desmond and I hadn't actually had sex, Maurice would not have appreciated me sharing space with another man like that. That fact alone made the whole weekend wrong, no matter how clean we managed to keep it. Why was I doing this mess, anyway? I thought about the up-and-down yo-yo of a relationship that Maurice and I had struggled to maintain for the last six years . . .

We originally met at *Hot Wheelz*, his tire and rims business that he owned near downtown. "The Shop," as Maurice and all the regulars referred to it, was the hangout for anyone who had or wanted baller status. Anyone that pushed a tricked out, overpriced luxury vehicle hung out there. It was the place to be and to be seen. Natalie, my best friend since we were kids, had just started dating Tarik, Maurice's best friend. That day, I went with her to the shop to meet Tarik.

In one of his songs, Tupac wondered if heaven had a ghetto. Well, if it does, there has to be a rim shop there called Hot Wheelz. And I was in ghetto heaven looking around at all the phat rides and cute guys dressed in the latest urban gear. It was summertime and a bunch of guys were standing out in the parking lot admiring a new Ninja motorcycle that one of the fellas had bought. But all attention turned to us when we got out of the car wearing our booty shorts and tight tops.

A big dark-skinned guy stepped away from the bike and embraced Natalie, and they began to converse. While she was talking, I scanned the group of guys, as they stared inquisitively back at me. Not knowing what else to do, I waved and said hello to the group. They all nervously muttered a response. I thought it very odd that the so-called 'players' suddenly clammed up when they were in the presence of a fine woman. And as far as I was concerned, I wasn't even in their league.

Their attention was not taken for long because soon, they went back to their original preoccupation with the bike. I looked around the parking lot at all the cars. There was hunter green and a navy-blue Lexus in the parking lot, as well as a black BMW, 740iL. There was also a brand-new gold suburban and a white Ford F150 truck. Standing in the parking lot was like being at a car show. All the cars had been carefully detailed and gleamed in the afternoon sunlight. They all had tinted windows and expensive tire rims, which had probably been purchased there.

In complete contrast to the expensive vehicles parked on the outside of the establishment, the shop itself was actually a very modest place on the empty corner of an old neighborhood shopping center. The name of the business along with the logo was painted in the window, and inside, there were samples of the different wheels and car rims displayed randomly throughout the shop. There was no cash register that I could see, nor did there seem to be any type of order in the place. The counter was littered with books and magazines about car detailing and accessories. The walls were a gallery of pimped out cars and scantily clad women. A couple of stools sat in front of the counter next to a bubble gum machine that appeared to have some very old bubble gum in it.

I doubted much business was being conducted in the cluttered little space. It had to be a drug front. At the least, a hang out spot for dope dealers to sit around a floss for one another, while they talked sports and told lies about their female exploits. Like the barbershop, almost. Whatever it was, I was completely here for all of it.

As I stood there taking in everything around me, I couldn't help but notice one guy in particular among the group. He was a lean 6'2, with a slightly muscular build. The first thing I noticed was his kicks. Sneakers have always been a great passion of mine, and he had on the flyest pair of Nikes I had ever seen. He had on long denim shorts and red graphic tee with a matching baseball cap. He had broad shoulders and beautiful, golden-brown skin, like a cookie fresh out of the oven. His hands were well manicured and clean for a man.

He also sported a dazzling diamond pinkie ring and a thick Cuban link bracelet.

He was urban, but not hood. Meticulously neat, like, his pants weren't hanging off of his butt and no out of shape Afro or braids in serious need of tightening up. And he wasn't flashy like the other guys, weighted down by ridiculously large Jesus pieces and huge rocks in their ears. Hell, his ears weren't even pierced. And he wasn't loud and animated like he was trying to be seen. Although it was his business, he allowed the other guys to hold court in his place while he hung back, doing more listening than talking.

His physical appearance and gentle mannerisms were working together to win me over. But there was one thing in particular that grabbed and held my attention to him, besides his shoes. That horribly beautiful scar taking over almost the entire left side of his face. It began just above his eye and ended just below his jaw line. It was the marking of a burn of some sort, and I shuddered at what hell he possibly suffered to get it. I also couldn't help but wonder if he had been bullied because of it.

The other side of his face was quite handsome, once you over the first shock of his unfortunate disfigurement. Maybe it was the intrigue of it being some bad boy badge of honor, like a bullet wound or a tear drop tattoo. Or maybe it was a feeling of overwhelming compassion I felt imagining all the physical and emotional pain he suffered as a result. But there was something about that scar that drew me to him and wouldn't let go, no matter how hard I tried not to stare. I did my best to play it off like I was looking around at everything else while I secretly took sneak peeks at him.

After Natalie and Tarik had been talking for a few minutes, she realized that she had just left me standing there.

"Oh, excuse my rudeness," she apologized, "This is my friend, Ericka. Ericka, this is Tarik, and this is Maurice." She did a general wave in the direction of the others. "And these are the guys."

I extended my hand to Tarik. He was fine, too. No scar, but fine, just the same.

"What's up, E? It's nice to meet you. Like Nat said, this is my man, Maurice." He nodded to the guy with the scar that I had been secretly admiring. "He owns this fine establishment. And this here is Will, Dre', Sonny, and Black." He pointed in the direction of each of the guys as he introduced them.

I shook Maurice's hand and nodded to the other three.

"Whose bike?" I asked.

Maurice spoke. "Mine. I just got it yesterday."

"That's tight," I said, admiring the bike. "I want me a bike so bad."

His interest was piqued.

"You ride?"

I nodded. "Learned when I was in the military."

"Oh, you were in the military? Say word. Army?"

"Yep," I beamed. "Still in the National Guard."

"You an Army chick, huh? So, you can put some hand-to-hand combat moves on me if I get out of hand," Maurice joked.

I chuckled. "I'll let you slide, if you take me for a ride sometime."

If I didn't know any better, I could have sworn he was blushing.

"Yeah, I'll take you riding. That ain't no problem. In fact, why don't you step into my office?"

I looked over at Nat, who was grinning like I was her kid and had just won a medal at school. She elbowed her boyfriend, Tarik in the ribs.

The other guys had broken off from us and started talking amongst themselves, not paying us any further attention. Or so I thought.

As we were walking off, I heard Will call behind us, "You

better had taken her in there because I was getting ready to give her my card!"

I leaned into him and whispered, "If he had, I wouldn't have taken it."

We both laughed and went into the shop.

Once inside and out of the scrutiny of the rest of the group, I gently probed him for information.

"You sure your girlfriend won't have something to say about you riding around other women?" I asked slyly. I would hate for my phone number to fall into the wrong hands."

He smiled. Nice teeth. "Nah, it ain't nothing like that."

"And I don't have to worry about anybody trying to run us off the road or shoot me off the back of your bike? I'm not trying to be the subject some crazy woman's jealous rampage," I pressed.

I was playing. But I was so serious. I wasn't so naïve that I didn't think he didn't have at least one woman stashed somewhere around. He was handsome and he looked like he did okay for himself, even in that ransacked shop. Scar face or not.

"No wife, girlfriend, or baby mama drama?" I asked, directly.

"Nope, no wife, no girlfriend, and no kids. I mean, I got friends, but you know, nothing serious."

Men kill me with that 'I got friends' crap. It's an insurance policy that covers them being able to sleep with everybody without having an infidelity charge brought against them. You can't cheat if you're not committed. I'd normally cut the conversation short after hearing such crap, but my attraction to him and that motorcycle wouldn't allow me to walk away. So, instead I shrugged it off, took the business card like a champ, and wrote down my number on the back of another card.

"Since you're single, can a girl get a date sometime and a motorcycle ride?" I asked, boldly.

He smiled, again. "Sure. We can go on a date on the motorcycle, if you want to."

I laughed.

"I'd like that. I hope to be hearing from you soon."

"You'll be hearing from me tonight."

Maurice held the door for me, and as I exited the shop. I gave a smug look to Natalie and Tarik, who were still grinning like fools.

As we drove off, Natalie was like, "You go, girl. Maurice has got it going on. That was his blue beamer in the parking lot. He is paid."

"Girl, that flashy stuff don't impress me. I mean, it's nice. But you can look at all them Negroes and tell they are a bunch of headaches. Flossing around town with expensive cars with big rims. I'll bet their girlfriends don't know they're single."

Natalie laughed. "Nope. I've seen a gang of girls at that shop. But I've never seen anybody's girlfriend."

"Not even Maurice's?" I asked, eyeing her suspiciously.

She shook her head. "No. He's really single. Divorced, actually. You like him, huh?" Again, with the grinning. I rolled my eyes but couldn't suppress the smile invading my own lips.

"What can I say? I like my men laid back. That calm spirit was pulling on me hard. There's just something about him."

She agreed. "Yeah, even with his face messed up and all, he's still fine."

I shrugged. "You forgot. I worked in a military hospital. Disfigurement don't bother me. He's still a man under all that scar tissue."

"Yeah, Ericka. But he's not a patient," reasons my superficial friend. "This is a dude you're checking for. Y'all will be in public together."

I thought about that for a minute. Would we get a negative reaction? Would people stare at us? Or did other women see his scar as an attraction like I did? He probably got more play than all those other guys put together. I bet that he was the biggest dog on the planet. I wondered if he had always had the scar, and if he ever got teased about it. The guys at the shop didn't seem to make a big deal out of it, but then again, guys were not as vain about appearance as females.

I asked Natalie, "What happened to him?"

"I'm not sure," she answered. "I heard he was hit by a car or something like that when he was little. It looks like he might have got drug or something."

"Damn. It looked like it must have hurt."

"Yep. You're a good one, because I couldn't be that close. He's cute and all, but you would kiss him?"

She didn't say it mean, she was honest, but I still thought that it was a messed-up thing to say. But I didn't say so.

Instead, I said, "Come on, Nat. It ain't that damn bad. It makes him look mysterious. Like a rival drug gang tied him up and dunked him in some boiling hot water to make him tell them where the stash was. In fact, when we get together, that's what I'm gonna tell people when they ask."

Natalie laughed until tears stained her cheeks.

"Everybody? Including your parents?"

"Yeah," I scoffed. "What they gonna do? I'm grown."

"Your dad's gonna shake his head because he already think you crazy. And your mom is gonna report you to CPS and take Tomika from you."

I feel like people put way too much emphasis on looks. Even the most handsome man's looks can be wiped away in an instant by an accident, a bullet, or anything. Besides, beauty can hide some ugly characteristics underneath. I had a sorry baby daddy to prove it.

Seriously, though," I asked Natalie, "what would you do if Tarik got caught in the face by a bullet and lived. You know that his face would be jacked up, but would you not want him, anymore because of it?"

She thought for a minute.

"Well, yeah, I would still be with him because I loved him. Changing his face on the outside doesn't stop him from being Tarik on the inside, you know."

"Yeah, I know. But think about what you said about Maurice. Are you saying that you wouldn't have got with Tarik if his face was messed up like Maurice's?"

"Well, yeah. It's different because I already know Tarik."

"So, are you saying that people like Maurice are not worth getting to know because his face is jacked up?"

She was getting flustered.

"Maurice is different because he still looks good, even though part of his face is messed up."

She wasn't making a bit of sense and we both knew it.

"So, what you're saying is that Maurice is an exception because only half of his face is jacked up and the other half is still fine."

She became indignant. "No, that's not what I'm saying at all! I just meant . . . I don't know what I meant. I swear, Ericka, you should have gone to law school. You have an answer for everything; or at least a question."

We both laughed.

Then she posed a question to me.

"Well, be honest. Would you have given Maurice any play if his whole face was messed up?"

I thought about it for a minute. "Honestly, I couldn't say for sure. It would depend on how bad it looked. I mean, let's keep it real. I don't do charity cases, and even though I might be a little lenient in the looks department, you still have to have some, however limited they might be."

"So, that would make you just as superficial as the rest of us, huh?" she laughed.

"Nope. You said it yourself. Maurice is cute, but his face still looks pretty bad on that side, no matter how cute he is. And you admitted that you wouldn't have talked to him. Though, I'm not claiming to be self-righteous by a long shot, you have to admit that I can look over flaws that other women can't."

"That's true. Remember that guy you dated that time that only had one leg? You are a regular equal opportunity employer."

We both cracked up at that.

"Girl, that boy could do things with me that other men couldn't do," I chuckled.

"Like what?" she wanted to know.

"Girl, he had mad upper body strength. That boy would bench press me like free weights at Gold's Gym."

Natalie was in tears.

"For real?"

"Yep. He was the bomb in bed."

Chapter 13

You Don't Know, Do You?

It was pitch black outside, so I couldn't see a thing as I knelt down on the ground to unzip my sleeping bag. The flannel sheet I layered it with this morning made it nice and cozy to slide into as I settled in after finishing a long, grueling guard duty shift. 'Dang, it's tight in here,' I thought, struggling to re-zip my bag. That sheet I put in here must have been thicker than I thought.

My scream was muffled by the generator that roared outside of my tent. I felt someone or something reach across me trying to finish zipping up my sleeping bag. Panic-stricken, I desperately scrounged around in the dark for my rifle, which I had leaned against my pack on the ground beside my make-shift bed. But the only thing I could come up with was my flashlight. Frantically, I snatched it on to see who or what had decided to share my bed tonight. I couldn't afford to miss by swinging at it in the dark.

Trembling, I slowly raised the flashlight toward the interloper, terrified of what I was about to unveil. A buffed male figure took shape in the light. I gasped.

"At ease, soldier," he whispered seductively.

I sighed heavily with relief.

"Desmond, you scared the hell out of me! How did you get in here?"

"I am wherever you will me to be, my love."

He reached around me again and in one smooth motion, zipped the bag over both our heads.

"No wonder this thing felt so small," I giggled. "I thought I had gained some weight."

"Your sheet made it warm, but I'm here to make it cozy. C'mere, let's start a fire."

Desmond reached down to help me unbutton my pants. As he did, my hand accidentally brushed against a very impatient erection.

"My, aren't we standing tall this evening?" I asked, smiling broadly.

"Yep." He nodded downward. "He is standing tall, and you are looking good."

I moaned with pleasure as he began to nuzzle my neck.

'Good thing that generator is so loud,' I thought . . .

I was jolted awake by the shrill ring of the telephone.

"Hello?" I mumbled, sleepily.

"Happy belated birthday." The voice on the other end was dripping with sarcasm. "You finally decided to come home, I see."

It was Maurice and he was pissed. *Damn.* I wasn't expecting him home until tomorrow night. I had completely forgotten about him until now. I tried to play it off.

"Hey, baby. Where you at?"

"I just left the shop on my way back to your house for about the tenth time since yesterday."

Uh-oh.

"I thought you weren't coming home until tomorrow, sometime."

"I wasn't, but I felt bad about canceling your birthday plans at the last minute. So, I called you back to ask you if you wanted to meet me at Myrtle Beach for Bike Week and celebrate. But I couldn't get in touch with you. You weren't answering the phone at home, or the cell phone. I figured you were mad at me, so I came home."

Guilt loomed over my head like a dark cloud. Since when did he care whether or not I was mad with him? If I had sat home all weekend, he would not have shown his face in Raleigh until late tomorrow. He just came back to make sure I hadn't found someone else to spend my birthday with. I resented the thought and felt smug about having done just that.

"I wasn't mad. I just found something else to do."

"Oh, yeah? Like what?" he asked, cautiously.

"I ended up at the beach, anyway." There was no need to say what beach. That would just bring up more questions. "I had intended to come back yesterday, but what for? I was only going to end up being bored by myself since everybody left me. So, I stayed the whole weekend. No sense moping around here by myself."

That shifted some of the guilt back on him.

Well, who did you go to the beach with?" he wanted to know.

You don't know, do you? "With myself," I lied. "Who else did I have to go with?"

"Well, why weren't you answering the phone? I could have stopped through on my way back from ATL. You didn't even have your cell on. You must not have wanted to be found," he said, suspiciously.

It pleased me to have him worried for a change.

"I didn't. I was considerate enough of everyone else's plans that I didn't make a big deal out of not having anyone to spend my birthday with. So, why would I want to spend my whole weekend talking on the phone to people who could have easily been there with me? You cancelled on me, remember?"

"Sorry, babe. You know I didn't want to be away from

you on your birthday. But Sonny would have been trying to put me out of business if I didn't track down those $10,000 spinners for his Escalade in time for the Essence Fest. You know how that nigga love to floss. Besides, if I hadn't tracked the order down, I wouldn't have been able to get your present. You know it's been kind of tight around the way, lately."

He had a point. Business was sluggish until the weather warmed up. Nobody wanted brand new chrome rims scratched up and dirty from ice and salt brine from driving in bad weather during winter months. And nobody was outside to notice your new 'twenties' in January. But soon as spring made an appearance, people started going to the car wash to get rid of the winter dirt. Then, it was time to go buy your baby a new pair of shoes and high side around town. Or for the less car savvy person, guys put new tires and rims on their cars to give it a more stylish look.

"It's all good," I said, squashing the subject. "So, where're you on your way to, now?"

"I'm coming over to see you, baby girl. And suit up. We going for a ride."

I jumped up like a little kid and started scrambling for my riding boots. Reese and I rarely went out together, but it was always an adventure. He hung around guys who drove big cars and motorcycles, threw around money like rich people, and stood around and looking arrogant and aloof when women approached. A bunch of wannabes, if you asked me. But if I didn't have a kid with responsibilities and bills, I'd be right there in the mix. Except I wouldn't be one of the thirsty chicks sweating some dude on a bike. I'd be the one chick with a bike doing burnouts in the parking lot. And all the dudes would be sweating me.

"Where're we going?" I asked.

"You'll see," he said. I'll be there in five minutes."

As I was tying my boot laces, I heard the doorknob turn. I had given Maurice a key a while back, but for the most part, he usually still rang the doorbell unless he was coming over late at night. He started doing that after I ran into him in the hallway one night on my way back from the bathroom. He almost gave me a heart attack.

"Where you at, Mama?" he called from the door.

"In my room," I called back.

Maurice appeared in the room looking good in an orange and blue Sean John tee shirt, knee length jean shorts, and an orange baseball cap. Damn, orange is his color. He came up behind me as I stood in the mirror, putting my hair in a ponytail. He squeezed me tight around the waist and covered my eyes with his hands.

"How you get in here? I told you not to come right now, because my man was on his way over. You gone get shot," I teased him.

He chuckled. "Yeah, right. I ain't worried about that dude. I got something for him if he comes up in here while I'm in here."

I turned around to face him with a mock look of surprise. "Oh hey, baby. I didn't know it was you."

"Whatever, man," he laughed. "You ready to go?"

I nodded and followed Maurice out into the yard.

Once outside, I noticed that there were two bikes on the back of his truck parked in my driveway. I recognized one of them to be his, but I had never seen the other one before. It looked to be brand new. It was a brand-new Kawasaki Ninja, red with metallic gold flecks in the paint.

"That other bike is tighter than yours, babe. Where'd it come from? Is somebody putting it in the shop to sell?" I said, admiringly.

"Oh, you like that, huh?" he asked, with a sneaky look on his face.

"Hell to the yeah! I'd ride that bad boy till the wheels fall off," I said, not taking my eyes off the bike.

Maurice could hardly contain himself. "Happy Birthday to you . . ." he began to sing.

I stared at him in disbelief. "Why are you playin'?" I asked.

"This is you, Ma," he confirmed.

"For real?" I leaped into his arms and began to scream. I couldn't believe it. Maurice had bought me a motorcycle for my birthday. I had always dreamed of having one, but didn't think I would be able to afford one until Tomika had grown up and moved out.

I scurried into the back of Maurice's truck to get a closer look. It was beautiful.

Maurice walked over to the side of truck, enjoying watching my excitement over my gift.

"Oh, thank you, baby! Thank you so much! I love you!" I leaped out of the truck bed into his arms again and began showering him with kisses. He relished his newfound affection.

"You're welcome. Sorry it's so late. I bought it from my boy in Atlanta, but he wasn't able to bring it until Monday. So, I met him in South Carolina so I could get it to you on time. I know you like them with a little kick, so I got you this Ninja hoping that you won't kill yourself."

"Boy, this is more than I ever hoped for, right here." I squeezed him again. "It could have been a Big Wheel, as long as it was from you."

He was blushing behind his shades. One of the things that attracted me to him from the very beginning was his low-key disposition. Maurice had really outdone himself this time, but he acted as though he had just picked me a dandelion.

Where did all this come from all of a sudden? Was it possible that he knew where I had been the whole weekend? Nah. If he did, I would've gotten a knot on my head for my birthday instead of a motorcycle. I wasn't expecting any of this, and now I felt really bad about what I had done.

"So, you didn't go down to Atlanta to track down no missing shipment, huh?" I asked.

"Naw, girl. Sonny's cheap behind ain't gonna spend ten thousand dollars on nothing, especially in my shop. That fool will argue over the price of an air freshener to hang in the dash of his car."

I laughed. "That's true."

"Kenny was actually supposed to bring me the bike, but he called me and told me that something came up and he wasn't going to be able to come on Friday like we planned. And I wanted you to have it on your birthday, so I lied to get out of our plans so I could go to South Carolina Thursday night and have it on your doorstep when you got home from work Friday. Then I was gonna take you back to Bike Week so we could ride and hang out together. But you didn't come home."

Damn! I missed the opportunity to ride with no helmet. I wondered if he could see the word 'guilty' written in cursive repeatedly all over my face.

"If I had known all that I would've just stayed home for my birthday."

"I know, but if I had told you, it wouldn't have been a surprise. But you got it, now, and I'm glad you like it. And you better stop kissing me like that before I pick you up, take you back in the house and make you thank me now instead of later."

I wiped the lip gloss off his mouth with my thumb and took a step back.

"So, you ready to ride, or you gonna stand there and look at it on the back of my truck?" he asked.

"Hell, naw! I'm ready to go!" I answered, exuberantly.

I got my motorcycle's license last year when Maurice got tired of me complaining about him never having time to ride me around. In an effort to shut me up, he offered to let me ride myself around on his bike as much as I wanted, if I took the two-day course at the DMV and get my license. The following week I signed up and passed the class. It was easy, considering that I'm the biggest tomboy on the planet and I've always ridden mopeds, dirt bikes, go-carts. You name it. I can ride it. He was shocked when I burst through the shop door with diploma and license and reluctantly relinquished his key. That had been over a year ago, and up till now Tomika and I rode his bike more than he did.

Maurice unhitched the motorcycle and rolled it down the ramp. I could hardly contain myself as I put on the black helmet I found in the passenger seat of the truck. It was the same color as the bike, and it had "E. Middle" airbrushed in cursive across the back.

I hopped on my new toy and took off like a shot to the top of my street. I made a right turn and tooled around the block to get the feel of my new ride. The engine growled like a ferocious tiger as I gunned it out on the open road.

When I got back from my test run, Maurice was busy making some adjustments to his helmet straps and putting on his riding gloves. He looked up as I rode up beside him and shook his head, smiling.

"Just couldn't wait, could you? I thought you had left me," he laughed.

"Naw, baby. I wouldn't pass up a chance to cruise these streets with you."

Chapter 14

His-and-Her Ninjas

We hit all the usual spots where people liked to cruise and park. First, we rode down New Bern Avenue to the Blue Whale car wash, the biggest car show in town during the summer months. It was on one of the main thoroughfares in the city and the perfect place to show off a new toy. There, we picked up a couple of shop regulars who were cruising on their bikes, then we all rode out to the BP station on Capital Boulevard, a popular hang-out spot for riders. It was right at dusk when we got there, and motorcycles had already lined the entire front end of the parking lot facing the street.

I spotted Natalie, who had ridden with Tarik on the back of his bike. Her eyes got real big when she saw me ride up beside Maurice.

"Girl, where'd you get that bike from? It's tight."

"Thanks, girl," I beamed. "This is my birthday present."

Her mouth dropped. "Your present from who?" she wanted to know.

I looked over at Maurice, who had gone over to talk to Tarik and a couple of other guys I didn't recognize.

She grabbed my hand and pulled me off to the side. "Girl, Reese bought you that bike?" she whispered, loudly.

I nodded, grinning widely.

"When did he give it to you?"

"He bought it by the house a little while ago. I haven't been too long got back in town," I told her.

"I know. I've been calling you all weekend. And so have Renee and Toy. Where you been? And don't lie because I know Reese had to leave town on business Thursday," she probed, accusingly.

"You must have been talking to Renee. Damn, she got a big ass mouth."

"Well, she wouldn't tell much. All she said was you decided to go to the beach at the last minute. She said that I would have to get the rest from you."

"She did right," I said.

"Well, who'd you go with?" she asked, softly.

I pulled her away from the growing crowd in the parking lot.

"If you tell anyone else other than Toy, I'm kicking your ass, for real," I threatened.

"Who else would I tell?" she asked, innocently.

"Your man, that's who," I knew that she sometimes confided in Tarik about the stuff that just we girls talked about. A couple of things that Renee had told us about her husband in confidence had come back to me from Maurice.

"Girl, you know I don't roll like that. Tarik and Reese are too close for me to be running my mouth about stuff like that. We're girls. You know that."

"I know. I trust you." I let my guard down for my friend. "I went with Desmond."

"You went with Desmond?" she shouted.

I grabbed her by the arm and squeezed it really tight. "Damn Nat, why you gotta tell everybody?"

"Oww!" She yelled, and then cupped her hand with her mouth.

"Sorry," she mouthed. "Desmond took you to the beach?" She stared at me in disbelief.

I peeked over her shoulder to make sure no one was listening. Maurice and his friends were checking out my bike so hard that they didn't notice that we had walked away from the group to engage in our own conversation.

She spoke again. "You talking about fine ass, married Desmond that you used to work with at Global Technology?"

I nodded, trying to hold in the smile that was invading my lips.

"Y'all have fun?"

"Yep."

"Was it good?"

"What?"

She smiled, knowingly. "Don't play dumb with me, chicken. You know what I'm talking about."

I couldn't help but laugh. "I don't know. It wasn't like that."

She got mad. "Stop lying. See you make me sick, Ericka. You tell Renee all the good shit, but you don't never tell us nothing."

My girls are so jealous of each other and always accusing each other of favoritism. If one person got let in on any type of info, you'd better not forget to tell the other two, or you got accused of playing favorites. Truthfully, I love them all the same. I'm an only child, and the three of them were the sisters I never had.

"That's because you jigs run your mouths too damn much," I joked. "But seriously, we didn't do anything."

"I don't believe that."

"Well, believe it. He was a total gentleman the entire time. We had a nice hotel suite, and he paid for everything. But he didn't ask for none, and I didn't offer."

"Damn," she said, wistfully. "Maurice must have sensed

that shit, because he bought you that motorcycle. Does he know you been anywhere?"

"Yep. He's been trying to call me the whole weekend, too."

"I know he was pissed off at you."

"Oh, well," I said, indignantly. "All I do is sit around and wait on his black ass when I'm at home; bout time he sat around waiting on me for a change."

"I heard that, girlfriend. I ain't mad." She quickly changed her tone. "Here they come," she whispered.

Maurice and Tarik approached, followed by Will, Sonny and their girlfriends.

"You think you can run with the big dogs, now, don't you, E?" Sonny asked.

"Boy, I was running with the big dogs when you were still a puppy," I said, matter-of-factly.

The whole group fell out, laughing.

"I told Reese that he making the rest of us look bad. Now we got to get bikes for our women so we can keep up with y'all," said Tarik, squeezing Natalie's shoulder.

"Yeah, nigga," said Will. "Whoever heard of his-and-hers Ninjas? Who you think you is, Jay-Z, or somebody?"

"Shit," said Sonny. "I ain't buying no bike for Kim to be riding with some other cat and his crew at bike week."

Kim swatted at Sonny. "Please, like y'all don't be riding females when we ain't nowhere around."

"I know that's right," I chimed in. "I saw a picture of some trick on the back of Sonny's bike at bike fest last year, and I know for a fact that Kim wasn't even there."

"Man, I think you better shut up while you got time," laughed Reese. "But I tell you what. If I see some man on or near that bike, I'ma shoot both of y'all off. I don't care where you at." He said, pointing at me.

"You ain't got to worry about that. I won't ride anybody except the little one," I said.

I cut my eye at Natalie, who was watching my expression at Maurice's comment.

"That's right. It's partially hers. I even got her a helmet with her name on it."

"Damn, nigga! Now, you making it a family affair. You killing us," Sonny balked.

Maurice laughed. "Man, chill. Ain't nothing wrong with it. Anyway, we came over here to see if you player hatin' women wanted to go to Bahama Breeze to eat."

"Whatever, Haters," said Natalie. "Let's go." And with that, we jumped on our respective means of transportation and headed to the restaurant.

I was having a great time. It wasn't very often that I got to hang out without Tomika in tow or a self-imposed curfew hanging over my head. It felt good to be part of some adult action for a change and not have to worry about always being on the clock as a parent. Her father had not seen her in over five years. So, she really was never in anyone else's care other than my own unless my mother volunteered to baby-sit. Tomika was the light of my life, and I enjoyed being a mother. But it was times like this that sometimes I missed being that free-spirited chick I was before I became somebody's mama. Words like 'spontaneity' and 'freedom' were just not in my vocabulary, anymore.

After dinner, the gang all went their separate ways and Maurice, and I went back to my house. It was such a beautiful night, and the stars lit up the sky with such brilliance, that we decided to sit outside and star gaze rather than go in the house. I went to the refrigerator and got the bottle of wine that the girls at the job gave me. I took the bottle and two wineglasses back to the front porch where Maurice had already perched. He lit a small votive candle, and it flickered on my patio table.

"You gonna have a drink with me?" I asked, partially in jest. Maurice was not a drinking man, which was something else that I liked about him. I had only known him to drink one other time since I had known him. And even then, it was a measly wine cooler that made him so drunk, and he ended up falling asleep on the floor in the living room. I wasn't much of a drinker, either, so it wasn't a big deal to him.

"Yeah, pour me a little bit in a glass," he said, smiling.

I raised my eyebrows. "What? You gonna have a little taste?"

"Yeah, why not? It's your birthday. And besides, it ain't nothing but some wine."

I poured him a glass and held up mine to toast. We clinked a toast, and I watched him down the little corner I poured in his glass, feeling as though I was contributing to his delinquency.

"I'm sorry I ruined your weekend," I said sincerely. "If I had known that you had all these plans for me, I seriously would have stayed home instead of going to the beach. I just went out of spite."

Maurice continued to look out at the street as he spoke. "Man don't sweat that. All I care about is whether or not you like your present. So, what, if you didn't get it on your birthday?"

"I loved it, Reese. I never would have guessed that you'd get me a motorcycle. I guess you really do love me, huh?"

I glanced sidelong at him to see what his reaction would be. The real surprise would be to finally get him to say it.

He chuckled, "Yeah, I guess it does, to hear you tell it."

Close enough.

I got up, went over and flopped down in his lap. "I knew it," I said, kissing him on the forehead. He wrapped his arm around my waist and buried his head in my chest. I stroked the top of his head and closed my eyes. A wave of euphoria swept gently across my total being. Why can't things be like this all the time?

Anything I could possibly think to say in such a perfect

space would kill the moment. So, I enjoyed it in silence. How sweetly strange that he would pick this particular time in our relationship to get soft on me. I silently wondered whether I was finally wearing him down. I spent six years trying to get him to commit. And when he finally agrees, it's mostly on his terms. I was still unhappy because nothing had really changed. But at least I had the man. That counted for something, right? Then I go traipsing off to spend the weekend with a married man, with Maurice's nonchalant attitude as justification. Now, suddenly Maurice had decided to develop a sweet spot. I didn't know whether to be happy or pissed off.

The infernal beep from his Nextel two-way gave me my emotion of choice.

Here we go, I thought.

"Yeah?" he barked into the receiver.

"Yo, man. Where you at?" the voice on the other end wanted to know.

"Poole Road."

"Oh, you coming through, or what?"

Maurice paused for a second. I held my breath.

"Yeah, I'll be through there. Where you at?"

I exhaled loudly, defeated.

"We at the shop, waiting on Tarik," the other voice answered.

"Alright. Y'all go ahead, and I'll just meet you down there."

"Alright. Peace." And they were gone.

I got up and started into the house.

Maurice was puzzled. "Where you going?" he wanted to know.

"Well, since you about to jet, I'm going to bed," I said, not turning to face him.

"I wasn't about to leave now, E. Dang, why you getting mad?"

"I'm not mad. I thought this was our night. I thought you were staying."

He followed me into the house.

"I am staying. I'm just going to hang out for a minute, then I'm coming right back. Why you tripping?"

"We just got here. What's the hurry?" I complained.

"I told the boys that I was gonna meet them at Thirty Plus." He sensed the disappointment I felt. "I won't be gone long. I promise I won't be long."

"Alright then," I muttered.

I picked my battles with Maurice, and this was one I knew I couldn't win. There was no such thing as a total package when dealing with men. You either got the love and affection from the broke ones. Or the ones that don't have time for you that try to buy you. It was simply asking too much to want it all. Suddenly, it occurred to me. Bitch, you did have it all this weekend. Even if it was just a birthday wish. The thought of my weekend with Desmond brought a faint smile to my lips.

He put his arm around me and gave me a stiff peck on the lips. "I'll call you when I'm on the way," he said. "Oh, and before you go to bed, put on that little thing I like for you to wear." He smiled, mischievously.

"Be careful," I managed to muster, instead of 'Go to hell.'

After he left, I took a hot shower and went to bed. My thoughts drifted back to where I had been the night before.

As though he'd been reading my mind, the phone rang.

"Hello?" I whispered.

"Hello to you." Desmond's voice was low and seductive. I immediately forgot about being mad.

"What's up, Stud Muffin?" I asked, giving him my own temporary pet name.

"Now, I've been a lot of things," Desmond began, "but I've never been a Stud Muffin."

We both laughed. At least somebody enjoyed my company.

"From what I saw over the weekend, you were a stud

muffin with a tall glass of whole milk on the side," I embellished.

I could hear him blushing through the phone.

"You know, you really have a way of stroking a man's ego."

"Because you're always stroking the hell out of mine," I answered.

He laughed again. Once again, Desmond had come to save the day.

We spoke on the phone for almost two hours, during which time I half-heartedly hoped that Maurice would beep in on the other line to tell me that he was on his way back from the club. He didn't.

After we I hung up, I took the half-empty bottle of wine back out on the porch to drown my sorrows. I re-lit my candle and set it down. It was after midnight and the activity had died down on my street.

I plopped down in my chair and struck another match to light a blunt from the stash Desmond gave me at the beach. I took a long drag and held it in so the smoke could fill my lungs. I exhaled slowly through nostrils and watched the smoke flow into the air before dissipating into the night.

I took a few more puffs, pouting as I stared out into space, before deciding that Maurice was not coming back to my house after he left the club.

Part II
Summer, 2009

Chapter 15

(Maurice)
I Know I'm Not Innocent

I know Ericka's probably cursing me out right now. I told her I was coming back to her house after I left the club. Truth is, I didn't even go to the club. I went to the shop and messed around for a few. Then I went to my own crib to think.

She swears I'm some kind of player with a bunch of women on the side. But really, I ain't never been strung out for no woman like I've been for her. I just can't get used to being stuck up under no female all the time at this point in my life. It's not that I don't love Ericka or nothing like that. That's my ride or die and I'll go to war over that one. But I'm just not ready to give up my space. Yeah, we've had our little share of drama just like everybody else. And because of that, I've got to be sure in my own mind that when we settle down it's going to be for keeps.

Besides, no matter how much you think you know a woman; she always got a trick up her sleeve. I don't care how much of a player a brother thinks he is, he won't ever have as much game as a woman. I know I'm not innocent by a long shot, but I know for a fact that Ericka Middleton got more game than me and all my boys put together. Not to say that she's running it on me, either, but I'm not trying to put myself out there to be hurt again. I've opened up more to her than I have any other woman. But I need more time. And the way things have been between us lately, it seems that time is something that I don't have a lot of.

Ericka's been sweating me about putting more time in with her. She says that all I want to do is hang out with the boys at the shop. But what's wrong with that? I mean, I could see her tripping if I was out there tricking with some other female. But she knows where I am. And she knows it's all about her. It's almost like she wants me around so she can put on a show for her little girlfriends. So, everybody can see she got a man, too. It don't make sense. She ain't wanted for nothing since we been together. I'd give her and little Tee Tee the world on a string, and she knew that. So, I like to kick it with the boys? I'm still taking care of home.

I guess I shouldn't be mad, though. She ain't always been needy. She used to not care what I did. But I messed around and got too comfortable. Dipping back and forth with my ex and got caught up. Now, she be trying to have me in a chokehold so tight, I can't hardly breathe. So, now I'm pulled between wanting to live my life and do what I want like I've been doing and giving in a little bit for the sake of being in love. That might sound like some old punk shit, but love is a word I didn't even think would ever be coming out of my mouth again until I met E. Middle.

When Ericka drove up to my shop with Natalie in them tight Calvin Klein cut-offs and that belly top, I thought she was just another chick. There was something about her, though. Females come in my shop every day. And they don't want to buy no damn rims, or get their car detailed, unless they can sucker me into doing it for free. I call them 'shop rats.' You know the same thing as a 'hood rat' but they just got a different name because they hang out at my place of business instead of in the hood.

They come in here switching their hot behinds in here in front of all my boys thinking they gonna get paid because my crew travel lavish. They see the jewelry around their necks and all them carats in their ears and these chicks swear that they've hit the jackpot. But with all the traffic I get in and out of my shop, if them niggas really had any intentions of spending any money, I would be paid enough to open a bigger shop and expand my business into car repairs, too. Hell, I could have bought E. a beamer for her birthday instead of that damn death trap motorcycle that she been talking about since I met her.

Anyway, I just took her number because the fellas would have been talking junk if I didn't take it. It's like an insult to their manhood if they can't trick some broad into giving them their phone number when they go somewhere. They think I'm soft because I don't jock women like that. But I'm not a thirsty dude, even with my messed up like this. It don't stroke my ego to have chicks in my face all the time. Women know how to boost you up to get what they want from you, no matter what they think about you.

I found that out when I got to junior high and started noticing girls for the first time. I was the man in sports. And my mom and sisters were always gassing my head up, so I've always been confident. All the little girls wanted to be close to me at school and call me on the phone. You know how it is. But the accident changed all that quick.

When I was twelve, I was riding my bike to go meet some of my friends to play ball. Some fool in a big, old Cadillac came out of nowhere and plowed right into me. Somehow, me and the bike got caught under the car. Among other things, I got third degree burns on my face and neck from the muffler and tailpipe. I stayed in the hospital for a whole year. They grafted skin from places I didn't even know I had skin.

Overall, they did a pretty decent job, but I'll have this scar on my face for the rest of my life. They probably could have made it look a lot better, but that was in the early seventies, and I guess technology wasn't what it is now. The doctor told me that they could work miracles with plastic surgery now. But after all this time, it doesn't even matter to me no more. So, what you see is what you get.

When I got back to school the next year, people at school acted different. Now, that I think about it, I was pretty freaked out about the whole thing, too. It was months before I could look in the mirror. My real friends were cool about it after they got over the initial shock. But you know how kids are. I got clowned big time. They had all kinds of names for me that I still can't bring myself to repeat after all these years. And the girls that would talk to me, wouldn't do it in public. Only on the telephone or after school when everybody else wasn't around.

It hurt, so to deal with it, I got heavy into sports. I was All-American all the way through school. I played basketball, football, baseball and I ran track. By the time I got to high school, it didn't matter what I looked like anymore, because I was the one carrying all the teams to the championships every year. I had more girls than LL Cool J. All the girls that snickered and called me ugly me behind my back was all up my grill. All the girls that didn't want to be seen with me in public suddenly wanted to be my date for the Homecoming dance. Man, women learn how to be scandalous early. But my mama didn't raise no fool. There was no way I was going to give none of them no play after being treated like a wet food stamp all. I had too much class to just diss them outright. So, I was just cool to everybody without playing anyone as a favorite. Besides, my parents didn't teach me to dog no women.

My family showed me a lot of love during my healing process. I'm the youngest of ten and the only boy. So, my sisters always treated me like I was their child instead of their brother. They took turns caring for me while I was in the hospital. They would sit with me all day and baby me, corn rowing my afro and reading Ebony and Jet magazine to me from cover to cover because I was too weak to open my eyes and look at the pictures. When I was finally released, they all went shopping and bought nice clothes to help boost me up since my confidence had been shattered along with my looks in that accident.

Going back to school was hard. I was thirteen and kids can be monsters. Even some of the kids that I was cool with went along with the other kids that picked on me. Only my boys Will and Tarik remained true friends during that time. They even took up for me when they heard other kids teasing. But it still didn't make my feelings hurt any less. I used to come home from school and cry because I just wanted to look normal again. My mom used to come to my room and try to cheer me up on those extra rough days. She would say, "Boy, I don't care what them other no count kids at that school say. You still my child, and your daddy and me didn't make no ugly kids. You hear me?"

My sisters loved to boost my head up. They'd act like I was Malcom-Jamal Warner in a Gordon Gartrell shirt when I got dressed for church and stuff like that. You wouldn't think that compliments from a dude's sister would have much weight. But I guess it's true that if you keep telling someone the same thing over and over, they start to believe it. Because pretty soon, all the love that my family lavished on me went straight to my head. I'm not stuck on myself or nothing, but I got mad confidence. I don't get excited when a fine woman step to me.

Even though my being good at sports caused me to get much play with the ladies, the only one that I took seriously was my ex-wife, Toni. Toni was different from the others because she wasn't flashy like the other chicks that used to always rub up on me after the games. I ain't never been too keen on women that show a lot of skin. I mean, I ain't no punk or nothing. I'll look, but when it comes to having a woman in my life it's certain things about her that I'm just not interested in sharing, you know? Toni was classy and was kind of quiet. Her parents kept a tight rein on her, so I knew she wasn't really out there with other dudes. And I liked the idea of marrying a virgin.

I loved Toni. I can't even lie. And she was good to me. She was supportive during my athletic career. I played semi-professional football for a couple of years after I graduated from junior college. She came to all my games, and she never tripped about me coming home late or being gone for weeks at a time. Toni cooked almost better than Moms did, and she kept the house so clean I would scold myself for leaving shit on the floor. And sometimes, deep down inside, I still miss her every now and then.

The biggest problem that I had with Toni was that she was just too damned perfect. And when you got that much of a woman, sooner or later you'll find out that stuff just ain't gonna balance out. Toni was the most passive lover I ever had. Don't get me wrong. Believe it or not, I can count on one hand the number of women I been with intimately. I told you, I wasn't raised to be no dog. But even with the limited experience I had in the bedroom, I knew that it just wasn't popping off like it was supposed to.

Toni had a banging body, and I got a rise just watching her do everyday tasks like mopping the floor. She was my queen, but I couldn't get her to understand that it was okay for her to open up to me as her husband. I never had the problem waiting till after we were married. It was just that afterwards, she never learned to put her trust in me when it came to sex. It was a trip, because I'm not even a freaky-deeky type brother. I wasn't trying to stand her on her head or beat her or no crazy shit like that. She just never learned to enjoy us being together.

I tried everything. I did the rose petals on the bed, the scented candles, you name it. But I couldn't get her to open up to me. And since we couldn't really consummate the marriage, we were never really able to connect as husband and wife. And since we really didn't have a relationship, I just stopped coming home. I had even stopped playing ball so I could spend more time with her and develop our relationship because I wanted to start working on a family. But once I came home for good and got a real job, things became even more strained. She started making up excuses not to have sex with me and when she would have sex, she would just lay there. I felt like I was screwing a corpse.

The last time I tried to be with her, I felt her body shivering under mine. I thought that maybe she was finally starting to come around a little. I was smiling on the inside because I thought that maybe this was the night that we could start having a real marriage. Thinking that progress was being made, I rose up to look into her eyes. It was then that I noticed that she wasn't throwing it back to me like I thought, but she was crying. Man, my little man just shriveled up and went on to sleep. I didn't get mad, but I just wanted her to talk to me so I could help. This was, after all the woman that I was gonna have to spend the rest of my life with, and I had no intention of stepping out on her when she had all I needed at home.

But I could never get her to tell me what was wrong. She just cried in my arms, and I held her until she fell asleep. After that I started sleeping in the spare bedroom. I thought that maybe I was putting too much pressure on her, and that she would come to me when she was ready. Well, about five months later, she did come to me; with some divorce papers. Shortly after that, she moved back home to her parents, and I had no choice but to move on.

I have a couple of theories why Toni couldn't sleep with me. At first, I thought that maybe she had been molested or something. But I could never picture her daddy doing nothing like that to her. He just didn't fit the profile, whatever that would be. And I can't recall her ever having any other men that would have access to her in her house like that. The only other thing that I could figure out was that it was worse having to look at my gruesome face that close up every night than she thought it would be. I really believe that she couldn't bear to be that close to me. I never asked her, though, because I was afraid that she might confirm it; afraid that she might be bold enough to admit it to me.

At first, the thought kind of bugged me to think that my own wife couldn't stand the sight of me. Why would you even get with me if my looks were going to bother you like that? She never let on that she felt like that when we were dating, because we were always comfortable around each other, and had a good relationship. But I guess with all the going out to movies sitting in the dark and having to come straight home after dates never prepared her for having to look at me all day and all night, too.

Okay, maybe I might sound a little paranoid to you, but I'm real. I've been living behind this face for almost twenty years. So long, in fact, that no reaction that I get from people seeing me for the first time surprises me, anymore. I admit my looks probably do take some getting used to. But the fact that my own wife may not have been able to get used to it don't make a brother feel good. But we all got to do what we need to do to get along in this world, and whatever Toni or anybody else thinks about how I look don't stop me from thinking that I'm still a handsome devil by my own standards and they can't take that away from me. Hell, it really doesn't stop women from approaching me, anyway.

I started kicking it with Cassandra after that. Cassandra was a rebound woman, and she knew it. And I hate to say it, but I fell for her too. We saw each other off and on for about two years. But I was scared of getting my heart broken again, so I wouldn't let her get close to me. Or rather, I let her think that she wasn't getting next to me. We had a good time, but I just wasn't trying to be serious with anyone else right then. But I wanted her to stay around until I got ready. But she didn't know that I had plans to get serious with her.

After about a year, Cassandra got tired of waiting and broke it off. She started seeing this other cat, and then I met Ericka. After that, we stopped seeing each other at all. About two years later, she called me one night after she had a fight with her boyfriend. She told me that she and that other dude was over and that she wanted to get back with me. At that time, Ericka and I had decided that we were going to be just friends (or rather I told her that I just wanted somebody to kick it with every now and then, and she agreed) so I went ahead and laid it down with Cassandra. I told myself that since Ericka went along with me so easily about being friends, maybe she wasn't really serious about me. Plus, I still kind of wanted to be with Cassandra. So, we got busy. And she got pregnant.

I was loving the fact that I was going to be a daddy. I was with her through the whole pregnancy. I was at every doctor visit and asked more questions than she did. I wasn't going to leave the mother of my child out there like that with my baby. I was going to support her because I wanted my son to have a good start like I did. Hell, I didn't come from no broken home. But Cassandra took it that we were going to get married and be a family. Eventually we probably would have because I wasn't trying to have any other man around my son, but me. I just wasn't ready right at the same moment when she was ready. My divorce from Toni was still a fresh wound. I tried to tell Cassandra that she wouldn't never have to worry about nothing as far as her or the baby was concerned. But hormones do strange things to a woman's mind when she is carrying a baby. Dealing with Cassandra's crazy ass during her pregnancy gave me a taste of why so many brothas leave their girlfriends and their kids. But it don't justify it for me, so I wasn't going nowhere.

Cassandra kept stressing me about moving in with her and getting married. When I told her I wasn't ready to get married, she broke it off with me and told me that she wasn't going to let me see my son. I know we had a kid on the way and everything, but I was doing everything that a man is supposed to do in a situation like that. I gave her whatever she asked for. I helped her with her bills and kept food in her hungry ass mouth because I didn't want my son's stomach to be growling inside hers, you know? And it pissed me off that she would insult my manhood after all the stuff I was doing for her just because I didn't want to get married. And it wasn't like I told her crazy ass that I wouldn't marry her at all; just not when she wanted me to. Shit, any other man would had told her to come and see them for a DNA after the baby was born before she could even get a dime.

I don't understand why women always try to play the marriage card, anyway, like that's going to make everything all right; knowing full well that if you're already having problems it's just going to make it worse. I mean, I'd already been hurt before so I would have never done nothing intentional to hurt her. And I always did right as far as my seed was concerned. But it wasn't enough. It never seems to be enough for some women. If I had married her knowing that I wasn't ready to be her husband and it didn't work out, I would have still been the bad guy. She wasn't going to let me win no matter what, so I made my decision and rode it out.

She threatened to move back to Maryland where she was originally from, so I couldn't see my baby every day and she would do stupid stuff like change her appointment time so I would be showing up at the wrong time looking stupid. She flat out gave me the wrong time for the ultrasound appointment; the one when you find out the sex of the baby. By the time I got there with my video camera, they told me that she had asked not to let anyone in the room. When I would go to her house to check on her sometimes, she would try to make me give her some, and then get mad because I wouldn't sleep with her. She would scream and cry, getting herself all worked up. She would throw shit like she was having a temper tantrum. I knew that wasn't good for the baby, so I would get pissed off and fly off the handle. Then she would lose it and scream and wile out for hours. And I would just sit there and listen in case she decided to try something crazy. I didn't want her to hurt herself or the baby. I didn't know what to do. But, despite all that, I was in the delivery room when my sons entered this world and haven't been too far behind him since.

After Cassandra had Lil' Reese, her hormones calmed down a little bit, but things were never really the same between us. I can't really explain it to you. I guess after going through all those changes, she just drained me of every emotion that I could have felt for her. I could never hate her, because she was the flower who bore my seed, but too many things had been said and done between us in those nine months and damage was done that could never be fixed. Our split was peaceful, and we are still cool to this day. We raise our son together like two adults should and we respect each other.

I guess she really was ready to settle down because she got with this cat she met at church, and they got married. I'm not going to lie. My feelings were hurt behind that one. I couldn't see another man being daddy to my son when I'm not around and getting to be around him more than me. I was jealous so then it was my turn to trip. San and I started arguing and I told her that she was stupid for marrying somebody else when she knew I would always take care of her no matter what. I told her that if anything happened to my son under that fool's care, I was going to kill both of them. Now

I realize that I was wrong. And even though I would prefer that Lil' Reese only had one male figure in his life; things have turned out pretty decent, so far. Sometimes I wonder if I could've avoided all this from happening if I had just married San from the beginning. I wonder if everything was all my fault for making the wrong decision when it came to my son's mother. I guess I'll never know. I always think about something Ericka says all the time. "It doesn't matter what choice you make, as long as you're able to live with your decision." And so far, this has been a pretty livable decision. I'm not cool about not being able to have my son around me every single day, but then again, if I had chosen to be with his mother, I would have lost Ericka.

But ever since my ex-wife, Toni, and me split up I've been sort of apprehensive about committing myself to another relationship. 'Apprehensive' is one of them one hundred dollar words I got from Ericka. She's a freaking egghead. I call her 'Encyclopedia Brown.' I love to tease her about using all them big words, but on the real, it's a big turn on for me. When E. hits you with one of those words you can tell she's not doing it to try to impress you or talk down to you. That's just how she talks. I used to try to trip her up by asking her what stuff meant all the time. And she would rattle off the definition without blinking. Now when I ask, I'm trying to learn something. My baby is smart and when you dealing with somebody of above average intelligence, you got to be willing to grow and learn. And keeping up with E. Middle is a full time job as it is without being a dummy on top of it all.

Like I said, earlier, when I met Ericka, I just thought she was another wannabe shop rat. She drove up with my best friend, Tarik's girl, Natalie one day. I saw her checking me out, but there are not too many women that don't stare at me for some reason or another. There are actually some women who are attracted to this damned scar on my face. Some chicks tell me that it gives me a thugged out look. And thug niggas seem to be in, right now. Go figure. So, when she kept ducking her eyes when I would look her way, I didn't think much of it. Or rather, I was trying to play it off like I didn't have the urge to grab her and bite her on the jaw. She was a straight dime piece and those Calvin Klein cut-offs she had on was showing her booty no mercy.

Ericka's got it going on, inside and out. She's a five-foot, six-inch tall Amazon. She's not a model type chick with a pale face and no booty that dudes seem to go for nowadays. E. is a real woman with big, childbearing hips and a firm back yard. She's got big legs and tight calves that cut up the booty just right when she wears high-heeled shoes. She's got milk chocolate skin and those little bitty tight eyes that close when she laughs and makes me weak when she looks at me. She's a wholesome beauty. She doesn't wear make-up too much and when she does, it's usually only eye liner and Chap Stick. She's got thick, shoulder length hair that she wears in a pony-tail, which I love. But what I love even more is that she didn't have to tussle with the pony for his tail. I can't stand women that wear weave. You can look in her face and tell that she's a deep thinker because she has that serious look. It's not a hateful look like a chicken head with an attitude, but a no nonsense air, like she about business.

My girl is a tomboy at heart, so she always got on jeans and sneakers. But she don't be sagging like the fellas. Her jeans always fit like the skin on a banana. And we got the same taste in shoes and shirts. It ain't nothing for me to look up and see her in one of my tee shirts or swallowed up in one of my throwbacks. It's a good thing we don't wear the same size shoe. She loves men's clothes, but her tomboyish look brings out her feminine side. It's kind of like watching your girl walking around the house in your pajama top and no bottoms. And unlike a lot of girls, rarely does she walk around with her butt hanging out; except those Calvin Klein cut-offs. I can't even get her to wear them, no more.

Before I saw her looking at me I wanted to step to her, but I knew at least two of them buzzards already that was standing outside the shop with me that day already had her locked in their sites as soon as she got out of the car. And didn't none of them really have no game, anyway. So, I wasn't gonna play myself by trying to out talk the rest of them. Not that I've got all of this tight game, either, but niggas that hang out in my shop talk too damned much. They play themselves by saying the stupid stuff they be saying. But when she walked up on me and started asking me questions about the engine and rpm's and stuff like that on the bike, I knew she wasn't no ordinary woman. I got nine sisters and don't none of them know the difference between a go-cart and a lawnmower, much less a Harley and a Ninja.

Even though Ericka didn't front about wanting to ride on my motorcycle, she also had a real interest in what kind of power it had and the new stuff that had been added to the new year model. It was funny hearing a female talk like that. Most chicks would have been asking stupid questions in an attempt to act interested so they can get in good. And they try to be slick and feel you out to see what they can get out of you. Stupid stuff, like 'how you gonna take somebody for a ride when you only got one helmet?' But baby girl loves a bike and she didn't have any problem telling me what she wanted from me. And when I told her that I would take her for a ride, all I was thinking about was how good those Calvin Klein cut-off shorts was going to look spread out behind me as I zoomed down the street. I didn't know all I was getting at the time.

Like I said before, not only is Erica fine as all outdoors, but she's smart. E. knows a little about everything so she can mix it up with people that most ordinary folks can't. She spent time in the military, so she's been around all types of people. That doctor that she works for is always taking her to these medical symposiums (another hundred dollar word) that they have at these high dollar restaurants like Angus Barn and Second Empire. Ericka will go in there and mingle with all them doctors and surgeons like she's got a medical degree herself. Then, she'll leave them and stop by the shop and shoot the shit with me and the boys like she ain't never left the hood.

And to top it off, my baby takes care of her baby all by herself. Tomika's nine and her father hasn't been in her life since she was two. The dude don't even pay child support or nothing. I just can't understand how any man can know he got kids in the world and act like they don't exist. I couldn't handle not being able to see my son every day. That's my dawg.

I remember one time I was at the Blue Whale cleaning my car. I push a white BMW 740 with twenty-inch deep dish chrome dips. Anyway, this cat who was checking out my ride happened to see Lil' Reese's car seat in the back. He was like, "Man, I don't be riding around with no car seat in my whip. Mama has to ride with that thing in her car." Like he ashamed for people to know he got a kid. Lil' Reese and Tomika won't ever cramp my style like that. If anything, I get more play with my kids in the car with me than I do when I'm by myself. Not that I'm looking for any play, right now, but I'm just saying. And yeah, I said 'kids.' I love Tomika just like she's mine. But anyway, he pissed me off and I let him know right then and there that I didn't have no problem rolling with the car seat. Niggas need to grow up and learn what it really means to be a man. When I do marry Ericka, I'll be the daddy that Tomika's sorry sperm donor could never be and we all going to have the same last name. Forget that step-crap. I hope that one day she'll call me 'Daddy' instead of Uncle Reese like she does now. I always wanted a little girl. I haven't told any of this to her mama, though. If I did, she would really start stressing me out.

It didn't take long for E. and I to get tight. We have most

of the same interests. A chick that has a genuine interest in cars, motorcycles, and sports is hard to come by. And it's even harder to find one that's got the same taste in kicks. It's weird because Ericka is more like my running partner than my girlfriend. It's almost like kicking with Kenny or Tarik; only she's softer and easier on the eyes. When she comes around the shop, she doesn't make the boys uncomfortable by acting all stank like somebody did something to her. She'll come in and start kicking it with the homies and talking shit, just like she one of us.

Sometimes she might even go in the Boom-Boom room and shoot dice, which tripped everybody out at first. I got a little area in the back of my shop that looks like a closet, but it opens up into an extra space that I let the boys gamble in after I close the shop. They don't even mind her shooting with them. And she be winning, too. But I had to make her stop going back there because a couple of dudes got robbed a while back leaving the shop. We used to just play for fun, but lately, a lot of money has been exchanging hands back there. I had to start packing some heat after that first stick-up and I don't want Ericka to get rolled on because some thug thinks she got some dough on her.

On the for real, for real, I ain't really all that cool with Ericka hanging out at Hot Wheelz, period. It's not like she spend a lot of time there, or nothing, but it's not the kind of place for a woman, especially my woman to be hanging out. Most of the dudes that hang out at the shop are cool, but they sneaky and scandalous, just like these chickens. I know they be looking at E. and trying to holla at her when they think I'm not paying attention. She handles herself well, so they don't mess around with her too much. Plus, she's too independent to run to me every time somebody steps to her. I haven't even said anything to her about any of this because then she would think I don't want her around because I'm trying to hide something and start popping up all the damn time. We been going through some things lately and I ain't trying to add fuel to the fire. And since she don't really hang around a lot, now it's easier just to act busy when I want to get her to leave. She says she don't like to be a distraction while I'm working, so she'll usually bounce. Or I just give her something to do. She's been helping me with some admin stuff in my office, so I just send her back there. Once she starts doing something, she don't stop until it's done, so that keeps her out of the limelight for a while.

That's another thing I like about her. She isn't really a nuisance like other chicks I've run into. Most of my boys can't stand to take their girls nowhere. In fact, they can't even stand to be around them most of the time because women expect to be right up under us every waking moment. They always want us to be up in their face, holding their hand or kissing their ass, or something. But E. is different. She actually has a life. She acts like a grown person with responsibilities other than trying to keep up with me. She's not desperate like the rest of these females out here. She's so laid back; she had me thinking she didn't want me. Until lately, she never even tripped about the long hours I kept at the shop or me hanging out with the fellas afterwards. I had a little too much room to breathe. That's what got me in the mess I'm in, now. I took all that rope I had and hung myself with it.

When I think about it, I actually have the ideal woman; fine, smart, well-rounded, fun to be with. But right now, this relationship thing is not so cool. Ericka has been riding me to death about not spending enough time with her. I told you when you think you got the ideal woman; something is not going to balance out. She swears out that I'm always out with the boys. I keep telling her I'm trying to get paid. Right now, other than her and my kids, that's all I care about. I've been trying to get her to understand that I don't get a paycheck every week like the rest of these cats that work for somebody else. And regardless of what my shop looks like on the outside, it ain't no drug front. If it wasn't for my kids, I might consider doing something illegal. It would be an easy way to make some real money. But I can't get locked up and leave my kids without a father. Tomika and Lil' Reese keep me honest. And since I'm the only one I can depend on for money, I got to go whenever the money calls. Sometimes that might mean that the shop stays open until eleven or twelve o'clock. If I have a slow week, I'll let the boys gamble in the back and cut the house. And as long as the shop is open, I got to be there. They my men's and them, but if anything happens to Hot Wheelz, and I'm not there, it's still on me. I know that gambling is illegal, too, but the police ain't trying to harass me about no petty dice game.

When we first got together, everything was cool. But I wasn't sure if she would ever mean anything to me, so I didn't spend a whole lot of time with her then, either. Plus, I was still messing around with Cassandra trying to figure out what she was going to do. Cassandra was stressing me out about the time thing, back then, too and I was thinking about cutting her loose, anyway. I was so impressed with Ericka's game after the first time I went to see her that I was already in. I used to make myself not go to her house or call her so I wouldn't seem all anxious, like Genuwine. She was the "around the way girl" that L.L. talked about in that song and I vibed better with her than I did with any other woman. She made me feel like she had a real interest in me; not just because she thought I was thugged out or because she thought I had some loot. And to top it off, she was cool with just being friends. She never hounded me about coming over and taking her out or nothing. And she was always glad to see me when I came. She just kind of went with the flow. That's what I used to love about E. She was laid back and not into all the drama that all other females seem to love. And just like a fool, I messed up the only other good thing I had in my life besides my son.

Chapter 16

(Maurice)

I Need my Jewels!

Even though E. and me weren't technically an item, I was still sloppy in letting her know about my son. I told you, I thought she was being nonchalant and just passing time with me. We had been together off and on for the last two or three years. She didn't really push the issue about us not taking the relationship any further, so like any other man; I didn't say nothing about it either. Honestly, I really did like her, but I didn't think she wanted to be serious. I was hoping that the subject wouldn't come up. So, when she didn't push it, I just took advantage of the situation.

One night about six months after my son was born, Ericka saw a picture of me holding him on the night stand. I admit sparing her the details about why I had been avoiding her for damn near a year, and I definitely didn't tell her that I had been screwing my ex, but I could've sworn that I told her that I had a son. I might be ashamed of the way I chose to handle the situation, but I ain't never been ashamed of my baby. But for some reason, Ericka didn't know that Cassandra had ever been pregnant.

I tried to reason with her, but hell, she wasn't trying to hear nothing I had to say. Lil' Reese was already six months into his life. It wasn't nothing nobody could do about that. We argued and I said something that really hurt her. I told her basically that she didn't have no reason to trip because she wasn't my girl. If I could've taken it back, I would have. That was a foul thing to say, especially since deep down I knew she really was my girl. But the way she started flipping on a brother, I guess I got nervous. She was acting like Cassandra used to act when she was pregnant. I could kinda see where she had a right to be mad, but it wasn't like I did the shit on purpose; not to tell her about the baby, I mean. I still believe that I really did tell her that I had a son on the way. Hell, I told everybody else. I would never say this to her, but she wasn't all that into me when the situation first came up. So, she pushed that little piece of information into the very back of her mind and forgot about it. She just took it out on me because she forgot.

Things got rough between us for a long time after that. In fact, I'm still getting fallout from all of this, right now. She wouldn't leave the house right after she found out that night. She just sat up with me looking through all of the baby's pictures. She spent the night, but she had to leave early the next morning for National Guard duty. I'll never forget the last thing she said before she turned her back on me and walked out. She was like; "I know I shouldn't be hurt because we're not really together. But deep down, I would have loved to think I'd made more of an impression on you than I apparently did." She told me that she needed time to get over it by herself and she would call me when she could face me again. And I stood in the door in my boxers, like a damn fool, wishing I had done right by her from the start. Because watching her leave and not knowing whether or not I would ever see her again, I suddenly realized that after two years of 'just kicking it' with this girl that she had me open like Miami Subs after the club closed.

I tried to tell myself that she was just mad and needed some cool off time, but then a couple of days of not hearing from her turned into a couple of weeks. I tried to act like I wasn't fazed but I couldn't let what we had go out like that. I wanted this woman more than anything, and even though I was playing it cool, I had to put my pride down and sweat her for a change.

And that hateful chick did not make it easy for me, either. She made me run her down, for real. I called. We talked. We argued. I went to her house. She wouldn't let me in. We'd fuss through the door. Ericka could be just as mean and evil, as she was sweet and easygoing. Hell, I almost threw up my hands to the whole thing. I ain't got time to be sweating no woman. But she wasn't just any woman. She was my woman. Or she could have been my woman, if I hadn't been trying to be hard. I played myself, just like them niggas at the shop do all the time.

Finally, one day out of the blue, on a day when I was really stressed, she called me on the phone and said, "I wanna see the baby."

Just like that. No 'hello,' or 'can we talk?' or nothing. I started to say, "Let me call you back," or something stupid like that. She caught me off guard and I was tired of her having the upper hand. She wouldn't take my calls. I thought she was gonna call the police on me when I tried to come to her house. She had completely shut down on me. Now, all of a sudden, she calls almost a year later giving me some instructions. So, I said, "All right. I'll bring him over this weekend." I ain't no fool. I had already played myself once and I wasn't about to do it again.

When I brought Lil' Reese to Ericka's house, I thought he was gonna tear down the joint. He was about eighteen months old and getting into everything. With Tomika being old enough to know better, E's house is not really child-proofed. She's got candles and knickknacks all over the place. My son could not stop touching everything he saw. I was nervous because I thought she was going to be mad about Cassandra's child up in her house messing up stuff. But she didn't. By the time we got ready to leave, she had him so spoiled that he didn't want to leave. He was all up in her lap and loving on her like he had known her the whole time. He wouldn't even look at me. And Tomika fell right into the big sister role. She pulled everything she owned out of her toy box so that he could play with it. I had to tell her to put most of it back because I could spend all of my cheddar at Toys R Us replacing Tomika's stuff. I think she liked the idea of being big sister so much, she didn't even mind the fact that Lil' Reese was demolishing her room like Godzilla let loose in Tokyo.

He played until he fell into a coma in Tomika's room from pure exhaustion. Tomika put him in her bed and then lay down on her stomach beside him to watch television, leaving me and Ericka in the room alone. We sat there, she on the couch, and I was on the floor at her feet. Nobody was saying anything. My stomach was in knots because I thought she was still pissed off at me and wanted to argue. *Here it comes*, I thought. A year was enough time to build up a volcano of shit, and though I missed her, I wasn't up for no fight. Any other cat would have thought I was taking the soft route for what I did next, but I didn't care. I knew that most of this was my fault. If nothing else, I had no business trying to play her and Cassandra at the same time. If I had just kept chilling with E., I wouldn't even be having to deal with this mess to start with.

I looked at her. She had this blank look on her face. I gave her the little tired, puppy dog eyes and tried to smile, but she just looked past me out the window. I took a deep breath, hunched my shoulders, and closed my eyes. She wasn't having it. The only thing left for me to do was to brace myself for a big-time tongue-lashing.

"He's handsome," she said to whatever had her attention in the window.

"Thanks," I said, trying not to say too much too fast.

She got up and walked toward the window.

"I guess when you assume, you really do make an ass out of yourself," she sighed.

"What you mean?"

"Well, even though we hadn't verbally committed to each other, I just naturally assumed that because things were so well between us, that you weren't sleeping with anyone else."

"Baby, I wasn't sleeping with nobody else."

She raised her eyebrows and turned her gaze from me toward the bedroom where Tomika and Lil' Reese were.

"So that baby in my daughter's room is a product of my over active imagination, just like me thinking I was the only woman in your life, right?" she scoffed.

Okay, so I said something stupid. I tried again.

"No, babe. I mean, I hadn't been before that night with Cassandra. When she called me to her house that night, I didn't really have any intention of doing anything but talking, for real. But I have to admit; I still had some feelings for her. I had some for you, too, but you know brothers ain't used to females who don't try to put them on lock down. You acted so cool about everything, I thought you didn't want me or you had somebody else. So, I figured since San wasn't with her man no more, then maybe I could go ahead and hook back up with her instead of waiting around to get dissed by you."

"Remember about a year ago when I told you that I thought I was about to get locked up behind some old charges from a bench warrant? Well, I was lying. I ain't never had no charges on me like that. That was the most believable lie I could come up with to buy me some time until I could get a handle on San's crazy ass. San was pregnant then, and her hormones had taken over. I was spending all of my free time trying to be there to support her till the baby came. She was trying to get married, but I didn't want to get married and mess up three lives."

She narrowed her eyes, remembering.

I kept talking.

"She knew it wasn't going to work but I guess she didn't want to be by herself with a baby, no matter how miserable she had to be."

"I stayed away from you because I didn't know how to tell you that I had got somebody else pregnant. And on top of that, I know how she is. She would have automatically seen you as a threat to her getting what she wanted, and y'all would have been at each other's throats. I know you wouldn't have been trying to stoop to her level, but San can be ruthless enough to make you wanna draw blood from her ass. And I couldn't have forgiven neither one of y'all if something happened to my baby over some bullshit while she was carrying him."

"Anyway, she started coming back to herself after Lil' Reese was born and things had actually been going pretty smooth between me and you, despite the fact that I had been carrying around this secret. I guess I should've given you a little more credit and just told you all of this before."

For the first time, I had to admit that I had been wrong. I really hadn't mentioned to her that I was about to become a father. I was so busy sneaking around trying to avoid her and trying to keep Cassandra from killing herself or me one, that I never considered telling the truth as a choice. Here we were, almost two years later discussing the situation all calm and uneventful. If she snapped and told me to get out and don't come back, it would have been good enough for my dumb ass.

Ericka had been listening real quiet and patient the whole

time I was talking. After I finished, she walked up on me so close, she couldn't have done nothing else but kiss me or slapped me. I stood stock-still and waited. She lifted her hand and pointed the long nail on her index finger so close to the tip of my nose she was almost touching it. I took a deep breath. *Damn.* I knew I was gonna have to fight this chick before the night was over. She opened her mouth to say something, but nothing came out. She withdrew her hand and took a step back.

"First of all," she began, "I take extreme pleasure in being right, so let me just say that I don't appreciate the manner in which you spoke to me on the night that I found out about Christopher in the beginning. So, I believe that an apology is in order, don't you?"

I hung my head. Erica automatically got proper on you when she started to read your ass. She sounded like that lady judge on TV. I felt like a condemned man. But if all she wanted was an apology, I was more than happy to give her one.

"Baby, I'm sorry for not handling my business with you. You know I would never hurt you on purpose."

I stepped up to her and tried to kiss her lips, but she held up her hand, so I ended up kissing the inside of her palm.

"And . . ." she continued unfazed by sudden display of affection, "you lied continuously to keep me from finding out about what you had done. You know, I'd relieve you of your scrotal sac and its contents, since that is what got us into this difficult situation in the beginning, except that the planet Jupiter would not be far enough away for me to run to get away from you once you fully recovered. Not to mention that I probably wouldn't be able to get within several miles of your genitals as long as I had scissors in my hand."

I winced. *Scissors?*

"Baby, I thought we were handling this like adults. C'mon, now. I need my jewels."

She had really lost it.

"What for? Are you planning to do this to me, again?" she asked, sarcastically.

"No, E. Middle. I promise it won't ever be nobody but you ever again. Can we please start over so things can go back to the way they were before all this happened?"

She looked at me with a cold stare.

"Things can never be like they were, Maurice. You made sure of that. You had a baby by another woman. That means I can never bear your first child. That means if we decide to have anymore, I can't name him Maurice, Jr. because you already have a Maurice. Even though we weren't together, you claim that you had feelings for me. You said you cared for me, but you cheated on me. Even though we weren't exclusive, I cared so much about you that I didn't want to be with nobody else. But you couldn't give me that same respect. Now, not only do I get to feel like a fool, I get to look like one in front of everybody because they know we've been together too long for you to have a baby that young by somebody else. Things will never be the same between us again."

She turned her back on me.

I spun her back around.

"Look at me, baby. Please, now. I didn't know you felt that way about me. God knows I didn't. If I did, I wouldn't even have answered my phone when San called me that night. I swear on my life, if I had known you wanted to be with me, I would never had gone to her house."

"Look. I know that I committed the ultimate disrespect. But you know that technically we weren't together. I know you don't like to hear me say that, but baby, that's real talk. But, now that I know that our feelings were mutual all along, you gotta give me a chance to show you how much I want to be with you. At least give me a chance to make things right with us."

She shook her head.

"I don't know, Reese. Too much has happened. When

you told me that you weren't really looking for a serious relationship, I gave you your space because I know you can't make anyone do anything until they're ready. As our friendship began to grow, I thought that you were coming around. I didn't think I would have to sweat you about being in a relationship. I was sure that you would come around on your own. Then to find out that all this time, I was being played . . ."

She stopped and closed her eyes like thinking it about was too much for her to bear.

"I have my pride, Maurice. And I have a problem with taking you back and having to worry about whether or not you out in some other woman's face because you think I'm losing interest."

"I can't do nothing about what happened, Ericka. All I can do is do what I can to make things work from here on out. I know it's not going to be easy. I know I'm going to have to win back your trust. And I know I'm going to be subject to interrogations when I get home late and all that. But, babe, you do whatever you need to do, okay? Because I need for you to trust me. Alright?"

She nodded her head, but she didn't look like she really believed me.

"If you say that I'm what you want, Reese, then I'm willing to give you the benefit of the doubt this one time. But you need to understand that whenever you get upset about me questioning your whereabouts that you brought all of this about with your sneaking around. Every time you want to fix your mouth and tell me to trust you, think about why it is that I don't. I'm not sure how long it will take me to get past this or if I ever will, but my feelings for you are strong enough to leave room in my heart to give you another chance. But understand that if you mess it up this time, it will be on you."

After she reluctantly took me back, things were decent between us for a long time after that. Then all of a sudden, I can't explain it, but I started slipping away from her, again. I wasn't kicking it with no other females, or nothing like that, but the situation with me and Ericka just got a little too comfortable. I started getting antsy. In a way, I started feeling smothered by her. She wasn't keeping tabs or nothing. I just felt like I was missing something by coming home to Ericka every day. Tarik and the boys would be hanging out during the week, and I would be at home watching television with Ericka and Tomika. It was cool, but it just wasn't me. So, I kind of got back out there a little bit. Really, all I'm doing is just putting in a little extra overtime at the shop. No big thing. But Ericka got used to me being home and now she is tripping. She says I don't spend no time with her. She even went so far as accusing me of being with Cassandra, of all people. We have been arguing a lot about it. I love her now, as much as I did before, but I just don't know how to make her understand that I need more room to breathe. I don't want to break up, or nothing. I'm just used to doing my own thing. But I'm afraid if I tell her that, she'll take it wrong and think I don't want to be with her. So, I spend most of my time avoiding her and the situation. But lately, I've had a strange feeling like our relationship was about to go through a major change. I just couldn't put my finger on what it could be.

Chapter 17

I Can't Tell You All My Secrets

Prior to the weekend that we spent together on my birthday, Desmond and I had talked on the phone almost every night around ten o'clock, after he completed his work on the warehouse floor. He'd call me from his office to keep him company while completed any receiving orders in the computer or responded to email. After that magical weekend, things basically went back to the way they had always been, which was fine with me because talking only on the phone alleviated the pressure of finishing what we started in Virginia Beach.

"So, how did your boyfriend make up for not spending your birthday with you?" Desmond asked me.

"He bought me a motorcycle," I responded, casually.

"Wow!"

Desmond was impressed, not because Maurice bought me a bike, but because I actually knew how to ride one.

"You know, the more we talk, the more I learn how interesting you really are," he commented.

"I can't tell you all of my secrets. If I do that, I'll lose my intrigue and your interest."

He laughed. "Not likely. There's enough intrigue in you

to keep me satisfied for a long time. And besides, your mystique is not the main thing that attracts me to you, anyway."

"Oh, really? Then what is it?"

"Your company," was his response. "It's these nightly conversations that bring me back to work every night."

"Well, my game must be really tight if I can give a man desire to get up and go to work, every day. That desire is usually motivated by necessity or greed. That's deep."

After a short pause, Desmond spoke again. "What's deeper is how hard it's becoming to stay away, especially since we only got to spend time together for the first time a couple of weeks ago. Your birthday weekend was like a hit of crack. Now, I want more. Hell, I even drove by your house last night."

My eyebrows went up in surprise. He was feenin' like Jodeci. And I didn't even have to give him none. Now, I was curious.

"Why didn't you stop?"

"Because I saw another car parked in your driveway, a BMW. I figured it was Maurice, so I kept driving. I don't want to start any drama. He doesn't even know I exist, does he?"

"Nope," I answered, dryly. "And he causes enough drama by himself. By spending every waking moment at that damned shop. It's usually after midnight before he gets here, if at all. And as far as him knowing anything about you, he'd actually have to be here during a decent hour to hear the phone ring; much less know who I'm talking to. I'm sorry. How do I look talking to you about my man problems?"

Desmond sighed. "It's cool. That's what friends do. We bitch about our problems to each other."

"Yeah, but you don't bitch to me about your wife."

"My wife's not the problem," he offered after a moment of awkward silence.

"So, you're saying you're the problem," I quipped.

Desmond cleared his throat, as he searched for the right way to frame his situation with minimal details.

"I'm saying all marital issues aren't situations where blame necessarily needs to be assigned."

It was never spoken that we didn't discuss his relationship with his wife. I never brought it up out of respect for him. And so, I wouldn't have to confront my willingness to have a fling with a married man. But in light of the closeness, we'd recently developed, I guess I needed him to tell me something that would give me a pass to continue. I needed his wife to be the one doing Desmond wrong, to make me feel better about his role in it, as well.

"So, it's nobody's fault that you planned a getaway with another woman while your wife thinks you're away on business?"

"You don't understand. It's not like that."

Not like what? If she was cheating on him, what was the big deal? That kind of thing happened all the time. Hell, he was cheating on her. But apparently, there was more to it than them just not getting along anymore. Maybe he had her tied up and gagged in the basement, or something. That would be about right, the way my luck ran with men.

"I know that you don't want to discuss this, but don't you think I have a right to know why I'm helping you cheat on your wife?"

"I'm not cheating on my wife. We haven't been sexually active. Even though you were loud and clear that's what you wanted."

"Well, we haven't slept together, but we have lain in the same bed, and we've kissed. That may not have amounted to much to you, but let's face it. I don't think your wife would have appreciated knowing that her husband was spending that kind of time with another woman, no matter how platonic you try to make it sound. And better yet, how would you feel if the shoe was on the other foot?"

Desmond was getting agitated. "Well, what would Maurice say?"

Ouch. "We're not talking about Maurice."

"And we're not talking about me, either. Besides, I haven't heard any complaints about my so-called infidelity until now."

"And I'm not complaining now. It's just hard to think a man as sincere and genuine as you would have a problem holding together his own marriage."

The tension was mounting, so I tried to clean it up.

"Look, Des. I know that you are a good dude. And I would like to think that you would never do anything intentionally to hurt anyone, that includes your wife and me. But let's be for real. You're spending time with me that you should be spending with your wife. I'd feel better if I knew that I didn't have a distorted view of the situation."

Desmond became defensive. "Oh, I get it. You want me to give you some sugarcoated excuse about why I have chosen to spend time with you rather than my wife to make you feel better about lusting after a married man. Well, I got news for you, Ericka. She's not cheating on me, okay? She's never cheated on me. She is a better wife than I could ever have hoped for. We're not in a contract marriage, nor did our parents arrange it a long time ago. She didn't marry me for my money or I for hers, and she didn't trick me into believing that she was pregnant and then fake a miscarriage. So, if you would like to continue our friendship, I suggest you find another way to soothe your guilty conscience instead of nagging me about the details of my marriage!"

"Damn, Desmond. I didn't mean to . . ."

"Yeah, I know. Look, I need to hang up, now. Bye, Ericka." And he was gone.

Shocked with a bruised ego, I hung up the phone, laid back and closed my eyes. Was it asking too much for me to know why he suddenly chose to spend his free time with me rather than with her? I didn't see anything wrong with trying to soothe my guilty conscience. And I couldn't help it if he didn't have one.

The phone must have rung in the middle of the night because I could hear Desmond on the other end talking in a low, muffled voice. He was apologizing and telling me that he wanted to come over and explain everything. I told him that everything was fine and that I wasn't mad at him for hanging up on me. He told me that everything was going to be alright now and that he had taken care of everything. I asked him what he was talking about, but he just kept telling me that he was coming over and to be awake when I got there. He hung up before I could protest.

I'm not sure how he got in. I just remember him climbing in bed next to me. He kissed my lips passionately, and I succumbed to his touch. When he entered my hot flesh, my whole body shivered with ecstasy. He made love to me, urgently, thrusting in and out, up and down, faster and faster. As both of our bodies shuddered in feverish climax, I heard a single gunshot. I screamed as Desmond's body lurched in pain and then lay still on top of me.

The room was pitch black, but I could see the evil in her face while she kneeled over me, shoving the barrel of her .380 between my chattering teeth.

"Did you really think that filing some divorce papers would get rid of me?" she hissed.

I lay there, terrified into silence. I prayed a silent prayer of repentance and braced for impact. Instead, she snatched the gun out of my mouth and violently clubbed me over my frontal lobe. I winced in pain. She was going to make me suffer. I screamed loud enough to wake up Desmond, but he just lay on top of me, motionless.

Maurice shook me like a rag doll as I continued to scream, uncontrollably. "Ericka, wake up, baby! What's wrong? Come on, baby, wake up!"

I balled up my fists and unconsciously began to pound Maurice, in a desperate attempt to fend off Desmond's wife's maniacal rampage.

"It's okay, E! I'm right here. I won't let anyone hurt you. Come on baby. Calm down. I'm right here, babe. Shhh . . ."

He wrapped his arms securely around me and began to rock me, soothingly. I stopped screaming, but still shook like a leaf as I held on to Maurice for dear life. It had only been a dream.

I sulked around the house most of the morning trying to avoid making eye contact with Maurice. He was completely taken off guard by my little episode and was frantic to know what I was dreaming about that would make me lose my mind like that. I really wasn't interested in going into the gory details about my nightmare. Nor did I want to give him any details about my 'friendship' with Desmond that might allude to how I really spent my birthday. I blew it off by saying I couldn't remember what I was dreaming about. He didn't seem satisfied with that answer but reluctantly dropped the issue at my request.

I thought about paging Desmond but decided against it. He really got pissed off at me for making inquiries about his marriage and I thought that I just needed to leave well enough alone. I walked around the rest of the day in a quiet funk.

I tried to make sense out of the terrible dream that I'd had the night before. It was so real. I thought I could actually feel her hot breath on my face as she held that gun to my head. I couldn't remember having a more vivid dream.

Was she psychotic? All my dreams about Desmond were usually full of passion and fire, not murder and mayhem. In those dreams, I was able to live out fantasies that our reality kept us from. I was always jerked away by the overwhelming lust that consumed me when he entered my dreams. But never had I been snatched back to reality overcome by fear. My mind must have been working overtime with guilt I carried around from carrying on this forbidden friendship in the first place.

Or maybe she really was an insanely jealous woman who would kill us both if she found out about us. Maybe he started an argument to end things so she wouldn't find out about us and come looking for me. Whatever they had going on, he obviously had no intention of telling me what it was. And in the wake of the worst nightmare I'd ever had, I resented being placed in a potentially dangerous situation without the courtesy of a forewarning.

I cared about Desmond, but I wasn't sure if I would be anxious to maintain the friendship if he continued to be so secretive about his life. Besides, I was already putting my own relationship on the line by flirting with the possibility of an impending affair. Things were not perfect between Maurice and me, but I had come too far to lose him over some get-back sex with a married man who couldn't even divulge what was making him cheat on his wife.

Chapter 18

Who is Dee?

More than a week went by and still no word from Desmond. Things had gone back to normal at my house. Tomika had returned from her vacation with my parents, and I went back to work. Apparently, the nightmare I had about Desmond scared Maurice almost as much as it did me. He started hanging around my house more since that night, cutting his days at the shop a lot closer. Rarely did he come over after nine or ten, now. He still acted like his normal self, but he prowled around the house after Tomika and I went to bed, like a restless lion. He fell asleep next to me but late into the night, I'd wake up to the television on in the living room. His side of the bed would be empty. I could often feel him staring at me on of his frequent checks on me while he was up.

It was nice to finally receive some extra attention from Maurice. But his over protectiveness was beginning to grate my nerves. I wasn't used to him being around all the time and had grown used to taking care of everyday tasks around the house, myself. Now all of a sudden, I was practically tripping over him. Everywhere I looked he was there, trying to wash clothes or put dishes away in the wrong cabinets. He was driving me nuts, but it was nice to have him around. To

think, all I had to do to get his attention was wake up screaming from a nightmare.

It wasn't until almost a month later when I figured out his
real motives for watching me so closely. Maurice came in the
house early one evening while I was on the phone talking to
Toy. I was on the cordless phone in the kitchen taking a pan
of brownies out of the oven for dessert.

"Oh, Toy, Maurice just came in the door. Let me call you
back," I said, hurrying her off the phone.

"Sup, Baby?" I asked, as I stood on my tiptoes to give
him a peck on the nose.

"Humph. Ain't nothing. What's up with you?"

The crease in his forehead let me know that something
was amiss.

"What's wrong with you?" I asked him, returning to my
preparation.

"Who is Dee?"

I stopped what I was doing and returned his frown.

"Dee who?"

"Well, who is Desmond, then?"

My heart dropped in my drawers. I played it off, but my
mind was going a mile a minute.

"Desmond Wright? Oh, that's a friend of mine from
Global Technology. Why?"

Maurice eyed me, suspiciously.

"Has that nigga been over here?" His voice was slightly
raised, which was extremely uncharacteristic for Maurice,
who was normally quite easy-going.

I was determined to hold it down. I wasn't sure what
he was driving at, but there was no way he was going to
get away with accusing me of anything, when I could never
account for his whereabouts with any certainty.

"So, that's why you been spending so much time over
here lately. I knew it was too good to be true," I sneered.

"You had a nigga up in here behind my back?" He was growing more agitated by the second.

I laughed. "You are trippin'."

"Don't try to play me, Ericka," he growled. "Just answer the damn question."

I took the defensive. "Look, don't be coming up in here accusing me of shit when all I do is go to work and come home. You're the one keeping all the late hours. Do you think if I was screwing someone else, I would bring them up in here when you got a key? At least gimme some credit for having half of a fucking brain!"

Maurice was pissing me off. Here I was thinking was concerned, when he was really just spying on me.

But where was he getting his intel? I hadn't heard from Desmond since we had that argument. I racked my brain trying to figure out what Maurice actually knew. If he had found out about my beach trip, I could kiss my ass goodbye. I wasn't prepared for what came next.

"Well, maybe if you turned that half of a fucking brain off before you went to bed at night, you wouldn't be calling out other niggas' names in your sleep!" Maurice was livid.

I winced at his last comment as though someone stole me in the face. That's impossible. I don't talk in my sleep. Maurice had even jokes about holding a mirror under my nose at night to make sure I'm still alive. Other than that outburst I had during that nightmare, I didn't even breathe heavily most of the time. Now, here I was being accused of calling out another man's name in my sleep. There must have been some kind of mistake.

My mind raced while I mentally searched for a way out.

"What the hell are you talking about, Maurice?"

"Ericka, you are really pissing me off with the innocent shit. I'm not stupid, hear?"

Calmly, I replied, "I didn't say nothing about you being

stupid, but wouldn't you say it was stupid to accuse some-body of something and not fill them in on what it was?"

"Okay, since you wanna continue to play dumb, here it is. That night you had that nightmare I heard you mumbling something like, 'Come on in, Dee,' like he was at the door, or something. A couple of minutes later, you started screaming like somebody was killing you up in here. I thought Tomika was gonna run in here thinking I was beating up her mama. But then when I tried to get you to tell me what had got you so upset, you wouldn't tell me. I wasn't sure if you had actually said 'Dee' or not, but I knew that if I stayed awake beside you long enough, you were going to say something else. That's why I started coming over here early, so I could be here when your ass went to bed. I knew you were gonna start talking again, or that nigga was gonna call here, one."

I stood mute, as he continued.

"A couple of nights ago, you said that name again. It was clearer this time. I heard you plain as day. Then last night while you were sleeping, some dude named Desmond called the house asking for you. I guess 'Dee' is short for Desmond, huh?"

I ignored that last comment.

"And? What did he say?"

"He didn't say nothing, but to tell you he called, and he would call you back later."

"Is that all?" I asked, trying to appear unaffected.

"Hell naw, that ain't all. I'm about to break your fucking jaw unless you can come up with a good reason why I shouldn't think you screwing around with somebody else when you calling out a nigga's name in your sleep that's calling this house!"

For a minute, he almost had me. Lucky for me, Maurice gave me all the ammunition I needed to counter.

If dealing with lying, cheating ass men all my life had done anything at all; it has helped me to develop my poker face. My daughter's father used to look me dead in the eye and lie so good that I was constantly second guessing my own better judgment. Even when I caught him in bed with another woman, he insisted that his intention was not even to have sex with her. He was so convincing, I almost believed him. I didn't, but I forgave him. Now, that's the game.

I looked at Maurice, as he elaborated on how he sat up in the middle of the night waiting on me to confess my infidelities in my sleep. The nerve of him to actually cop to finally relenting to my request to spend time with me so he could catch me cheating. I'd spent the last six years begging him like a desperate fool to be a real boyfriend. Even stayed around after finding out he had a baby by another chick after we started seeing each other. Now, he's mad and ready for war over something that not only was easily preventable, but virtually nothing, as far as drama went. Shit. I should've let Desmond bend my ass over the balcony in that hotel suite. That would've at least made this shit I was dealing with both these ninjas worth my time.

I looked Maurice square in the eye and said, "I met Desmond a whole year before I met you. If there was something going on between me and him, why the hell am I still hanging around here after six years taking shit off of you? I went to my old job to have lunch with some girls I used to work with. That's how we ran into each other. And on top of that, Desmond's been happily married since way before I knew anything about him. So, if I'm always tripping about you never having enough time to spend with me and you're supposed to be my man, then what sense would it make for me to take some leftovers from somebody's wife? You sound crazy."

I rolled my eyes in disgust while Maurice fiddled for a response.

"Oh, so what you saying? You got a thing for him, but instead of sleeping with him, you just dream about him?"

He was determined to be right.

"Do you think that my life revolves around an orgasm? I don't get all up in your business and ask you about all the tricks that hang around the shop that I know ain't spending no money. Nor do I say anything about the ones always beeping in on your Nextel. The one I don't even have the number to."

At this point, I had completely dismantled Reese's argument, and he went from threatening to break my jaw to snapping his shut. He stood there, quiet and defeated, clearly sorry he'd picked this battle with me. I delivered a finishing blow.

"But since you must know, the last time I talked to Desmond, he called while I was watching the news. There was a story about a guy found dead between cars in a night club parking lot in Durham. I told Desmond about my what happened to my boyfriend. A lot of the details were similar to what happened to him."

Maurice knew that shootings had a great impact on me since my high school sweetheart was gunned down right in front of me at a club we used to frequent close to the end of our senior year. A guy he had beef with bumped into him on purpose to start a fight. But security saw the whole thing and kicked dude out. As we were on our way out, the guy, his ex-friend approached my boyfriend from behind as he held the car door for me to get in. I can still hear him gurgling as he drowned in his own blood waiting for the paramedics to get there. His killer was never caught.

I continued.

"I really couldn't remember what I was dreaming about, but I figure that news story must have been triggering. And it didn't take a genius to figure out that I was having a nightmare that night, not a wet dream."

Maurice hung his head in shame.

"I'm sorry, E. Okay? I'm sorry. I didn't know. Stuff like that stays with you. I'm sorry I came off on you like that. And you did scare the hell out of me. And I'm sorry I thought you were doing dirt."

He lifted up my chin and gave me his best puppy dog look. The scarring on his face gave him an extra forlorn look, giving him an unfair advantage in the argument. My ice on my heart started to melt, but I couldn't let him know that.

"You forgive me?" he pleaded, enveloping me in a bear hug.

"Yes, I forgive you. But you know I don't want anyone else," I lied. And you know what you need to do for things to be right between us. What's wrong with you? You sneaking around here like Deputy Dawg, or somebody, trying to create some bullshit. What? You got a guilty conscience?"

"Naw, baby. I just don't want you to go out and be with somebody else because you think I'm cheating on you. You know I ain't nowhere but at the shop hustling trying to get this paper. Or kicking it with the fellas. Don't you always get me when you call me? I keep telling you that you don't have nothing to worry about. I'm not going nowhere."

That was the problem. He wasn't going anywhere; at least with me, anyway.

"I know that, Reese. But why do you always have to be at the shop with them fools? You act like you like them better than me. We can't ever do anything because you always put what they want in front of what I want. I'm tired of doing stuff by myself. And when I'm out, men approach me all the time, wanting to know if I have a man. I might as well say 'no.'"

He looked at me, thoughtfully.

"Is that what you want to tell them, E.?"

"No, but if things don't change, we both need to start doing something different."

He sighed.

"Look, I'm feeling what you saying, babe. But, it's gonna take some time for me to let go of them streets. You know what I'm sayin'? It's in my blood, baby. But I will try harder, okay?"

"That's all I ask," I said, mentally patting myself on the back for successfully averting a potential disaster.

"I gotta go back to the shop and tie up some loose ends, but I'll be back before ten. Do you need something while I'm out?"

"No. I'm straight for right now. You want to take a plate with you back to the shop?"

"Nah. I'll eat when I get back."

"Okay. Be careful out there."

"Alright," he said.

He gave me a quick peck on the lips, and he was gone.

Whew. That was too damn close. I laughed out loud in spite of myself. Maurice came over thinking he had caught me dead to rights. But in less than ten minutes I had him apologizing. We're taught to learn from our mistakes. Getting involved with Tomika's father was probably my biggest. But I swear, sometimes his bullshit came in handy. Dealing with Lance also turned out to be one of my greatest learning experiences.

As I set the table, I couldn't help but wonder if Maurice was really going back to the shop to work. Maybe that was just the player in me.

So, Desmond finally decided to take his ass off his shoulders and stop being mad at me, huh? He probably thought that he had caused some drama between Maurice and me and was waiting for me to call when the coast was clear. Well, I wasn't exactly through being pissed off at him, either, so I decided to give him a couple more days to get over himself. I still had no clue what had actually set him off and hadn't decided which way to approach him. I set two places at the table, while plotting my next move.

Chapter 19

Just My Luck

My car had been giving me problems the previous week. I could start the engine, but it hesitated at stoplights and going up hills. I put fuel injector cleaner in it at Maurice's request thinking that would help. But by this morning, black smoke had begun billowing from the tail pipe. I went in to work and called Maurice after narrowly reaching the safety of my office parking lot.

"Good morning, Sunshine," I cooed.

"Mornin." His early morning voice rumbled deep inside his chest, seducing me through the line.

"You sound like you still in bed. I should've called out."

He chuckled. "Naw. I wish. I've already been to the shop and to Durham to pick up two sets of tires."

"Okay, then! Business is booming. That's right, Daddy. You better make me some money." I teased.

He laughed. "I think I might make you a little bit, today. How much do you want?"

"I am not going to be greedy," I answered. "Can I just get enough to buy a new car? It doesn't even have to be brand new. I'll take a certified pre-owned."

The seriousness came back into his voice.

"Your truck still tripping?"

"Yes. Now there's black smoke coming out the back," I replied, pitifully.

He paused. "Did you drive it this morning?"

"Yeah."

Another pause.

"I'm going to give Mr. Frank a call this morning. Can you get one of your girls to follow you so you can drop it off to him? Because I won't have a chance to come and get it until later."

"Yeah, I'll get Toy to do it. We were supposed to have lunch today, anyway."

"That'll work. After you drop the car off, have her take you by Hot Wheelz and get my car so you can have something to drive until yours is ready. Then I'll take you back to Mr. Frank's to pick it up. That sound cool with you?"

Was it cool? I was going to get to roll in the 740 with the brand-new rims, not to mention the new system he had just put in with a DVD player in the front console. I would say that was very cool.

"Yeah, that's cool," I said, trying to stifle my enthusiasm. I couldn't fool him, though.

"I'll meet you at the shop at 5:30, sharp! That's more than enough time for you to make it to the shop from work. Don't have none of your cluck head friends in my car. Don't be messing with the settings on my radio. And absolutely no parallel parking!"

I rolled my eyes upward.

"Yeah, yeah. Who do you think you're talking to, Tomika, or somebody?" I asked, indignantly.

"I wouldn't have to give Tomika this type of instruction because she knows how to act," he said.

"Whatever," I balked.

The only thing Maurice loved more than that car was Lil' Reese and Tomika.

I could hardly wait for five o'clock to come so I could go for a joyride in the BMW. I called Reece to let him know I was going to be a couple of minutes off schedule to pick up a few things from the store. That way he wouldn't be trying to report the car stolen before I got here. I knew he would be timing me from the moment I left work until the time I pulled into the shop.

Just as I suspected, his truck still was not out front when I pulled up, even though I was late. I called him on his mobile phone to see where he was. He was actually nowhere near the shop. He was on the other side of town having some rims put on a customer's car, and it would be another hour before he would make it back. Tomika's had Girl Scouts, so I called Renee to let her know that I might be late picking Tomika up from her house afterwards.

I ran my errands and made a couple of laps around town to kill time before meeting up with Maurice back at Hot Wheelz. It was my original plan to ride around and be seen a little bit, but my plan was thwarted by the lack of people out and about. Even on a late summer afternoon when most folks are getting off work and most street entrepreneurs are just waking up, nobody seemed to be out.

The party was apparently at Hot Wheelz. The parking lot was full by the time I got back. I don't normally go inside the shop when there are a bunch of guys hanging around. Most of them are trifling and are in my face as soon as Maurice turns his back. But since I recognized Tarik and Will's cars outside, I went in to wait. They were most likely in the back shooting dice or playing cards. So, I could just go into Maurice's office and finish up an organization project that I had started earlier in the month for him.

The front entrance was locked, signaling a dice game was going on in the rear of the building. I knocked, and Tarik poked his head from around the corner. He stood in the door for a minute, mute, sporting a cheesy, lopsided grin as I yelled at him from outside to open the door. The goofy act only lasted a few seconds, and he opened the door and hugged me.

"Get off me, fool," I laughed, hitting him in the arm. "It's hot as hell out here and you playing."

"What's up, girl?" He looked out the window over my shoulder. "I thought your husband was with you."

I rolled my eyes. "I'm not sure where my husband is. Maurice is out on Capital Blvd. putting some rims on somebody's car. I'm waiting for him to come and get me and take me to my truck."

"Where is it at?" he wanted to know.

"At Mr. Frank's. Spark plug went bad in it."

"Oh, ok. That Negro let you drive his precious beamer?" It even sounded incredulous to his best friend that he would let me drive that damned car. "You wearing that man down, E," he laughed.

"Is that right? I can't tell," I said.

"Well, he called a few minutes ago and said he'd be here in about fifteen minutes."

You would think that Maurice and Tarik were in a relationship. He never thought to call me, who was sitting here waiting on him because that was my job. It would have been pointless to mention any of this to Tarik, so I made a joke, instead.

"Alright. Don't y'all hoodlums be back there tearing down my man's place of business. This is how he keeps me in Prada, Fendi, Gucci, and them," I joked.

Tarik laughed. "I got them under control back there, E. Middle. You know I'm gonna keep my boy's back."

I nodded and went into Maurice's office and closed the door. I turned on the CD player to drown out the noise in the back. As R. Kelly began asking me about getting up on a room, I wondered why the hell a man would be listening to TP-2 during the course of any workday. I shook the devil off and pulled out a stack of invoices to add up the charges.

Reese often asked me to perform office tasks that he couldn't be bothered with like entering his sales into the computer and making bank deposits. Maurice stayed so busy during the day that he actually needed someone in the office at least three times a week. But I was cheaper. In the middle of my calculations, I had a thought to check the file cabinet to make sure he hadn't haphazardly left any checks to deposit or deliveries to schedule. I noticed the noise rise significantly in the back as I crossed the room.

I turned and tipped back to the door to listen. I was used to guys talking loud and yelling when they won. The usual male bonding and posturing was typical here. But this was different. The yelling had an angry tone. Like the snarl of wild animals. Trouble was brewing. I knew I should've took one more lap around town.

I carefully cracked the office door to see if I could figure out exactly what was going on and if I could get out before anything bad really happened. Just my luck, two guys were in each other's face daring the other to make a move. Tarik was standing in between them in an attempt at preventing them from tearing one another apart. There was so much commotion, I couldn't make out completely what was going on. All I could make out was something about cheating and seven thousand dollars in the pot.

If the fact that these deadbeats had seven thousand dollars to piss away in a dice game wasn't bad enough, I noticed that one of the guys involved in the fight was my childhood nemesis, Chris, a.k.a. Candy Cane, or Cane, for short. He was a wannabe dope boy who went for bad. Back in the day, my high school boyfriend, Kevin befriended him out of compassion. And they were close until Kevin finally realized the same thing the rest of us kids already knew. He was just plain bad news. Always had been. And apparently, nothing had changed. These dice games have gone on in the back of Maurice's shop without drama for years. Reese was easy going, but mess with his business and he became an entirely different person. The guys who hung out there regularly knew it and respected it. Chris never had respect for anything or anyone in his life. I wondered what he was even doing in here and if Reese knew him.

I continued to watch the confrontation spilled out onto the showroom floor and Tarik was doing his best to diffuse the situation, while Will started herding everyone else outside. It appeared that they had everything under control. People were leaving, although a couple of guys stayed back to help Tarik break up the fight. Tarik had the other guy in a bear hug, trying to drag him outside. The guy was so mad, he was foaming at the mouth, screaming for Tarik to let him at Cane. As he continued to yell, Cane got past the remaining dudes and sucker punched the guy. Tarik instantly let him go, to prevent Cane from continuing to get the drop on him. The other guy began to fight back. He grabbed Cane around his throat and with one hand, sent him soaring into one of the shop's display cases. The sound of glass shattering reverberated throughout the room, and for a split second everything seemed frozen in time.

Tarik, who had been the only rational person in the group, began to lose control.

"Man, what the fuck is wrong with y'all?" he yelled. "How you gonna come up in here and tear up my boy's shop? Take this shit outside. Now!" His voice was high pitched and strained.

The aggressive dude got up in Tarik's face. He spoke in an even tone that sent a shiver down my spine.

"Nigga, fuck you and your boy. I want my motherfuckin' money or I'm about to break more than that goddamned display case."

As delighted as I was to see Cane tote an ass whuppin, I decided that now would be a good time to make a break for the door. Maybe I could just slip right past them, and no one would notice me. But the fight stood in my way of safety. '*Where the hell was Maurice?*' I thought, as I tried to maneuver towards the door as discreetly as possible. Tarik and I made eye contact as I passed between the two adversaries amid the broken glass, but didn't say anything. I detected a faint look of relief on his face as I made my way to the door.

Maurice rushed just as I passed between Cane and the other guy. I was both mad as hell and elated to see him at once. As he crossed the threshold into the shop, a look of utter disbelief came over his face. I knew he was furious. I wanted to tell him to let the insurance company worry about it, but he wasn't hearing it right then. He was yelling something at me, but it was drowned out by the sound of a small explosion that came out of nowhere behind me.

An intense white-hot sensation ripped through the flesh of my right leg, stopping me in my tracks. I opened my mouth to scream, but before I could get the sound out, another pain stabbed me in my left shoulder blade. The ground came rushing forward, but Maurice broke my fall. Although there was a fire raging in my leg and back, my body felt cold and limp. Maurice's mouth was moving frantically, but I couldn't make out the words. An expression of complete horror had taken over his face. I asked him why he was looking at me like that. I tried to tell him that everything would be okay, but he didn't hear me; or he didn't believe me . . .

Chapter 20

(Maurice)

Mo' Money, Mo' Problems

I was supposed to meet E. at the shop so I could take her to Mr. Frank's to pick up her car. But I got tied up putting some rims on a customer's car. Then I took my time coming back because I knew she probably wouldn't be there when I got there. She had been dying for a chance to drive my car. And since I had just finished pimping it out with some new chrome 22's and some new boom in the system, I knew she was going to want to high side around town to be seen. I still told her to come straight to the shop after work because if I didn't give her a time limit, I'd be stuck taking the CAT bus home. But really, I don't mind her driving it. And most of Raleigh knows my car so if she's driving it, ain't nobody gonna mess with her. She think she's the shit when she push- ings my beamer, anyway. So, if driving my car makes her feel like a mini-baller makes her happy, then I'm happy.

I was kind of surprised to see my car pulled up in front of the shop. I just knew she was somewhere cruising the hood or at the car wash. The fact that she was inside the shop when it was a crowd of dudes inside was kind of odd because she normally won't hang around if there's a bunch of guys. She can't stand a crowd of dudes, especially the ones that hang out at Hot Wheelz.

People started rushing outside but were focused on something inside the shop window. I saw Will and walked over to him.

"What's the deal?" I asked him, puzzled.

Will seemed troubled. "Man, some niggas went to blows in the shop about some dice money. They in there tearing up shit. I just got everybody outside, and Tarik is in there trying to break it up."

My heart started pounding.

"Man, where's my girl?"

Will shrugged. "I ain't seen her. Why?"

I pointed to my car parked right at the door.

"She's driving my car!"

I burst through the door just in time to see Ericka trying to ease her way past the two guys squared off in the middle of the floor. There was glass all over the place and one of the guys was lying on the floor in the middle of what used to be my large display case, like a turtle turned over on his back. Tarik was standing between them and was watching Ericka as she maneuvered carefully towards the door.

Tarik turned in my direction as I came in. He didn't say anything, but I could tell that his main concern was getting Ericka out of the middle of that conflict.

I couldn't believe what was going down in my business while I was out. Tarik and Will were my boys, so I never had a problem shooting out to take care of business as long as one of them was there. I didn't have anybody to help, and I was out a lot. So, it was easier to leave them there so at least there would be someone there to greet a customer if one came in. It's bad for business to have to close the shop every time I have to leave. Now, I regretted leaving these niggas in my store.

I ain't never had no trouble in here. The boys always played dice in the shop. At first, it started out as something we did for fun more than anything. The bets would be something small, a dollar here or five there. Then, as time went on, cats started putting their egos in it and the bets started growing. Niggas started walking out of my shop with thousands of dollars from a game of cee-lo, and I wouldn't have made a dime that day in legitimate business. So, I started taking a cut for the house. It's a decent chunk of change when business is slow.

But like Biggie used to say, "Mo' money, mo' problems." Word got around that all this money was flowing in my shop, and everybody trying to get paid. They think that I'm balling out of control just because they see some nice cars parked outside. But if I had access to the kind of money that some of these cats that be hanging at the shop have, I would just open up a casino in Vegas instead of letting them shoot dice in the back of my business and risk going to jail. One of my boys got robbed leaving the shop one night. I swear, people just lose their minds when a little money enters the picture. But other than a few minor scuffles, I hadn't had anybody just roll up in my place and act a complete fool. That is, until now.

I was kinda pissed about Ericka being in Hot Wheelz with all those dudes in the first place. But I was ready for war when I saw how they tore up my shop. And to top it off, the cat laying on the floor was that punk-ass-wannabe-hustler nigga, Kane. I can't stand his trouble making ass. Word on the street is that he was the one who pulled stick-up outside of the shop a couple of months ago. And he knew that I knew it, too, so I don't even know where he got the nuts to waltz up in my shop from, anyway.

Me and Ericka locked eyes for a minute, but I didn't say nothing because I didn't want anything to hinder her from getting out of that shop. These dudes obviously didn't have no respect for me or my shop, so I know they didn't give a damn about my lady. This shit was about to get ugly, but I had to make sure E. Middle was out of harm's way, first.

As she approached the door, I stepped to the side to give her room to get out of the door. That's when I saw Kane go for his waist. Before I could move, he started blasting. He was trying to hit the other dude, but he dived for cover, and Ericka got hit in the back of the leg. She froze and gave me this shocked look. I caught her as she went down from a second bullet she took in the back.

I held her tight and rocked her.

"Oh, shit! Baby, I'm so sorry. I'm sorry, E. I'm so sorry."

She was whispering something, but I couldn't hear her.

"Shhh. Don't try to talk, baby. You gonna be all right. I got you."

Kane was startled by the fact that he had shot E. instead of the dude he was fighting. In that split second pause, Tarik dived on top of him and punched Kane in the face. He grabbed the gun, got back to his feet and kicked that nigga in the head. Then he ran to the door.

"Will, call 9-1-1, man. E. is hit!"

The other cat had got out of the shop and was running through the parking lot.

He turned back to us.

"Is she breathing, man?

Ericka didn't look too good. She was breathing heavy and fast like a panting dog. She wasn't trying to talk anymore. Her eyes were closed, and her skin was all clammy.

"Yeah, man," I said, "but she struggling." I was trying to keep cool, but I was scared that my baby was going to die right there in my arms.

"Will! Sonny! I need one of y'all to get in here and help, a'ight?"

Will and Sonny both came in the door, looking expectantly.

"Will, go back there and get some towels out the storage

room and bring them back. Hurry up! Son, go outside and tell the boys to let him go. Let the police think he got away in the madness. Later on, we'll pick the nigga up and take him for a ride."

Sonny grinned an evil grin. "Oh, fo' sho." Then he turned to Kane on the floor. "Don't worry punk. You gonna get to go, too." Sonny was the evil henchman in our crew. This nut was so far gone, that he would take care of our beef himself just to have something to get into. He was a scary dude, like Tupac's character, Bishop in "Juice."

Then he patted my shoulder. "Don't worry, man. She gonna be alright."

He looked at Kane.

"Man, I ought to fuck your ass up! But I got to go to the hospital and make sure my girl is okay. But I'm coming for you. So, you better use that head start, wisely. Punk ass nigga."

Kane wasn't saying nothing. His head was still spinning from that last kick he got from Tarik.

Will came back with the towels and kneeled down beside Ericka and me.

Tarik spoke to me, again. "Turn her on her side a little bit, man. We got to put some pressure on the holes, so she won't lose so much blood. Come on, man. It's gonna be alright."

I lay down completely on the floor and while Will helped me turn her on her side. Her head rested in my lap, while Sonny held the towel firmly against her back. Blood was pouring out of her like water coming out of a faucet. My nephew, Montez applied pressure to her leg. Tarik stood as a look out for the ambulance while he held the gun trained on Kane in case he breathed too hard.

Tarik looked at me. "Hey. Be strong, nigga. She gonna make it through. You got a ride or die chick."

He grinned.

"Boy, ain't nobody dying in here, today!"

I shook my head. "Man, I thought she was out riding around. That's why I took my time coming back." It was getting harder to hold back the tears.

"Stop tripping. You didn't know she was here. She got here after I talked to you on the phone. And I let Kane's punk ass stay once I found out he was here. I should have known his black ass was gonna start some trouble."

"Fuck that nigga. I'm gonna handle him as soon as I make sure E. is gonna be alright." Talking about getting this punk back for shooting my girl took away my urge to cry. If E. Middle hadn't been laying motionless in my lap, I would have finished his punk ass right there before the police got there.

Sonny spoke again.

"Naw, Reese. I got his ass. You can't be catching no case over this fool. You got too much to lose. Besides, if you go to jail, where we gonna hang out at?"

I looked at this fool wondering if he knew how stupid he sounded. If he went to the pen for killing either one of these clowns, didn't he realize that he wouldn't get to hang out here, either?

Us talking regular like it was just an ordinary day was helping calm me down. I didn't have a chance to think about how long it was taking the ambulance to get there. My boys always came through for me in a crunch.

Tarik said, "Yo. The police is gonna be trying to shut your shit down for that dice game, man. So, when they get here, you don't say shit, alright? Just let me do all the talking. You just need to concentrate on being there for E. Middle."

I nodded, weakly.

Kane had started to come to. A knot had raised up on his head the size of a baseball and his eye was swollen shut.

Tarik kneeled beside him and got right in his face, nose to nose.

"And nigga, your statement better not include no dice game, either. Or I'm gonna scalp you, myself, punk."

The police bust through the door with guns drawn.

"Drop your weapon and get your hands up!"

Tarik put up his hands in surrender and bent over slowly to put the gun down.

"Officer, there's your shooter right there," he said, pointing at Kane. "I was holding this fool, so he wouldn't try to run."

The police looked at us, hesitantly.

"Yeah, man," I said, weakly. "That's his gun Tarik just put down. He ran up on him from behind after the second shot."

The other officer rushed over and put Kane in handcuffs. The first officer spoke again.

"What the hell's going on in here, fellas?"

I looked at Tarik and then back at the police.

"Man, I was out making a run for my business and when I walked in, this nigga right here and another dude was squared off in the middle of my store."

As I was speaking, the paramedics had pulled up and flew in to start working on Ericka. Tarik had to help them pry me away so they could get to her. I couldn't bring myself to let her go. It was my fault she was lying in my arms covered in blood in the first place. If I hadn't been so overprotective of that damn car, she would have still been out riding around while I was out on that job. Damn! Why did she have to pick today of all days to listen to anything I said?

I couldn't stand to see her laying there all helpless but I couldn't take my eyes off her. My lack of attention to her got her two bullets in her beautiful body. Blood was trickling out of her mouth and her skin was gray and ashy looking. I struggled to control the urge to smooth down her hair. My baby couldn't stand for her hair to be out of place.

As I stood by watching the medics do their thing, the lead cop walked up on me, again. He acted like he had an attitude.

"So, you are the owner of this establishment?" he asked, suspiciously.

"Yes," I said, matter-of-factly. I wasn't about to let him intimidate me.

"What's your name, sir?"

"Maurice Council."

He started writing something on his little pad. I couldn't see what it was, but it was taking a long time for him just to be writing my name.

The officer was standing in front of me with his back to the guys working on Ericka so I could look through him and see what they were doing to her.

"Some of the guys outside said there was a dice game going on in here. You do know that gambling is illegal in this state, right?"

He was pissing me off.

"Man, if they were in here gambling, I don't know nothing about it. I left my boy, Tarik in here while I made a run because I was expecting a customer at six and I didn't want to miss him. Instead of you over here asking me about this bullshit, you need to be throwing that nigga, Kane up under the jail. That's my girl laying behind you full of holes!"

By that time, they were loading her up on the stretcher. I brushed past him.

"Look, man. I'm not going to let my girl go to the hospital by herself, so if I'm under arrest, then do your thing. Otherwise, back up off me."

The officer began to back down a little.

"No, Mr. Council, you're not under arrest. But we will be at the hospital later to get a statement from you."

"Yeah, you do that." I said without turning around.

Chapter 21

(Maurice)

Who You S'posed to Be?

The paramedics wouldn't let me ride in the back with Ericka, so I rode with the driver while the other dude worked on her behind us. They had done a pretty good job controlling the bleeding, even though she had already lost a lot before they got there. She was stable and semiconscious, but she wasn't saying anything. I stayed turned around in my seat the whole time trying to see what they were doing to her, and I kept talking to her from the front to let her know I was still there with her. It seemed like it took forever for us to get to the hospital. When we finally got there, they whisked her in the back of the emergency room to prep her for surgery, and a couple of attendants ushered me out into the waiting area before I could protest.

Nat, Toy, Renee, and Ericka's parents rushed me as soon as I walked into the waiting room. I explained to them what happened as best I could, even though I really didn't know what had gone down before I got to the shop. I never even got a chance to prepare to face her parents. I hadn't really had too many dealings with them in the past, so I thought they were going to blame me for what happened to her. But they actually turned out to be pretty cool in spite of the situation. Her dad wanted to know if I knew who shot her. I told him how the police had got the shooter, but the other guy involved in the altercation got away before the police got there. Her mom was grateful that we stayed with E. rather than going after him and getting ourselves in trouble behind it. I didn't tell her that we planned to hunt that ass down like an animal as soon as I could leave the damn hospital.

Tarik had called Nat right after we left to come to the hospital, and she had called Renee and Toy. Renee left Tomika with her husband and kids since she was already at her house for their Girl Scout meeting. I went up to Renee to thank her for taking care of Tomika and she snapped on me.

"If you had been taking care of your business, Ericka wouldn't be laying back there fighting for her life, Nigga! She has spent the last six years waiting on you to do right by her, and for what? Two fucking bullets in her ass! I told her to leave your sorry ass alone a long time ago. I hope you're satisfied!"

Out of all her friends, I couldn't stand Renee's black ass. She was a freaking meddler, and she thought she knew what was best for everybody. She had ground her husband's manhood in the dust a long time ago with her all her relentless temper tantrums and mood swings. She didn't know I knew it, but her ass had been talking against me since day one. I wanted to punch her fucking lights out.

"Look, Renee. I'm not gonna help you disrespect Ericka's parents by having this conversation with you out here in front of all these people. So, you need to back up off of me and stay out of my business," I said to her as calm as I could muster. That was just like Renée. She loved to make a scene.

"Why can't we discuss it, Reese? You scared that her parents gonna find out how you've been dogging their daughter all this time and that you're the reason why she's laying in this hospital full of holes! Dammit, she was waiting for you to pick her up and take her to get her truck! Where were you?"

Our altercation was apparently more interesting than what was happening on the waiting room television, and people were getting involved in our argument like they were at a tennis match. Everybody's eyes were suddenly on me. I would not disappoint.

"I was working. And Ericka knew I was working, so you putting in your two cents about what happened today don't mean shit, Renee, cuz you weren't there, okay? And furthermore, Ericka don't spend all of her free time trying to castrate me like you do Terrell. So, stop hating on me because she don't feel like she got to run my fucking life!"

Natalie grabbed my arm.

"Reese! That's enough! Y'all cut it, right now! This is not helping her. And Renee, as usual, you're out of line. Come with me to the cafeteria to get something to drink. You need to cool off. Reese, stay here in case the doctor comes out or Tarik and them come."

I nodded, flopped down in a chair and put my head in my hands. I couldn't believe this shit was happening. Renee was a bitch, but she was right.

This shit was all my fault. I thought about all the times Ericka complained about me staying at the shop late into the night and the times that I would leave her to go hang out with the boys at Friday's or the club. I never asked her if she wanted to come. And I would hang out all night and be bored as hell. I should have been spending all that time with my woman. All she was trying to do was be close to me and show me some love. But I was too busy trying not to let my guard down. And for what? Ericka was a good woman. She was always straight up with me. And even though we weren't married, she always took me for better or for worse. She loved me for me. She was the only woman to ever take me just like I was, and now there was a big chance that I was getting ready to lose her. I couldn't hold back the tears that had begun to roll down my face. I didn't love her like she needed to be loved and now I was going to lose her.

Ericka's mom walked over and put her hand on my shoulder.

"It's going to be alright, son," she said to me.

I looked up at her, and she was smiling.

"I'm sorry, Mrs. Middleton," I said, sniffling. "I didn't know she was going to be at my shop waiting for me. The only reason why I took so long was because I knew she wanted to drive my car. I swear, I would never let nothing happen to E. I love her."

She took my hand.

"I know you wouldn't, baby. You're all she talks about. She loves you, too. Nobody else may understand the relationship you two have. But as long as you understand it, that is all that matters. If I thought you were mistreating my daughter, don't you think I would have said something by now?"

She chuckled and nodded over to Ericka's dad who was flipping through a magazine in the opposite corner.

"And I've got a big, black husband over there that won't hesitate to back me up if I need him."

I smiled at her. She and Ericka looked almost like twins.

"Come on. We're getting ready to pray."

Natalie and Renee had come back from the cafeteria, followed by Tarik, Will, and some cat that I had never seen before. We all got in a circle and held hands.

"Let us pray," Ericka's father began.

While he prayed, I prayed a silent prayer of my own.

'Lord, please forgive me for not honoring the blessing of Ericka's love. I ask you to spare her life and bring her back to all the people here who love her, even if it means taking her away from me.'

After Mr. Middleton finished praying, he came over

and hugged me. He was a strong black man who never said too much, unless he was talking about a car or his favorite women. But he loved the women in his life, and it was understood that you did not disrespect them, or you would have to answer to him.

"You know, Ericka tells me everything about you, good and bad," he said.

I hung my head.

He continued.

"But I was a young man one time, too. So, I realize that some of the complaints she has are really just a maturity issue on your part. Deep down, I believe that you really love my daughter. Now, you see the hard way how important it is to make the most of the time you have with the people you love. My daughter is stubborn and impatient just like her Ma. To tell you the truth, I don't know how you lasted this long."

We both laughed.

But you know when you get her back, this time, it will be totally on you."

"Yes sir, I know."

He patted me on the shoulder and walked away without another word.

As I was about to get up and go over to Tarik and the rest of the group, the nurse paged for the Middleton family over the loudspeaker. Then she ushered us all into a small conference room where the doctor was waiting.

"Is she okay, Doc?" her dad asked. "Can we see her now?"

The doctor shook his hand and introduced himself. His name was Dr. Covington, and he had just finished Ericka's surgery.

"We were able to successfully remove the bullet from Ericka's leg. It had lodged in the back of her thigh muscle. We had to repair some torn tendons and muscle tissue, but with some physical therapy she should be as good as new."

"However, the bullet in her back was a little trickier. We were able to remove it, but in doing so, there was some trauma caused to her spinal cord. We won't know for a few days how much damage has been done."

The room got really quiet, and everybody had this look like the man had just said she died. It was then I noticed that guy from the prayer circle, again. Who was this cat, and why hadn't anybody introduced him to me?

Her mom asked, "Are you saying she might not be able to walk again?"

No, he couldn't be saying that. She had to be able to go skating with Baby Girl like she always did on Saturdays. She just got that motorcycle. She hadn't even really had a chance to ride it. What about all the things I planned for us to do like us taking our motorcycles to bike week together next year? Or taking her to Jamaica for our honeymoon? She couldn't be paralyzed. Her life was just beginning.

I kept quiet, scared that if I opened my mouth, I would lose it.

The doctor spoke again.

"There is a fifty percent chance that your daughter might never walk again. But right now, there is so much swelling from the gunshot and the surgery to remove the bullet, it is impossible to tell. Ericka narrowly escaped this thing without having to have a blood transfusion. The loss of blood was significant. Because of the position of the bullet in her back, the trauma also caused her right lung to collapse. We had to put her on a ventilator for the time being. She's not out of the woods yet, but there is a great possibility that she is going to make it through this."

Ventilator? What the fuck had I done?

Toy spoke up.

"Can we see her?"

"She's in ICU, so you can only go in two or three at a time. There is a waiting room up there like this where you can sit while you take turns going in. Try not to stay in there longer than a couple of minutes at a time."

When we got to the ICU, Ericka's parents went in first. Me and the rest of the group went into the waiting area to sit. But the mystery dude didn't come in with us. He kept on past the waiting room and made a stop at the nurses' station before disappearing in another room down the hall.

"Yo Rik, man, who is that dude that's been hanging around here since before we left the emergency room?" I asked Tarik.

"I don't know, man," he said, scratching his chin. "I thought maybe he was somebody in the family. He spoke to her parents, though. Why? Where'd he go?"

"He went into one of those rooms down there."

"You want me to check it out for you?" Tarik asked.

"Naw, man. I'll find out for myself. It might not be nothing."

"Alright, dawg. Let me know if you need me."

I purposely waited for everyone else to go in first. I wanted to be able to take my time without someone else waiting for me to come out so they could go in. Plus, I sort of hung back to see whether or not that unknown brother was going to come back and try to see Ericka, too. If he did, that would be my time to find out exactly who he was.

I admired the way Ericka's parents were able to be so strong when I knew it was tearing them up on the inside to see their daughter all jacked up. Hell, they had to comfort the rest of the group. Natalie held it down until she left the room, but she collapsed as soon as she got out into the hallway. And the other two were crying like she was dead. Ericka's mom was consoling them, and it was her daughter that was in the hospital. I was standing there thinking how thankful I was that E. apparently took her strong personality from her peeps. She hardly got ruffled about anything. I can't stand no weak ass woman.

Tarik took the girls out to get something to eat and to give me a chance to be by myself with Ericka. When everybody left, I made my way toward her room door. I peeked inside, kind of scared of what might be waiting on me. The light in the room was real dim, so I couldn't really see her at first. I could hear the beeping of all those machines and that ventilator that was helping her breathe. I walked real slow toward her because I dreaded coming that close to reality. I wanted to see my baby, but I didn't want to see her like that.

When I got up to the bed, I tried to smile away the tears that were threatening to fall down my face. I didn't want her to wake up and see me looking like no bitch standing over her. It hurt me to see her laying there with that tube forced down her throat and her hair all messed up. I reached down to smooth it back on the pillow. She would have been trying to primp right there in the bed if she thought I was anywhere near. I chuckled at the thought. Her skin was pale and ashy, probably from all the blood she lost, but she looked so beautiful and peaceful laying there, anyway. I took her hand and kissed it.

I pulled up a chair and sat real close to the head of the bed. For a minute, I just lay my head real close to her body. She used to always complain that she didn't have enough cuddle time in bed with me. When I did spend the night there, she would get as close up under me as she could, and she would curve her body to fit mine however I was lying. She liked the closeness of just having me in bed with her at night. She said it made her feel warm and secure. I used to get mad and purposely go home at night because I thought she was trying to lock me down. Now, I wanted to feel that same feeling of warm security she talked about all the time. I couldn't understand where she was coming from before. Now I would have given anything to be able to curl up at home in the bed with her right then. But the only feeling I got from her right then was the cold ass air coming from the vents in that hospital room and Ericka's body heaving up and down from the ventilator pumping air in and out of her mouth.

She lay there, still like a rock. She wasn't moving. She wasn't doing nothing. I wanted her to wake up so I could talk to her. I had so much to tell her. Before when she used to try to talk to me, I would sit there and play stupid. I would let her do all the talking and not say nothing. Then when she would ask me stuff; I would act like I didn't understand what she meant. She would get so pissed off at me. I wanted to tell her that I loved her. That I was just scared if I put myself out there, she would hurt me. I was scared to tell her that I really wanted to marry her and have a ton of kids. I didn't want her to know how good it actually felt having her around. And that I would have gladly told them niggas at the shop to get them some business if I wasn't so scared that she would stop loving me if she knew that she really had me sprung. Instead, I went out of my way to not spend any time with her. I always put the boys before her. I basically fed her with a long-handled spoon. I did just enough to keep her around; nothing more, nothing less. And apparently, she really did love me because she put up with all of my shit like we had been married for thirty years.

I tried to think of one good reason why after all this time I deserved to be with a woman as good as Ericka. I couldn't think of any. I took a deep breath and just began to tell her everything that was on my mind. I wasn't sure if she could hear me. But I had to tell her right then, in case I never got to say them again. I had wasted enough time being stupid. It was time to put up or shut up. I rose up and took a deep breath.

"Hey, E. Middle. I know you would be having a fit about the nurses leaving you in here with your hair looking all crazy, so I smoothed it back for you. I guess they lost your ponytail holder on the way over here. I'll bring you some more from the house later, okay? But you know you look good to me, whether your hair is done or not, right?

Baby, I'm sorry for letting this happen to you. You know I would never let anybody hurt you. I would kill a nigga before I let them do something to you. I know you think I just left you out there today like I always do. But it was different, this time, I swear. I just took my time because I knew you wanted to drive my car. I know you like rolling in the Beamer. I just wanted to give you a chance to high side and try out the new system and floss with the new twenty-two's. I know you like stuff like that, too. I was just trying to make you happy. Because I know you been unhappy with me lately, and I wanted to try to make it up to you. I didn't know you were going to come back to the shop and get mixed up in all that shit that was going on. I would have killed everybody in there to keep anything from happening to you.

I love you, girl. I know I ain't never said it before. I'm sorry that you almost had to lose your life to make me realize how much you mean to me. But I love you, girl. I've always loved you. And I don't care who know it. I don't give a kitty about them dudes at the shop or nothing else. All I want is you. And if I have to spend the rest of my life trying to make this shit up to you, I will. I just want you to be okay, baby. Please come back to me."

This time, I couldn't stop the single tear that rolled down my face. Forget being a player. That 'trying to be a player' shit don't get you nowhere in the middle of the night when you all alone in an empty bed feeling empty as hell on the inside. Being a player didn't get me nowhere when I needed somebody to help me organize my office at Hot Wheelz. Ericka is the one that handles most of my finances, balances my checkbook at my shop, and keeps money in the bank so I don't blow it all. And being a player damn sure ain't going to get me nowhere when I don't have nobody to rub the back of my head at night when I'm tired until I fall asleep. Or scratch my back with them long ass nails, or pop popcorn and bake cookies for us to eat while we watch James Bond movies.

I had said all I could say, so I bent over to kiss her forehead one more time before I left. I looked at her for another minute or so, hating to say goodbye. As I tried to let go, I felt her squeeze my hand just a little. She had been so still the whole time I was there, the sensation felt strange. I froze and studied her face again. But her eyes were still closed and other than that slight squeeze, she hadn't moved.

"I knew you wouldn't leave me," I said, smiling.

I let her hand go and left the room.

"Thank you, God," I whispered looking up at the ceiling.

I walked right into the unknown brother as I was leaving the room.

"My bad, bruh," he said to me, patting me on the shoulder.

I backed away from him, kind of flexing a little. It was about time dude identified himself.

"Bruh, I been seeing you hanging around my girl's room ever since we got here and none of our peeps seem to know who you are. Wassup? Who you s'posed to be?"

He smiled.

"You must be Maurice. We finally get to meet."

He reached out to shake my hand, but I just looked at it.

"Okay, so it's obvious that you know me. Now you gonna tell me who you are or what?

"Sorry, man. It's just that Ericka has told me so much about you. I feel like we could be boys. I'm a good friend of hers. I'm Desmond. Call me D."

So, this was the infamous De that made the women yell out his name in their sleep. This punk must have had a set of bronze balls to show his face around here when he had something going on with my woman. Ericka said that they were just friends, but I still had my suspicions. I heard her call his name with my own ears. And she had stopped complaining so much about me not coming around, so I couldn't be sure that she was spending all of her lonely nights at home, either.

"How you know she was here, man?" I asked, suspiciously. "And why you been lurking around here being all secretive and shit?"

"Look man, I didn't mean no disrespect. I introduced myself to her parents, so they knew who I was. And I stayed quiet out of respect for all of y'all. It would have been too distracting to be trying to do introductions in the midst of all that was happening. I was taking the scenic route back from the cafeteria for coffee when they brought Ericka in. I recognized her on the gurney and followed the commotion into the ER. That's how I knew she was here."

I looked at him like he was crazy.

"So, what? You strolling around the hospital for exercise, or something? You sound like a stalker to me."

"Naw, man. I'm no stalker. I've been here for the last few days with my wife. She is down the hall."

I relaxed my posture a little bit.

"Your wife? Is she alright?"

"No, man. She's not doing too good. Lapsed into a coma late last night."

"Damn, man. I'm sorry to hear that. What's wrong with her?"

Desmond shook his head.

"Thanks, man. The doctor couldn't get her blood pressure to go down after she lost our last baby, and she's been under round the clock care ever since. She spiked a fever earlier this week and the doctor put her back in the hospital. It's been kind of downhill ever since."

I felt kind of sorry for the dude. But that still didn't explain what he was doing hanging out around here. Why was he in here trying to see about Ericka when his own wife was in here bout to take her last breath? I couldn't help but think he still had a hidden agenda. But I tried to be cool about it.

"Man, I'm sorry about your wife, you know what I'm saying? I guess I kinda know what you going through."

"Yeah, thanks man," Desmond said, sighing. "Things are kind of rough for you right now, too. At least I don't have people flipping out on me like you do, though. Her home girl was out of line for stepping to you like that in the ER."

I was trying to stand my ground because I wanted to confront him about being with my girl. But this cat was actually pretty cool. He wasn't trying to step on my toes or nothing. Under any other circumstances, we probably would have been partners.

"Yeah, man. I ain't sweatin' that shit. It's always somebody out there that don't want to see you happy, you know."

"I feel you on that," Desmond said.

I got the feeling that maybe I had the wrong impression of D. But I still needed to see if I could find out for sure whether or not he and Ericka had been messing around. I tried to approach as cautiously as I could without letting him know I suspected anything.

"Man, it's good to meet you, and everything, but I have to admit Ericka really hasn't ever mentioned you to me. I'm not trying to be funny, but how do you know her, and why is it that you know enough about her to figure out who I was?"

Desmond looked at me like he was thinking hard about something. Maybe he was trying to think of a quick lie to save his ass.

Then, he said, "Ericka and I used to work together at Global Technology. I always thought she was good people, so I kept in touch with her after she left. We lost contact for a while, but I ran into her again a few months ago when she came by to see some girls she was tight with at the job. We exchanged numbers again and we have been speaking on the phone at least three times a week ever since."

I was starting to get a little heated. This cat had been talking on the phone to my girl three times a week for the last few months, and I didn't even know nothing about it. And he was standing up there all smug like they had been pulling something over on me. I was trying to be cool, but it was hard.

"What?" I asked him, not wanting to believe what he was saying. "Why do you and my girl have so much to talk about?"

Desmond didn't even flinch.

"Look, Reese. Don't take this the wrong way, alright? It's not even like that."

"Not like what, nigga? Before I heard my girl call out your name in her sleep a couple of weeks ago, I didn't even know you existed. Now, you standing here with a straight face trying to tell me that y'all been conversating on the phone three times a week for the past few months? Well, I need to know, what is like, then?"

"Look, Reese, man. Me and Ericka are just friends. There's nothing going on between us, nor has there ever been. We just clicked on the job and got tight, that's all. She a good person to talk to and frankly, I enjoy her company. But I love my wife and Ericka loves you. Neither one of us is trying to jeopardize our relationships. We are just mad cool, that's it. I swear."

This dude must think I was born yesterday. Even if it wasn't nothing going on with him and E., he couldn't tell me that he hadn't thought about the possibility.

"So, how does your wife feel about the little friendship you got going on with E.?"

"Honestly, my wife has been semiconscious for the last six months. That's why I work at night so I can be home to take care of her during the day. I talk to Ericka on the phone before I leave work at night and go home to my wife. Ericka has been my diversion from my home situation. She doesn't even know my wife is sick. I didn't tell her because I needed someone to talk to that wouldn't spend all my free time telling me how sorry they were about my situation. I don't need pity, I just need some real conversation every now and then, you know? My wife didn't know Ericka before, but even if she did, I don't believe she would have a problem with us being friends."

"Well, the problem I have with you is that you are a man. And you say you love your wife and all that but come on. You can't tell me that you ain't never thought about trying to get with my girl. It's not like your wife would know."

I probably stepped over the line with that one. But who did this brother think he was fooling? How you gonna use my girl as your substitute wife? That shit still wasn't flying with me.

Not to be one upped, Desmond came back with, "Hell yeah, man. I thought about it a million times. No matter how much time my wife has left, she'll never come back to me again. And I love her, but I need to find not only a way to move on, but also the right time. I would never disrespect my wife like that, comatose, or not. As for me trying to get with your girl, if that's all I wanted to do, bruh, I had plenty of chances to do that. Don't try to play that loving boyfriend bullshit with me. You standing here trying to make it seem like Ericka was hiding some kind of affair we were having or something. The only reason you didn't know about me was because you were never around when she needed you to be there. I've called that house plenty of times at different times of the day and night. And you've only been there one time that I know of. I used to tease Ericka and tell her that she must have made you up because y'all never spent any time together. Hell, I talked to your girl more than you did. You tried to buy your way into her heart when all she really wanted was for you to pay her a little attention. Now that she's all shot up in there, you want to lay all up under her and cry and shit. It's not even about her, now, is it? It's about you trying to ease your guilty conscience, right? She was sitting at the shop waiting on you to pick her up. Isn't that what you told her parents? And as for her calling out my name in her sleep, I'm not gonna even acknowledge that bullshit."

I wanted to beat the hell out of D. for what he was saying, but causing a big scene wouldn't solve nothing. Plus, he was right. That time he called, and I answered was the first thing I knew about her receiving calls from other dudes. It was about six in the evening, and had I not felt bad about not spending no time over there in the first place, I would never have known. Hell, she could have been leading a double life as far as I knew. I just took it for granted that she was so in love with me, she wouldn't even be looking at nobody else.

Noticing that we had started to get kind of loud, Desmond asked me to come into the lounge where we could finish talking. After we stepped out of public view, he continued.

"Look, Maurice. I'm not going to lie to you. I'm attracted to Ericka. She's beautiful. She's intelligent. And most of all, you gave me open access to your woman. Sometimes, I would call at just the right moment. Like those times when you would have just left her to meet the fellas at the club. Or when you would call her at the last minute to tell her that you wouldn't be able to make it over that night because you were too busy bullshitting at the shop. I could swear sometimes when she answered the phone, she had been crying. Any other man would have pounced at the chance to make her feel better, to make her feel wanted. I was the one who took her to the beach for her birthday. You virtually gave me permission to get the panties. You never had any use for them."

I started to see red. This nigga was standing in my face talking about how he could have taken what was mine. I got up in his face nose to nose.

"So, what, man? You been banging my girl?"

Desmond didn't back down. He stood his ground looking dead in my eyes.

"Naw, man. I didn't bang your girl. I respect her. I know

she don't roll like that. So, I never even brought it up. What? You wanna hit me for noticing something you haven't been paying attention to for six years? Take your best shot."

I wanted to hit him. I wanted to knock his fucking block off. I willed my arm to move, but it wouldn't. The truth hurts, and my ass was in a lot of pain right then. I took a step back.

He grunted.

"Yeah, that's what I thought."

I turned my back to him.

"Man, I tried to give her everything that she wanted."

"If you really wanted to give her what she wanted, you would have listened to what she had been trying to say instead of dismissing it as bitching. She didn't want that material shit, man. She wanted you. She thought something might be wrong with her."

I gave him a puzzled look.

"She thought something was wrong with her? Wrong with her like what?"

"Man, she thought that she was doing something wrong because she couldn't get you to come out of them streets."

I sat down, shaking my head. My mind went back to the days when I was married to Toni, and I felt like Toni couldn't stand the sight of me. I remember Toni making me feel inadequate by never wanting me to touch her. And I had been making Ericka feel the same way. And I was too stupid to figure it out for myself. I had to hear it from another man about how I was fucking up in my own relationship. And dude had to be sincere, because if he had been one of them grimy dudes I'm used to dealing with, they would have just taken advantage of Ericka feeling bad about herself, screwed her, and then gloated to my face. I was grateful that he came to me like a man, but my pride was hurt because no man wants to hear that they are not satisfying their woman. And they especially don't want to hear it from another man. I couldn't even look up at him. I couldn't believe it had all come down to this.

"Look man," said Desmond. "You need to understand that this isn't about me having beef with you or trying to hurt your pride or nothing. I don't know you like that. Nor am I trying to protect your best interests. Personally, I thought she should have bounced a long time ago. I shouldn't even be telling you any of this. But for whatever reason, she loves you, and I'm tired of seeing her hurt. My wife is lying in the room next to hers and the doctors have already told me that the next breath she takes could very well be her last. But my wife knew before she went into that coma that I loved her. And I have no regrets. Can you honestly say that Ericka knew that about you?"

I couldn't bring myself to say the truth out loud.

"Man, I feel what you saying," I said, defeated.

"Look, Maurice. You knew when you met Ericka that she was different than the rest of the females out there. You should have known that what worked for everybody else wasn't going to work for her. She did everything she could to get you to want to be with her and you kept giving her the brush off. I don't know how she's going to feel towards you when she wakes up and realizes what happened to her. But I do know that if you plan on keeping her around, you better step up your game because she's got a reason to be tired of your ass, for real, now. I gotta get back to my wife. It's on you, bruh."

With that, he turned and walked out.

Chapter 22

(Maurice)

Revenge in Your Eyes

The police passed Desmond on his way out, as they came in to ask more questions about what happened at the shop. After the conversation I had just finished with Desmond, I sure as hell wasn't in the mood to be asked the same shit over and over by the police; especially when I didn't even know anything.

I stood, like I was preparing for a fight.

One of the cops was a guy that I played football with in high school. His name was Kelvin Bryant, and he patrolled the area where my shop was. We stayed pretty cool through the years, and he always paid special attention to my business. I was pretty sure he knew that the fellows shot dice in the back. But if he did, he never said anything. I was kind of relieved when I saw that it was him handling the investigation. If nothing else, I knew he would make sure that Kane's ass would be taken care of.

The other officer was the same dude that was asking all the questions before the ambulance got there. He had kind of pissed me off, so I still had my guard up towards him.

Bryant shook my hand and gave me a bro hug.

"Reese man, I'm sorry about your girl," he said, with genuine sympathy. "Is she gonna be okay?"

I shook my head.

"I'on know, man. She's on a ventilator. Doctor said she might be paralyzed."

"Damn, that's rough. I'm sorry to have to barge in on you like this. But you know I got to do my job, right?" he asked, apologetically.

I nodded my head.

He pulled out his little notepad and began to write.

"What was going on when you pulled up to the shop?" he asked.

I took a deep breath.

"Man, when I got there, it was a bunch of people standing around outside. I asked Will what was going on and he said some dudes were squared off in the shop. I ran in because I saw my car parked outside and my girl had my car today. I was trying to make sure that she didn't get caught in the middle of no mess. I didn't know if these guys were packing heat or what."

I told him about how Kane was laying in my display case and how he shot Ericka in front of us, trying to shoot that other cat.

The other officer cut in on the conversation.

"Do you know what the argument was about, Mr. Council?"

I rolled my eyes in the air.

"Look, man. I told you the fight had already started before I got there? How am I supposed to know what the beef was?"

"Nobody told you what happened afterwards?"

"Now, if I told you what somebody else told me, that would be hearsay, wouldn't it?" I shot back, sarcastically.

"Mr. Council, I'd watch myself if I were you," the white

officer said, coolly. "We already have enough evidence to get a search warrant for your place of business."

"A search warrant for what?" I asked, indignantly.

"You tell us, "The white officer said, smoothly.

Bryant was getting uncomfortable over our exchange. He cleared his throat.

"Um, Matthews, step outside, let me holla at you for a sec."

While they stood outside the door talking low, I wondered what the hell else would happen today.

Bryant came back in the room alone.

"Sorry about that, Reese. Matthews is just with me temporarily until my regular partner, Officer James comes back. You remember James, don't you?"

I knew James. He was also a brother, and he was cool, too.

Bryant continued.

"Man, look. I think one of your boys that was in the shop dimed you out about the dice game. I don't think it was personal. I just believe that somebody up in there had some warrants and started singing so they wouldn't get locked up. But don't worry about that. I'll take care of it as long as you can assure me that your shit is on the up and up."

I threw up my hands.

"My shit has always been on the ups, man. You know, I let the fellas play every now and then when business is slow, but that's it. And if that was such a big deal to you, you would have been locked me up. C'mon, you know me better than that."

Officer Bryant paused for a minute.

"Yeah, you right. Drugs and shit ain't really your style. It's all good. But I need to ask you one more thing."

"What's up?" I asked.

"That cat that Kane was shooting at? Let him live. He's

got two strikes and when we get him, he's going down as a habitual felon, anyway."

I played dumb.

"Man, what you talking about?"

"Don't play me, Reese. I hear that evil nigga Sonny is going looking for him. And it's been too much bloodshed, already. Let us handle it, from here. We know who he is, and we'll get him."

I turned my back, but didn't say nothing. It was his fault that my baby was in the hospital. He had better hope Sonny got to his ass before I did. And Kane better be glad he was already locked up.

Officer Bryant put his hand on my shoulder.

"Yo. You can turn your back on me, but you can't hide that revenge in your eyes. I know you're pissed off because he tore up your shop and the bullets went into your girlfriend instead of him, but you need to let us handle it. It's not worth your freedom, man."

I turned to face him, again.

"Well, what if you don't get him? You know y'all ain't gonna really look for him, anyway. You got the shooter. And Kane will probably be out in eighteen months or less. You know the system don't care when stuff happens to us."

"That's not altogether true, Reese. And even if it were, your way of handling it is not right. Now, I'm only gonna say it one more time. Let me do my job. If anything happens to that dude before we get to him, you're gonna take the fall for it. You got that?"

"Yeah, man, whatever," I said, without really meaning it.

"You got the number," he said, reaching to shake my hand. "Call me if anything else comes up. And I'm gonna be praying for Ericka."

"Thanks, man," I said, taking his hand.

Chapter 23

(Maurice)

Somebody Had to Die That Night

I left the hospital that night with murder on my mind. I really wanted to kill Desmond for trying to push up on my girl. But deep in my heart I knew he hadn't, really. If nothing else, I knew that Ericka wasn't that kind of woman. And even if things hadn't been that good with us, lately, she still wouldn't have cheated on me. I knew that all this mess was my fault for not paying her any attention.

Even still, I couldn't shake the thought of her laughing and talking with this man on the phone like she did with me. That is, whenever I had time to talk to her on the phone. And I had to make myself not think about her being at the beach with him for a whole weekend. How could I have been so damn stupid? I tried my best to blame him for everything that had gone wrong in my relationship. When that didn't work, I tried to blame it all on her. But no matter how I tried to point the finger at somebody else, it still kept turning back to point at me. At that moment, though, I didn't care. I just wanted to put some of this hurt that I was carrying on somebody else.

They had already taken Kane's thug ass downtown. I

probably could've called in a favor to some of my boys in the county lock up. But chances were they already knew what had gone down before I did and were waiting on Kane to get processed in so they could get to him. That made me feel a little better, but I didn't want the fellas at the county to get all of my action.

I knew the other dude got away after Ericka got shot. So that meant his punk ass was still out there, somewhere. It must have been my lucky night. His sorry ass luck was about to run out. I didn't know his name, but I had seen him hanging out in the housing project right near downtown. He didn't shoot my girl, but he started the fight that damn near got her killed.

That punk must have been crazy to think that he could come up in my store with some bullshit and get away with it. Black folks are our own worst enemy. They always want to blame the white man for keeping them down, yet whenever black business owners lose out, it's usually at the hands of another black person. That's why we can't keep no decent clubs around here. Sooner or later, niggas will get bored with what's happening inside and start wilin' out. And Raleigh PD is quick to shut your shit down for good.

That's why I just let them hang out at my spot, so they could be somewhere where they could just chill and hang out without the police sweatin' them. And all I asked in return is that they respect my shit. But instead, not only did they disrespect my place of business; they tried to kill my girl in the process. So, somebody had to die that night.

Ericka was right. I did put them dudes in front of her and look what happened. But never again. From now on, no more hustling. Everything would be straight on the up and up from this day forward. Soon as I killed this nigga.

The more I thought about Ericka laying in that bed with that tube down her throat, the hotter I got. I rode up and down the little side streets and alleys hoping to catch a glimpse of the dude that Kane was fighting. I circled Lane Street and rode past St. Aug. It was late so, there weren't a lot of people out. There were a few standing around the corner here and there, but the block was quiet. I rode down through Washington Terrace and then through Worthdale, but still came up empty. I had just about given up when the phone rang. It was Sonny.

"What up, Son?" I asked.

"Yo, Reese, man. Where you at?"

His voice was cool and even, like he had just smoked some bud. But I knew better. His voice had a chill to it that made the hair on the back of my neck stand up.

"I'm headed to the crib. Why? Wassup?"

"Meet me downtown by the old warehouse near the train tracks. Down past Five Star. I got something for you."

I paused.

I didn't have to ask what it was. I tried to stay cool, but I knew he could hear how anxious I was sounding over the phone.

"Yo, Son. What you do, man?"

Sonny ignored me.

"Reese, hurry up, man. I ain't got all fucking night."

Then he hung up.

Shit.

I hit the accelerator and gunned the engine. I knew that crazy ass Sonny was about to do some shit we'd all be sorry for, if he hadn't already. Nobody would have ever thought that less than an hour ago, I was looking to kill somebody. Now that it appeared that he was already dead, it wasn't even worth it. Ericka was still trying to hold on in the hospital and I had still fucked up my relationship. And now to top it all off, I was about to catch a case for a punk that I didn't even get a chance to swing on. Could this day get any fucking worse?

A set of headlights flicked twice as I approached the warehouse. I felt like I was in a damn movie or something. What the hell had Sonny done and why the hell did he want me to meet him in this dark ass place? That nigga was crazy. I cut my lights and drove up slowly beside his car. Sonny opened my car door for me, and I got out.

"How your baby girl doing, man?" he asked solemnly.

"She's fucked up, man. She got tubes down her throat and shit. Doctor said she might not walk again.

I hung my head after I said it. The weight of the thought made my head too heavy to hold up.

"Yo, Reese. I know you was out looking for that nigga tonight. That's why I called. You gotta be there for your girl, man. You can't be pulling no time while your wifey is sick. So, I took care of that for you."

He motioned for me to follow him toward the back of the car. When he popped the trunk, there was the guy that I had been looking for all night hog-tied, his mouth covered with duct tape. His eyes were opened wide, and he looked scared as hell. Thank God, he didn't look like Sonny had hurt him yet.

"Yo, Son. I know you'll do anything in the world for me, man. And you know I got your back. But I don't want you to go jail, especially not for no murder. Man, they gonna put your ass on death row for this shit."

Sonny grinned that even platinum grin.

"Please. You my boy and everything, but I don't love you like that to go back on no lockdown. I just wanted to make him sweat a little bit."

Me and the dude in the trunk sighed real deep at the same time.

"Well fool, why you got him all tied up in the trunk of your car like you the 'Transporter' or some shit?"

Now, I was getting ill.

"And what you call me out here to do? You know he gon'

tell soon as you let him go. Then you gon' catch a kidnapping charge. And come to think of it, I am too, nigga!"

I wanted to smack this fool.

"Naw, Reese, man. All the rest of the cats at the shop bounced as soon as they saw the police coming. And word on the street is that Kane is downtown trying to say that 'Rik was the one who shot baby girl. He told them you was runnin' an illegal gambling and after hours spot out of Hot Wheelz.

And even though you and 'Rik both saw him shoot, your credibility is fucked up because of that dice game. And since mostly everybody else got warrants and shit, they ain't trying to get involved. So that means we ain't got no witnesses.

And if that nigga Kane can cast doubt down at the precinct, they might not convict his ass at trial. Or worse, he could plead out and do a few months and be back in these streets. So, I bought you out here to help me convince this punk to testify against Kane so the judge can go ahead and give him his third strike."

For a crazy dude, Sonny made a lot of sense. He looked at the dude in the car.

Sonny reached down and snatched the tape savagely away from his mouth. The guy yelled out in pain.

"You ready to talk, punk?" Sonny asked.

The guy bobbed his head up and down, frantically.

Sonny bent down and got right in his face. He pointed at me.

"You see my boy right here? He been at the hospital all day with his girl that took a bullet that was meant for your ass. If she lives, she might not be able to walk again. Do you think it's fair that she gotta ride around in a wheelchair while your legs still work, nigga?"

The guy stammered.

"Sonny, man, I didn't mean for it to go down like that. That nigga Kane owe me like fifteen g's. He tried to get me in that dice game."

"Fuck that money, Yo. You almost got somebody killed that didn't have nothing to do with that shit. Look, from where I'm standing, I saved your sorry ass life. My man been riding around here all night looking for you so he could put your fucking lights out. So, the way I see it is, you owe me a favor."

The guy in the trunk was breathing hard.

"What you want me to do, man?"

Sonny smiled.

"Oh, that's easy. You're gonna go tell Raleigh PD that Reese didn't have nothing to do with no dice game. And then you gonna tell them that Kane was shooting at you at Hot Wheelz, not Tarik."

That nigga, Sonny was smoother than Jack McCoy on Law and Order.

"C'mon, Sonny, man," the dude whined, "I can't be all up in the police face like that. I got warrants here and in New York."

Sonny rose to his feet.

"Alright, mothafucka. Since you more scared of the police than the niggas that's got you tied up and stuffed in the trunk of a fucking car, here's how we gonna run this.

You don't want to return the favor so I'ma take you out of my car and toss your ass in the back of my man's truck and act like I ain't seen you."

He shrugged his shoulders and looked at me.

"Reese, you got him, man. Help me get him in your truck."

I was enjoying every minute of watching him sweat. Not to be left out, I lifted up my shirt and revealed the butt of my nine-millimeter in my waistband.

"Fuck that," I said, trying to imitate Sonny's evil smile. "I don't want his DNA in my damn truck. I'ma do his ass right here."

"No, wait!" the guy screamed like a little bitch. "Alright,

Reese, you got it, man. I'll do it. Okay? You can even drop me in front of the precinct. Just please, untie me, okay?"

Sonny sighed, almost disappointed that the dude had agreed to his list of demands.

"Alright, alright. Bitch ass nigga."

He bent over to untie him.

"Wait," I said to Sonny. "How do we know we can trust this nigga to do what he said? He could skip town tonight."

"Oh, he'll do it and he ain't going nowhere," Sonny reassured me. "Because if he don't do it, then he'll be double crossing me. And I might not kill him for you, but I damn sure ain't gonna let him fuck over me.

And besides, nigga, I got your wallet and your id with your baby's mama's address on it. I would hate to have to pay her and the kids a visit in the middle of the night like I did your punk ass. But she might not be as lucky as your sorry ass."

The dude looked like he had just seen a ghost.

"C'mon, Sonny man. You ain't got to get my girl involved in this. She pregnant, and . . ."

Sonny cut him off.

"Do you think I give a damn about your mongrel ass kids? My man's girl might die and leave their kid without no mama. So, you better not be playing me, punk."

The guy nodded wearily.

I helped Sonny untie him, and then we both got in our vehicles and left the guy in the deserted spot, leaving him standing in the dark by himself.

Chapter 24

No Little Green Men

I finally woke up from this weird long dream, only to find out that I wasn't dreaming. It was indeed very real that I was lying in a bed hooked up to all kinds of tubes and machines. The darkness that my eyes had grown accustomed to was suddenly being invaded by the light forcing its way in. I blinked rapidly, trying to focus in on where I was, exactly. I tried to sit up to look around, but my body seemed to be bolted to the bed. The best I could do was to raise my left index finger. So, I lay there, stiff, darting my eyes back and forth around the room in an attempt to make sense of my surroundings.

It appeared that I was in the hospital for something, although for the life of me I couldn't figure out for what. The room was pretty festive for a hospital room. It was painted a soft pink, and big, brightly colored balloons floated in almost every corner. Flowers sat on every table and shelf. And someone had even taken care to hang get-well-soon cards on the walls. A picture of Tomika and I sat on the bedside table at the foot of my bed. It looked like someone had been planning a party.

A dull pounding inside my skull interrupted my thoughts. A tube had been shoved down my throat at some point, leaving my throat really dry and sore. Had I had surgery? Or worse, maybe someone had kidnapped me and stolen one of my kidneys. I wanted some water. I tried to call out for someone, but my lips didn't seem to be working either. In fact, nothing was working from the neck down, with the exception of the finger that I managed to wiggle. Trying to take in so much at one time was exhausting, even though I really couldn't move. I could feel the sweat beads forming on my brow. The room was beginning to spin. I closed my eyes and tried to take a deep breath. I had to figure out what was going on and why I was strapped down to this bed.

I tried to think back to the last place that I remembered being. But my head was pounding. I couldn't focus. What time was it? Where was everybody? Maybe this was one of those alien abductions. My mind was going in a hundred different directions. But since no one else seemed to be around, all I could do was wait.

I fell asleep again and started to dream. I dreamt that everyone had gathered for a party in my honor. They had been waiting a long time for me to come through the door so they could surprise me. But I could already see them from where I was standing outside the door. I knocked and knocked, but no one seemed to hear me. Oddly enough, no one really seemed to be in a partying mood, either. Everyone seemed so sad. All my family and friends were there. Even Desmond and Maurice were there together. And they were talking just like they knew each other.

I was tired of sleeping. And I was tired of lying in that bed. I had to get someone in there to get me some water and get me a mirror. I'm sure my hair was a hot mess if I had been lying in this bed for any extended period of time. I hated for my hair to be all over my head, especially when other people could see it. I prayed that when I opened my eyes this time a nurse or somebody would be there. And hopefully they would read my mind and get me what I wanted since it appeared that at this point, I couldn't tell them.

The light wasn't as bright when I opened my eyes this time, so it didn't take long for me to focus. Fortunately, there were no little green men lurking around my room. And to my sheer delight, everyone that I loved was there with me this time. I could see my dad standing by the door talking to Tomika. My mom and Renee, Natalie, and Toy were all talking quietly. They didn't seem to notice that I was awake. I opened my mouth to say something, but again, my vocal cords wouldn't cooperate. So, I lay there enjoying watching my family interact with one another.

Shortly after I opened my eyes, I saw Maurice walk through the door. He shook my dad's hand, and then scooped Tomika up in his arms and she gave him a big kiss on the cheek. He smiled brightly, as they chatted about something I couldn't really hear. As he put her back down on the floor, he handed her a big bag full of coloring books and crayons. She happily took them to another bedside table that had been brought in and lowered for her to color on.

Maurice briefly spoke to my dad and then made his way towards me. Before he could cross the room, someone called a greeting from outside the door. It was Desmond. To my amazement, Maurice and Desmond shook hands and gave each other a little bro hug. You know the ones they give each other where their shoulders are in each other's way, so they don't touch. I wondered how and when all of this came about seeing how Desmond and Maurice didn't even know each other existed as far as I knew. I wasn't sure how they became pals all of a sudden. And I wasn't sure if I wanted to find out. But I couldn't speak, so I had no choice but to lay there and see what happened next.

I'm not sure how long I lay there, but I guess I had been sleeping for so long my family had grown accustomed to going on about their normal routine while I slept. No one seemed to realize that I was now awake and absolutely parched. Finally, my baby girl came over to my bed with her coloring book. I didn't know if she could see the smile welling up on the inside of me or not. She was coming to show me the picture she had been working on.

"Mommy, I colored this picture for you," she said, propping herself on the edge of my bed and holding up her picture.

It was beautiful and she had stayed inside the lines. My baby was really artistic. She could draw pretty well, too.

She saw my eyes open and began to talk to me just like she had just spoken to me earlier that day. She kissed me on my forehead.

"Did you have a good nap?" she asked.

My mother looked up.

"Tomika, baby, don't lay on Mommy like that. You might pull some of her tubes loose. Come back over to the table with your book."

"But Mimi. I just wanted to show Mommy my picture."

"I know, sugar. But Mommy can't look at it right now. She's sleeping. You can show it to her when she wakes up."

Tomika was adamant.

"But Mimi. Mommy is awake. See?"

Everyone in the room stopped. My mom rushed to the edge and stared at me.

Then she smiled.

"Hi, my baby. We missed you."

She took my hand, and I tried with all my might to squeeze it. It felt so good that everyone finally noticed I was awake.

Desmond rushed out of the room to get the nurse. Everyone crowded around the bed peering at me like I was a ghost.

Ok, can I get some water, now?

When the nurse came in, everyone moved away from the bed so she could get to me. She stared at the monitors beeping around my bed and began to write furiously. Then she leaned over the bed and smiled.

"It's about time you woke up and joined us," she said, jokingly.

She shined a bright light in both of my eyes. I blinked rapidly.

"Her pupils are responding. Yep, I'd say she's back, alright," said the nurse.

Just then, the doctor and another nurse came into the room. They poked and prodded and manipulated, but nobody brought me any water.

Everybody took turns hugging me and kissing me.

The doctor told my family that I had been through quite an ordeal and that I was a very lucky young lady. But nothing from that statement gave me any clue, still, about what had happened to me. He told them that they could take the tube out of my throat once they were sure that I could breathe on my own.

My mother went out of the room to finish praising the Lord for bringing me back. The rest of the crew followed the doctor out so that they could finish talking about what would happen now that I was awake and alert.

A few minutes later, Maurice returned alone. He was smiling. He was still handsome, even though his face looked aged and weary like he hadn't been sleeping at night. He bent down next to me, carefully taking my hand and rubbing it gently across his face. I squeezed his hand with all the strength I could muster. I was glad he was there with me. He looked at me and smiled again.

"I love you, E. Middle," he whispered.

I must be dying; I thought to myself. In six years, Reese has never told me that he loved me before. So, this must be serious business.

I had so many questions. What happened to me? Why couldn't I get out of this bed? Why couldn't I talk? I opened my mouth to say something. Anything. I managed to utter a little groan. Whew. My vocal cords were finally starting to work.

Maurice looked at me, startled.

"What you trying to say, baby. Talk to your man! What's on your mind, E. Middle?

I gave it one more try.

"M-m-my hair okay?" I whispered, breathlessly.

Chapter 25

Alone with My Guilty Conscience

It felt good to have all my family and friends around to support me while I recovered in the hospital. In addition to the nurses that were always coming in to do something or another to me, there was always someone from my family there to help or just to keep me company.

My dad, who had recently retired, would come in about nine or so and stay till about three or four. Then my mom came over from work with Tomika in tow after five. Tomika did her homework at the hospital, or she drew pictures to decorate my room with. My mom took her home about six thirty to start getting her ready for the next day.

Natalie was a nurse at the hospital, so she popped up anytime during the day or night, depending on how her schedule went. Toy usually came in the evenings after she closed the collision center where she was an autobody technician, and after her daily basketball game at the gym. And Renee's mom took over the daycare in the afternoons two days a week and Renee relieved my dad so that he could have some time to take care of things around the house.

Ironically, Desmond had a close relative who was also admitted into ICU a couple of days before I did, which I was told is how he and Reese had their first introduction. I also understood that their first meeting was not pleasant, but they had somehow managed to resolve whatever beef they had and incredibly become more than civil to each other. I had my suspicions about their fight, but I had too much other stuff on my plate at the time to care.

Desmond came in on the days Renee couldn't. He hung out with me until Maurice closed the shop and came to see me. Sometimes Reese stayed all night. On the nights that he went home, Desmond would stick his head back in the door and check on me later in the night, since he was already there with his own family member. He never gave much detail about them or their condition. I just knew that they were gravely ill, and the doctors had done all that they could do for them.

I didn't press him about it because I wasn't quite up to taking on someone else's health issues along with my own. In addition to a collapsed lung, I also had a major femur fracture that they had a devil of a time trying to piece back together. I supposed the next time I went to the club or the courthouse, I would probably be treated like a terrorist because I had so much metal in my body now, including the bullet that teetered dangerously on the edge of my spinal cord. The doctors were afraid to move it for fear they might paralyze me in the process. And even if it didn't, my leg was in such a mess that it would be months before I could even try to walk, again, anyway.

I tried to focus on one thing at a time. I couldn't be worried too much about my legs right then because I couldn't feel them. But I could feel the crushing pain in my chest every time I tried to take anything other than a normal breath. Breathing was a major event, anyway; especially with the plastic tube they had shoved into my chest to re-inflate my lung and the ventilator down my throat. I was kept under heavy sedation the first few weeks to aid in keeping my excitement level to a minimum. Anything that caused me to take more than a half of a breath would send me such an excruciating pain, I would nearly faint. I guess that was a good enough reason that my loved ones chose to keep certain things from me until they felt that I was strong enough to handle them.

It was strange having Maurice around. I wasn't used to seeing this much of him. It made me a little sad to know that I almost had to lose my life for him to decide that he wanted to be around me. Later, the sadness gave way to resentment because it made me feel like he stayed out of guilt. I ultimately decided that he was indeed guilty. Not because he never actually spent any time with me before I got shot. But because he felt responsible for me actually having been shot in the first place. Again, this wasn't even about me. He was just pacifying himself by staying in my face all the time. We would see how much longer he would stay around once I got out of here.

The first few weeks were slow and grueling. Since it was mandatory for me to still be heavily sedated for the most part, the only thing that I could really do was lie there in a drug induced fog. I saw my family and friends come and go. I even talked to some of them, I suppose. But other than that, I don't remember much about the time right after I woke up in the hospital.

Once my lung capacity had increased to sixty-five percent, much of the pain I was in began to lessen and the doctors began to wean me off some of the sedatives that I had been on. And I was able to stay awake a little bit longer and visit with my family.

When I was stronger, Desmond and I resumed our friendship as if nothing happened. We hadn't discussed the argument we had about his wife the last time we spoke before I was shot. I guessed that he was trying to keep everything on a positive note, which was fine with me. I was just glad that we weren't mad at each other anymore.

It was a funny thing, though. The more I started to come around, the less I began to see of him. Sometimes I would catch him standing over me in the middle of the night when I was half-asleep. But during the day he was MIA most of the time. I never mentioned it because I just figured that his family member must have gotten worse, and he would tell me what was going on when he was ready. He must have really been under a lot of stress trying to work and look out for this person by himself. I wondered where his wife was and why she wasn't pitching in to help. I still didn't have a clue as to what type of relationship they had. If they were still together, she should at least have the decency to support her husband while his family member was sick. I couldn't imagine having a husband and not being there for him during a time like that. The thought of her being so selfish made me feel angry and protective over my friend. I wished that I were able to be more supportive of him.

A couple of nights before I was due to be transferred into a regular room from critical care, I awoke to a huge commotion on the floor and a code blue announcement over the hospital intercom. I thought it was coming from the direction of Desmond's family member's room. I prayed that the person had been able to make it through the night.

About three o'clock the next afternoon, I received an unexpected visit from Dr. Curtis. I hadn't seen her since the day I had been shot. I was told that she had been in quite a few times before I woke up, but this was the first time that I would get to see her.

She looked weary and haggard, like she had had a rough delivery. I wondered who delivered a baby today. She smiled when she saw me awake.

"Boy, you sure are a sight for sore eyes," she said, trying to mask her fatigue.

"So are you," I said. "I never thought that I would ever say that I was ready to go back to work."

She laughed.

"I have a stack of charts piled on top of your desk waiting for your attention."

"Well, it's nice to know that you're still holding my job."

She sighed and sat down on a chair near my bed.

"So, how're you holding up? You're looking well, considering."

We talked about the status of the shooter's trial, how Reese was doing and how glad Tomika must be to have me back. Then we began to talk about which patients had babies that were due this month, who had twins, whose labor went the longest. That's when I got the news.

"So, I see you got your scrubs on," I inquired. "Somebody go into premature labor? This isn't a surgery day for you."

She sighed deeply.

My heart began to beat a little faster.

"What's wrong?" I asked.

"Sonia Perry arrested a few hours ago. She didn't make it."

I was stunned. I knew that Sonia had been in failing health since she delivered her last baby stillborn, but I had no idea that she had been that sick.

"How?" was all I could manage.

"Well, she'd been in a vegetative state since earlier in the year. That's why she hasn't been in. She was admitted to critical care the week before they bought you in. In fact, she's been right next door to you the whole time."

What? I couldn't believe she was right next to me, and I never even got a chance to say good-bye. Sonia and I had clicked really well. We had even gone to lunch a few times; just the two of us. How did all of this manage to get past me?

Sensing my confusion, Dr. Curtis said, "Well, I figured you must have known. Her husband was in your room talking to your family the night you were shot. In fact, I was here several times before you woke up, and he was here every time except for one. He told me that you all used to work together, and you were good friends."

It couldn't be.

"Desmond Wright? But . . . but Sonia's last name is Perry," I stammered.

"Yeah, I know. Sonia kept her maiden name because her real estate business had already started to take off before she got married, so she kept her maiden name for business purposes."

A wave of sadness and guilt swept over me. So, this was the big secret that Desmond had been keeping about his wife. She was dying. That's how he was able to spend his birthday with me. That's why he never had anything bad to say about her. She wasn't cheating on him. She was sick and he was taking care of her. And I had known who she was the whole time.

Dr. Curtis thought that I was grieving for a lost patient and friend. But little did she know that my emotions not only included sadness, but also guilt and remorse. She talked a little more about Sonia, but I wasn't listening, anymore.

How could Desmond have spent all that time with me in good conscience knowing his wife's life was slipping away? I didn't know if I could live with the fact that I had been lusting after a dying woman's husband. He even split his time between us when she was on her last leg. How could he?

Dr. Curtis wound up her visit to go finish up her paperwork for the morgue. Then she left me all alone with my guilty conscience.

Chapter 26

The Bed That I Made

My life had officially hit rock bottom. I had been lusting after a dying woman's husband. I had infringed on her right to be cared for by the man that she thought would take care of her through sickness and in health during the time when she needed him the most. While she lay in that bed fighting for her life, I was at the beach with her husband frolicking like a foolish teenage girl. What the hell was I thinking? Even though I knew that Desmond was also to blame for all of this, I still couldn't hide from the fact that it had been my own low self-esteem that was the driving force in this whole ugly mess.

I had come to rely on Desmond to be there for me when I felt shunned by Maurice. And I felt guilty that I had taken precious time away from his dying wife all for the sake of being granted a stupid birthday wish. And to make matters worse, I knew and respected this woman. She had been my patient. But I was too busy wallowing in my own self-pity, I hadn't even been able to put two and two together and figure it all out. It was at that moment when Dr. Curtis told me the news about Sonia Perry that the ugly truth about my life slowly became clearer.

Lying in that hospital bed, I had finally come to the realization that my so-called boyfriend had no real desire to be with me in all the years we had been together. In fact, we spent more time together since I had been in the hospital than the entire six years we had been a couple. And now he was only around out of guilt. It seemed that I had waited my whole life to be able to have this kind of one-on-one with Maurice. But it was kind of hard to enjoy it lying in a hospital bed with a tube shoved into my chest and two bullets in my ass.

I finally understood that it was again my low opinion of myself that landed me in the hospital in the first place. But Maurice took it upon himself to carry the blame. He knew that the only reason that I had been at Hot Wheelz in the first place was because he had not been there ready to take me to pick up my truck from the mechanics like he was supposed to. And he knew that I had spent the better part of my relationship waiting for him in some form or fashion. But the reality was that it was I who made the decision to put up with him never being around. I was the one who decided that it was okay to stay in an unfulfilling relationship, even after six long years.

I had made some really bad choices and now I was sleeping in the bed that I had made. And if my life couldn't get any worse at that moment, my doctor had come into the room earlier that week to inform me that he was unsure whether or not I would be able to walk again.

I lay there trying to process all the negativity that was my life. I was a mess and there was nothing that I could do about it. Hell, I couldn't even get out of bed to pee. Up until that moment, I had been doing pretty well at keeping the physical pain, the emotional hurt, and the extreme guilt that I was carrying bottled up on the inside. Everyone thought I was so strong willed and brave. But they couldn't see how messed up I really was. And with so many people in and out of my room all the time, I felt that I always had to put up a brave front. Now, Dr. Curtis was gone, and I was all alone for once. I let the tears fall. They fell freely as if they were washing the ugly stains from my life. It was no longer important to put on a brave front for my family and friends. I sobbed uncontrollably and soon my sobs gave way to wailing. I cried long and loud. The tears seemed never ending. I felt that I had been crying for hours, and then I abruptly stopped.

I blew my nose and looked around, feeling a little silly to have spent time crying like a little kid. But it made me feel better. In fact, I felt better than I had felt in years. I actually chuckled to myself and then gave a hearty laugh out loud.

Despite everything that had been going on in my life, from the death of my high school sweetheart to Vince's denial of Tomika, and Maurice's act of infidelity, it never occurred to me to cry. Not once.

But having that good cry made me feel like a new woman on the inside. My soul felt like the air outside after a hard rain on a spring day. I felt much lighter, like a great burden had been lifted. Opening the floodgates and letting the tears go was the first step towards fixing my life.

Yes, I had to admit that my life was screwed up. But as much as I wanted the pain to go away, the alternative to feeling the pain was feeling nothing at all. And I knew that in order for someone to feel nothing at all, they had to be dead. And since I had no desire to be dead, either, I knew that I had to find a way to get my life back together so that I could feel something else besides pain.

Chapter 27

You Still Got Some Left

About a week after my visit from Dr. Curtis, Desmond showed up at my hospital room door with a bunch of fresh flowers. He was smiling, but his eyes looked weary. As soon as I saw him, my heart began to ache. I wished that there was something I could say to make things all right with him. He leaned over and kissed me on the cheek before taking a seat right next to my bed.

"How you feeling, missy?" he asked, trying to sound cheerful.

"Oh, everyday above ground is a good day," I said before realizing that it had been something Sonia used to say whenever you asked her how she was feeling. Desmond smiled at me weakly and rested his chin next to my leg like a loyal puppy. I began to gently stroke his head in comfort. We stayed that way for a while, too overwhelmed to say or do anything else.

"I'm gonna miss her, too," I said to him, softly.

He looked up at me. Large tears had welled up in his eyes, threatening to fall.

"I knew the night after she went into labor that we

wouldn't have much more time together," his voice cracked. "I guess I just wasn't as prepared to say good-bye as I thought."

His shoulders trembled as he buried his head back into my hospital blanket. Each muffled sob tore my heart into a million pieces. I continued to soothingly stroke his hair in silence, patiently waiting for him to finish crying. Once he was done, I handed him a Kleenex.

After a long silence, I spoke.

"Why didn't you tell me?" I asked, as non-intrusively as I could. I didn't want to make matters worse by badgering him about things that really didn't matter at this point, anyway, except to satisfy my own curiosity.

"Because it was tough enough just having to look at her waste away to nothing. It got to the point that I couldn't handle people always asking about her and having to continuously give a play by play of my wife dying. The less people who knew, the fewer times that I would have to keep reliving my nightmare.

"Her parents were both deceased before we met and she didn't really have any other family, except for an aunt that she wasn't in close contact with. It sounds rough, but it made it easier for me to handle everything. No complicated family dynamics.

We had discussed how we wanted to handle it if one of us got in an accident or something happened that required us to be kept alive on a machine, or something. And we both agreed to take care of each other for better or for worse. And she knew that I would have never pulled the plug on her, regardless even if she wanted me to. I loved her."

He sighed and went on.

"Only our closest friends and my immediate family knew how bad off she really was. On the job, the human resources department was bound by confidentiality, so nobody at the job really knew. I even asked Dr. Curtis to be scarce about the details she gave after the delivery, and apparently, she respected my wishes because you never knew. Although, I'm not sure how it got passed you since the office had access to her records."

I frowned, trying to remember how I missed the whole ordeal. I knew that she had been in the hospital. The office had even sent flowers to her room. I guess I just took it for granted that she had gotten better and gone home because no one had told me otherwise. And I knew she had lost another baby, so when she never came back for a follow-up, I just thought it would take her some time to grieve. Unfortunately, it had happened to her so many times it never occurred to me that anything else had gone wrong. While I was deep in thought, Desmond continued.

"I got in touch with Sonia's long-lost aunt right before she had the baby. I wanted to surprise her. I thought she would like the idea of having her only blood relative around to see the baby grow up. Her aunt decided to move back to the area for good, to be close to Sonia since she hadn't seen her since she was a baby. And after Sonia took a turn for the worse, her aunt asked if she could move in with us and help take care of Sonia to avoid putting her in one of those nursing facilities. I agreed, and so she's been taking care of her with an aide in the evenings while I work second shift."

The more he talked, the more sense Desmond began to make. It amazed me how he had kept up such a brave front all this time. I had questions, but I patiently held my tongue because I didn't want to miss anything he had to say.

"You and I got reacquainted about a month after she got really bad off. I always thought that you were good people, and I love talking with you. You're so smart and have such an interesting insight into things. You became a welcome distraction. And you treated me like a normal person. You didn't know what was going on, so you didn't know to take pity on me."

He stopped and looked far away, as if remembering one prying person in particular.

"Is that why you got mad at me that night when I asked you what was going on with you and your wife?" I asked.

He nodded.

"I wasn't mad at you, really. I wanted to tell you. I consider you to be a very close friend and I wanted to spill my guts about everything that had been going on in my life for the past year. But you had problems of your own and I didn't think it was fair for me to overburden you with my issues.

"And besides, when I talked to you, I all but forgot about how much I already missed my wife and how much I was struggling not to be angry with God for taking her away from me. Whenever you were anywhere around, I could be just plain old Desmond, again. I guess you might say I didn't tell you because I was trying to protect the little piece of sanity that talking to you gave me. I'm sorry I hid it from you all this time."

I was glad that Desmond had been able to look to me for strength during such a rough time in his life. And I was relieved that neither of us had done anything to disgrace his wedding vows. But I was still ashamed that I had more than given it some serious thought. Desmond really did love his wife. He wasn't cheating on her. I had taken his platonic fondness for me completely out of context. I silently wondered how many more times I had to be the fool this year.

"I can't apologize to her, anymore, but I still owe you one," I said, finally, with my head bowed.

He looked puzzled.

"Why would you say that?"

"Because I literally threw myself at you like some desperate chick. And now that I know who you really are, I feel so bad and so stupid. I just pushed myself off on you because I was too weak to let Maurice go instead of continuing to allow myself to feel less of a woman from his lack of affection. I never should have said I wanted you for my birthday. And I damn sure didn't have any business staying in a hotel with you at the beach. I just used your attention as an ego stroke when I couldn't get what I wanted from Reese. And I did all of that at the expense of a dying woman."

Before I could finish my thought, Desmond was adamantly shaking his head.

"No," he said with a little bass in his voice. "I'm not going to let you do this to yourself. First of all, this was not a one-sided thing. The attraction was mutual. Yeah, I was married. And I loved my wife. But let's face it. She wasn't coming back. And I knew that. I lived with it every day. And then, over here I've got the finest female friend in the city that I gotta talk to on the phone because I'm afraid that if I see her, I'll be tempted to cheat on my dying wife. So, instead I flirt with you on the phone with no shame in my game until you get comfortable enough to tell me how you feel. And out of that conversation, we both got a chance to spend some quality time with a quality person and a chance to get away from our problems for a little while. So, if you want to think about it in those terms, then we used each other. And we both got what we wanted, warmth and comfort that neither of us could get at home. And as an added bonus, we did it without disrespecting ourselves or anyone else. So, do we really have anything to be sorry about?"

I wasn't so sure.

"But what about our weekend at the beach?" I wanted to know. "We spent the weekend together in a hotel suite alone."

"True. I was doing something nice for a friend for her birthday. I'm guilty. You came out and enjoyed yourself. You're guilty. What else?"

I couldn't get him to see where I was coming from.

"Don't you feel the least bit guilty about all the time we

spent together while your wife was at home sick?" I asked, frustrated.

"I used to, Ericka. But not for what you think. I felt guilty because I knew that it wasn't safe for Sonia to keep trying to have a baby. But she really wanted one bad, and I just couldn't tell her no. After the third miscarriage, I wanted to stop. It was just too much for both of us, emotionally. But she kept telling me, 'Just one more time, baby. We can make it this time. I just know it.' But every pregnancy just got worse and worse. But I didn't have the heart to put my foot down and say no more. So, part of this whole thing is my fault. As her husband, I was supposed to protect her. But I was torn between protecting her and making her happy. And she was happy as long as she could look forward to being a mom.

"I begged and pleaded with her before she got pregnant the last time to stop pushing the issue. I told her that we could adopt. I even agreed to look into a surrogate. But she insisted that she wanted to do it herself. She said that she wanted to rebuild her family, since all her family was gone. You know Sonia was syrupy sweet, but she was the most pig-headed woman I'd ever met."

He smiled weakly to himself, and then continued.

"So, I agreed to go along with it one more time. But I told her that this was the absolute last time and that I wasn't willing to risk her life or health anymore to have a baby. She said 'okay' and joked that maybe I was using her health as an excuse for my own selfishness and just didn't want to share her with anybody else.

"She knew that wasn't the truth. And she knew that I loved her more than life itself. And I knew she knew it. That's why I don't have to feel guilty about anything that went down after she went into that coma. Because she knew that I was going to take damn good care of her as long as she was here.

"And I would have never disrespected her. That's why I didn't go there with you at the beach. Oh, trust me, part of me wanted to. And I tried to rationalize that I needed to move on. But it wasn't time, and I just couldn't bring myself to do anything like that while she was still here. But it was nice having a warm body next to me for a change."

"But Desmond," I said, "if you couldn't bring yourself to be with me, why did you even put yourself in that position in the first place? And you got away clean when you had to leave the next morning. But you came back. Why?"

"Ericka, I already had some business to attend to there and I just figured that while I was there, I could do something nice for you for your birthday."

"Yeah, you told me that you were there on business for Global Technology," I said.

"Well, not exactly," he answered. For the first time during the conversation, he appeared to cheer up a little.

Now, I was really confused.

"Not exactly?"

"The reason I was there is because I was supposed to close on a beach house that Friday. Sonia and I originally planned to move there after the baby was born. I thought about rescinding my offer. But I decided to go ahead and get it and maybe use it for rental property, or maybe renovate it and resell it."

Desmond and Sonia's businesses coincided because while Sonia was in the real estate business, Desmond bought old houses and flipped them on the side.

"I closed on the house before you got into town. I was still kind of undecided about what to do with it until we went for that walk on the beach that Friday night. You were talking about how much you loved the beach and how you wanted to move there, but it was expensive.

"So, the next morning while you were sleeping, I met with a contractor friend of mine in the area and had him meet me at the house so that we could make plans to convert it into a two family. I figured that whenever you got ready to move you and Tomika would have somewhere affordable to live."

I looked at him in disbelief.

"Desmond, what are you saying?"

He smiled even brighter.

"I'm saying that I decided to do something extra nice for my friend. You know how Sonia was. My wife was always surprising people with stuff and doing things that were way out of the ordinary. So, I wanted to keep her memory alive by doing something she probably would have done. I turned our dream house into a luxury duplex and decided to give you first crack at it when you decided to move."

I returned his broad grin.

"Boy, you know you're something else, don't you? And how did you know that I was really going to move? I hadn't given you a definite answer."

"Yeah, I know. But I heard the passion in your voice when you talked about moving. I thought you might take it a little more seriously if you knew you had somewhere to go."

"Oh, you know I would have jumped at the chance. I wish I had known about all of this sooner," I said, regretfully.

"What do you mean? My offer still stands. It's not too late," Desmond said.

I raised my eyebrows at him.

"Well, it doesn't appear that I'll be going anywhere for a while," I said, sarcastically.

"Well, you won't be in here forever, either. Have you even thought about what's going to happen when you get out of here?"

I really hadn't. I had been too busy feeling sorry for myself.

"No, but even when I get out, I probably won't be in any shape to move. Well, I could move, but I can't get a job if I can't walk. And I need a job to pay rent."

"I've been thinking about that, too. So, I came up with

a plan. Why don't you accept the duplex and go ahead and move? I'll take care of everything. You need a new start after everything that's happened. In fact, we both do."

"Yeah, that's true. But I don't know if I'll be able to do much for myself right now. And I'm not comfortable leaving my support system behind in the shape that I'm in right now."

"I know," Desmond said, confidently. "I thought about that, too. I'm going to be right next door. So, I can be there to take care of you while you and Tomika could still have your own private space. You could kick me out whenever you get tired of me. And the hospital there has an excellent rehab program."

Unbelievable.

"You've really got this whole thing planned out, huh? I don't know what to say."

"Well, you don't have to decide right now. I just wanted you to know that regardless of how bad things look to you right now, you still have options. A disability, whether it's temporary or permanent doesn't have to ruin your life."

I smiled at him.

"Thanks, Desmond. I'm flattered that you would go through all this trouble for me."

Desmond kissed me gently on the forehead.

"That's your problem, missy. You've convinced yourself that you're not worthy of good treatment. But nobody's more deserving to be treated like a queen, than you, your highness."

I blushed. Desmond always made me feel like a queen.

"You need to start thinking that about yourself. And I know that you're Miss Independent and don't need anything from anybody, but it's okay for you to accept help from others sometimes.

He tilted my chin toward him.

"This is not a time to be proud, okay? Everybody supports you and we just want to help. Let us help, okay?"

I nodded. I knew I needed to rely on help from other people, now. But it was still a scary thought that I may have to be at someone else's mercy for the rest of my life.

Desmond continued to lay out the plan he devised for after I was discharged from the hospital. He had checked into the hospital resources at the local hospital in that area. I could have someone come into my home and workout extensively until I worked my way up to actually going to the center to work. He talked to Dr. Curtis, who had agreed to handle my long-term disability so I could still be covered while I recovered from my injuries.

He even had both of the duplexes customized for wheelchair access complete with a removable ramp just in case I didn't need it for long. He had a moving company on standby and had even checked into the school that Tomika would be going to during the year.

I was amazed that he had a mind to think of all these things and take care of his wife.

"Desmond, I don't know what to say," I said, bowing my head, humbly.

He lifted my chin again and looked into my eyes.

"Just say 'yes' to life, baby, since you still got some left."

Chapter 28

What Do You Mean, 'We'?

Like all the get-well cards on my windowsill and my bedside table, Maurice was becoming more and more of a fixture around my hospital room these days. I couldn't seem to get rid of him lately. I still had mixed emotions about suddenly seeing so much of him. I liked the idea of having him around. I'd seen more of him since I got shot than I had the whole time we had been a couple. But while before I thought I could have stood seeing him every day, now I wasn't so sure. He actually was getting on my nerves, sort of. I guess I had become so accustomed to not having him around, without realizing it, I stopped needing him, really. I wondered why it took me so long to figure that out.

This particular night after everyone else had left to go home, Maurice still lingered around all quiet like something was up. He had been moody and fidgety all evening, like he wanted to talk to me about something but didn't quite know how to bring it up. I really wasn't in the mood for any deep conversation. So, I lay there in silence pretending to watch television, hoping he would get the picture and leave and go home. He didn't.

The nurse came in, asked how I was doing, and whether

or not I needed anything. I told her that I was fine. Then she asked Maurice if he was going to be spending the night. He told her that he hadn't decided yet. Suspicious, I decided that whatever it was he was getting ready to hit me with would determine whether or not he would be tolerated overnight. I rolled my eyes in the air, exasperated at the thought of a pending argument with everything else that was going on around here.

After she left, Maurice was ready to talk.

"E. Middle, have the doctors started talking to you about when they're gonna let you go home?" he tried to ask casually.

"Not really," I responded. "They want to keep me here and do some more tests to see if the feeling starts to come back in my legs. And I'll have to stay in rehab for a while, until I finish therapy."

"Oh," he said, thoughtfully. He looked a little sad.

"Why? What's wrong?"

"Oh, nothing. I was just thinking about what we're gonna do when you get ready to come home. You need someone there to look after you. And I'm just trying to figure out how we're going to handle it, that's all."

I narrowed my eyes at him.

"What do you mean, 'we'?" I asked, cautiously. I had no idea where all this was coming from all of a sudden.

"I mean all of us, baby. Me, you, your parents, Baby Girl, and your girls. We're all in this together. And I'm ready for you to come home, so I'm trying to start thinking about how we gonna get you home and take as good of care of you as we possibly can."

Yeah, right, I thought. Something was going on in his little mind. This was just a smoke screen to mask what was really going on.

"Reese, what are you talking about? You know good and well that none of y'all, including my parents, can afford to stay home and take care of me. And there's no telling how long it might be before I can do anything for myself."

Maurice shook his head.

"Man, please. 'Rehab Hospital' is just a fancy way of saying 'nursing home.' And I'm not trying to have you cooped up in no nursing home for who knows how long. You need to be at home where family can look out for you."

"Reese, you're being unreasonable. How are you gonna stay at home and take care of me? What are you gonna do, close down the shop? Because after what happened up in there, you sure as hell can't trust anybody to run it while you're home playing nurse to me. And besides, you couldn't be still around me for five minutes before I got shot, so how do you figure that you've settled down so much all of a sudden that you can stay home and take care of me when I'm sick? And in particular, give up your precious freedom to chase that elusive, almighty dollar that you love so much. Even I know better than that."

I shook my head and rolled my eyes. He was taking this concerned boyfriend shit to the extreme. And I was tired of waiting for the real Maurice to hurry up and take over so he could do what he did best; disappear so that I could get on with my life. I had had enough attention from him to last me a lifetime. And oddly enough, I really didn't have as much use for it as I thought I did.

Reese was adamant.

"Look, E. Middle. Let me worry about that, okay? I'm just trying to do what's best for you."

I sighed.

"I know you are, Maurice. And I appreciate that. For real. But I've been doing some thinking about this, myself, and I'm the one who's going to make the decision about what happens after I leave here, okay? I'm paralyzed, not brain dead. So, let's not do this, right now, please? I haven't even had this discussion with my folks."

"Okay, E. damn, I'm not trying to start no argument. I'm just trying to take care of what's mine that's all. At least let me feel like I'm being of some help, okay? You're my responsibility."

My patience was starting to wear a little thin from all this sudden display of overprotection from Maurice. I gritted my teeth and continued my attempt at civility. After years of yearning for Maurice to act like he was interested, it finally seemed to be happening. I was currently getting more attention than my fragile little ego could handle. But something inside me had changed. I no longer felt the need or the longing for him to be close to me. In fact, this whole conversation was making me tired, and I was suddenly feeling suffocated by Maurice. And like a dog backed into a corner, I bared my teeth and prepared to attack.

"Why you so interested in what happens to me all of a sudden?"

Maurice chuckled, nervously.

"I've always cared, E. Middle. Why you trippin'?"

When in doubt, turn on the charm. Maurice was so predictable. And obviously he thought I was, too. This was the point in the conversation that I was supposed to melt because he showed a little emotion toward me. And then I was supposed to give him back control of the relationship. Not a chance. I had wanted to address some things with him for a while but hadn't really had the urge to rock the boat until now.

"You're the one trippin', Reese. Don't you think it's a little too late to try and pull this Kevin Costner, bodyguard routine? Do I look like Whitney to you? Especially when we both know that you've never been all that interested in being around me for extended periods of time from the jump."

"C'mon, Ericka, why you always gotta keep going there? I know I ain't always made time to spend with you in the past. My bad, okay? But can't you stop being mad about that shit long enough to let me try and fix it?"

"But that's just it, Maurice. You can't fix it. You can't turn back time so you can show up before them niggas started brawling in Hot Wheelz. You can't bring back the feeling in my legs . . ."

Reese rolled his eyes like, 'here we go with this shit again.'

"Okay, Ericka. You made your point. I can't fix it. Is that what you want me to say? There, I said it. All this shit is my fault. I fucked up. But if I can't fix it, at least let me show you that I want to do right by you right now."

That would have been cool, except that I didn't feel like that right then. He should have caught me a couple of months ago. I folded my arms, defiantly.

"You know what? For the last six years you've made it painfully obvious that I'm not your number one priority. Hell, I'm not even in the top five. And I did everything to try and convince you that I was worthy of your time. But I could never get your attention. I know you love me. You're just not in love with me. And I was bitter about that for a long time. I couldn't understand why we could never seem to really connect. How could you be closer to some guys that hang out in the shop than your own girlfriend? You didn't even have the decency enough to call me and tell me that you were running late that day. But you called Tarik, and he told you that I was there waiting for you. He was the one who told me that you got held up."

Maurice was sitting there with his head bowed like he was deep in thought. He didn't say anything. He just shook his head adamantly, periodically in disagreement with most of what I was saying. I kept talking.

"You hate for me to come around that shop when it's full of guys. But it was okay for me to be there that day because you wanted me to park that damn BMW more than you didn't want me at that shop. Let's see. You come first. Lil'

Reese is second. The shop is third. The car is fourth. Your friends are fifth."

I shook my head and smiled cynically to myself.

"Told you. I'm not even in the top five. I never had a fighting chance."

Reese was getting agitated.

"See, E., now you just reaching for shit. You know it's not even like that. You always got to blow stuff out of proportion. You try to make it seem like I'm some evil nigga that treat you like a fucking dog when you know I always took care of you and Baby Girl since day one."

I waved my hand, dismissively.

"Listen, Reese. I never asked you to spend anything other than a little bit of your time every now and then. I never asked you for a damn dime. So, you can save the 'after all I've done for you' speech, okay?"

"So, that's what you been sitting around here pouting for all this time for, huh? Because you blaming all this shit on me like I set it up. Well, if that's how you feel, then that's how you feel. Blame me for everything that ever went wrong in your life, if it will make you feel better. But if you say that I've been neglecting you all this time, why not give me one more chance to love you and take care of you like I was supposed to from the beginning. I'm here now and I'm telling you that I wanna help, E. Middle. C'mon, now."

He reached down and kissed my cheek.

I rolled my eyes and gave his tired little speech a sarcastic clap.

"That's very noble of you, Reese, except for one thing. I don't need your damn help. And I don't need or want your twisted, thugged out version of love. It took my pride, my self-respect, and two bullets in my ass to figure out that being with you wasn't all that serious from the beginning. The dudes you hang out with must really look up to you for having your girl so much in check that you never get questioned about being in the street all the damned time. And I must seem like a real sucker to you because no matter how tired I claimed to be of your bullshit, I still take it like a champ on the regular. But guess what? I'm over the fact that you just weren't into me. 'Because you know why? I got enough love for me for both of us. So, you can tell your loyal subjects that King Maurice is back, and they can have you all to themselves. Not that you ever left, of course. I hereby relinquish my position on the throne. There wasn't enough room for a queen, anyway."

Maurice sighed deeply and rubbed his head like he wasn't sure what he should do. He sat there for a few minutes while he contemplated his next move.

Satisfied at having laid all my cards on the table, I didn't even pull a Martin Lawrence and tell him to "Get to steppin'!" I just sunk back into my pillows and began to watch television like he wasn't in the room. It would have taken too much energy to try and make him leave before he was ready. And after all that bitching, I was spent.

After a few more minutes of sitting there like an idiot, Maurice finally stood to leave. He looked at me for a long time, but I pretended to be engrossed in a *Law and Order* rerun. He broke his stare, leaned over my bed, and kissed me on the top of my head.

"I'll see you tomorrow," he said, simply, as if the conversation we'd just had never took place.

I rolled my eyes at him and turned my head to look out the window.

I'm sorry, did I just miss something?

Chapter 29

(Maurice)

She Wouldn't Do It with Me

"I'm not playing with you, Reese. I'm through playing with you, okay? Don't bring your ass back here. I'm sick of your shit," she yelled at my back.

I jerked around to face her.

"Or what, Ericka? I'm sick of your shit, too, okay? How long you gone keep trying to punish me? You been sitting around here with your ass on your shoulders ever since you woke up. Nigga, I love you, okay? You keep accusing me of putting everything else ahead of you. If that's the case, why am I up in here with your sullen ass taking this bullshit? Stop blaming me for all the fucking misery in your life! Yeah, I fucked up a lot since we been together. I ain't perfect. So, you keep telling me. But keep it funky. Why did you even stay with me for six years if I was making you so miserable?"

Ericka rolled her eyes at me. She didn't want to hear what I was saying, but she knew I was telling the truth. I wasn't in the habit of talking to my girl like that and I felt bad about it, seeing how she had been going through so much these last couple of months. But I was tired of her trying to make me out to be some cold-hearted nigga that never gave a damn about her. She was hell bent on making everybody think that she was some saint for letting 'dog-ass Maurice' get away with taking her for granted all these years. She was too busy being mad about everything she felt I did to her over the last six years that she let her pride get in the way of any of my attempts at reconciliation. I was through being the bad guy. I needed to make her see that I really did love her. I needed her to know that what I had been showing her wasn't necessarily the way that things were.

"I stayed because I've been waiting on you to notice me," she said, quietly. "I kept thinking that if I just hung around a little while longer that the spark we had when we first got together would come back. So, I waited. But it never did. And it seemed like the closer I kept trying to get to you, the further you would move away from me. I was already in too deep to just walk away. And I didn't want to risk leaving before you changed your mind about playing an active role in the relationship."

Ericka really had that drama queen act down to a science with all them dramatic pauses and whatnot. I'd had enough of that shit, too.

"Oh, yeah?" I asked, sarcastically. "If you were so stuck on me, then what's up with you and the married dude, E. Middle?"

She rolled her eyes up in the air.

"Please. Desmond and I were just friends and that's it. The only time that I called him was when I couldn't get up with you. And since you were never around, we just got to be mad cool. But it was safe for me to keep up the friendship because I knew that he would never do anything to jeopardize his marriage. And besides, all we did was talked on the phone."

"And you went to the beach with that nigga on your birthday. Don't forget that."

She looked like a little kid with their hand caught in the cookie jar, but she maintained.

"Nothing happened," she replied, coolly.

"Y'all had separate rooms?" I asked.

She hesitated.

"Never mind," I answered for her. "What were you about to say?"

"I know it was foul, but I split my time between the two of you, and I used him to pick up your slack. I was wrong, but I didn't know how else to get your attention. In a way, I kind of wanted you to find out because I wanted you to be jealous. I wanted you to think somebody else was taking what was yours so that you would notice me and come back around. I figured that you would start staying around me more so nobody else could move in on your territory."

I glared at her. My worst nightmare had been coming true right in front of me, but I had been too busy ducking Ericka to pay attention. I was trying to stay calm, but my blood was starting to boil.

"Stop the madness," I said to her, as calm as I could. "And tell the truth. You caught feelings for this nigga, didn't you?"

She shook her head no, but I didn't believe her. I wanted to, but Ericka had been carrying that bitterness around like a badge of honor for a long time. And I knew that if nothing else, she had indulged that nigga in some way just to get back at me. But because I went so long without handling my business, I also had some fault in this. I didn't really want to, but I didn't have a choice but to accept what she said as truth.

"Look, babe. You don't have to lie to me about none of this no more. I know why you did it. And I accept the truth whichever way it comes. I'm a man. I'ma be alright."

"But, there's no need for us to keep going over and over this stuff, Reese," she said. "It's like beating a dead horse. It doesn't even matter, anymore. I don't want to talk about it."

I looked at her.

"What 'chu mean it don't matter? It does matter. I'm trying to fix my freakin' mess, here."

She shook her head.

"You can't fix it, Reese."

"I can, if you let me."

"Reese, I love you. But in six years, you never gave me a chance. You kept pushing me away. Now, I give up. You got what you wanted. Why don't you just leave it alone?"

I ignored her request to leave it alone. I had left it alone for too long as it was. And it looked like it was too late. But it was time to act, regardless of how things ended up.

"Because I don't want to leave it alone. Look, E. Middle. We been playing this game long enough. I've been taking you for granted for years. And you been kicking it with this other cat for I don't know how long. And we both ended up getting hurt. So, that makes us even. Can we just put this all behind us and work this out? We been together too long to just give up on each other, now. I want you to be in my life and I'm trying to take care of you when you come home. I want to move in with you and Tomika and help you get back on your feet. What you say, babe? Let me prove to you how much I want this."

She got quiet for a few minutes. She looked like she was considering what I had just said. I felt relieved because I thought that she would give in.

She sighed, heavily.

"Look, I really appreciate you wanting to help. And I guess now, we are even. But things have changed since I've been in here. When I woke up from that coma and found out that I couldn't move, I realized how much time I wasted waiting on you to complete me. I also realize that it's not you that I should be mad with, I should be mad at myself. And now that I have a second chance, I think I need to be spending time getting reacquainted with me. So, now instead of trying to convince you that this is where you need to be, I feel like I need to let you go so that we can both move on with our lives. We've made each other miserable long enough."

I hung my head.

"Well, at least let me help you till you get strong enough to stay in your apartment by yourself."

She smiled, weakly.

"No, thanks. I won't be staying in my apartment when I leave the hospital. I've decided to move to Virginia Beach."

I looked at her.

"Move to Virginia Beach? With who?"

"I'm not moving with anybody. I was offered a townhouse by the beach and a job, and I decided to take it."

I couldn't believe she was talking about moving and she didn't even know whether or not she would be able to walk. Ericka had really lost it.

"How you gon' take care of you and Tomika while you're out there all by yourself? And how you gon' pay your bills? You ain't in no condition to be trying to work!"

She got quiet.

I was getting irritated.

"What? You can't talk to me, now, E?"

"Desmond made all the arrangements," she said really quiet.

"What did you say?" I asked in disbelief.

She looked at me directly and spoke again.

"Desmond offered me the place and the job. He's even arranged for therapy to come to the house until I got strong enough to do stuff for myself."

I literally felt the knife slice into my back.

So, I guess that was my confirmation right there. If there had been any doubt in my mind about Ericka sleeping with this cat, Desmond, it was all gone, now. Why else would he offer to move her all the way to Virginia and put her up in her own place?

"Oh, I get it. So, you have been fucking that nigga. For somebody that was so in love with me, you sure didn't have a problem letting somebody else take over my leftovers. And you were even good enough to get him to take care of you, too."

"That's enough!" she yelled at me. "You got some nerve accusing me of sleeping with somebody else! You gave Desmond the motive and the opportunity. You were the one who came up with every excuse in the world about why we couldn't ever do anything together. You haven't given me as much as a second glance in the last four years and now you mad because somebody else paid me some attention? Well, unlike them niggas that you love so good at that damn shop, Desmond respects you. He ain't never stepped to me wrong, which is more than I can say for half of them! Yeah, I was wrong for spending time with Desmond that I should have been spending with you. But I never slept with him. He's my friend, and just like you, he wants to help. And I want his help. Don't get mad because I decided to stop running behind you for a change. This ain't got nothing to do with sex."

The heat was rising in my shirt collar.

"No, but it's got everything to do with you being a fuckin' liar. And then you got a nerve to blame this bullshit on me. You got me walking around here feeling guilty and shit, when your hands are just as dirty as mine. If you thought that I was treating you so damn bad, you could have left. I didn't have no damn chains on you. Why you didn't call him when your car broke down? Maybe if you had, you wouldn't have me to blame for you laying up in this hospital."

"Because I didn't want him, I wanted you," she said. Tears were streaming down her face, but I wasn't feeling those damn crocodile tears. Ericka had turned out to be scandalous just like the rest of the chicks.

"I can't tell," I said, dryly.

"Well neither could I, but that didn't mean that I could

just decide not to be in love with you anymore, Reese. Even though I had to be a damned attempted murder victim to pique your interest, I never lost interest in you. But as much shit as I put up with, you want to hold a grudge because of something you think I did to you? Well, that just makes this a whole lot easier for the both of us. We both fucked over each other and now we can just break up and move on. Now, I don't have to feel guilty about moving and you don't have to feel obligated to take care of me."

She turned her face away from me and stared out the window like I was already gone, and she was in the room by herself.

"Man, whatever," I said, and stormed out the door. I didn't need this bullshit, anymore.

On the drive home, I couldn't stop thinking about what she had said to me. I knew that for years I had been neglecting Ericka in some way. Most of the time I didn't do it on purpose, but I had to admit that sometimes she could be too much woman. And I was overwhelmed with the responsibility of keeping her happy. It was like I was afraid to try and be happy with her. I was never happy with any of the women that I had been in serious relationships with.

Everything would be okay until we decided to make things official. My wife Toni and I were cool until after we got married. When we were dating, we saw each other a lot but never really spent every minute in each other's faces till we moved in together. It was the same with me and Cassandra. As long as we were just kind of kicking it, things were straight. But things changed when she got pregnant. And me and E. Middle were a'ight till she started talking this exclusive commitment bull.

And the whole commitment thing scared me, honestly. Well, I guess it wasn't commitment, really. It was the women that scared me. Because women don't really know what it is that they want. And every woman I had been with claimed that they wanted to be with me, but when we got together, their actions said something different. We always had to go through some kind of drama and strife. Whether it was Toni's scared ass crying when I tried to have sex with her or San's crazy ass cutting the fool and throwing tantrums when she couldn't get what she wanted from me. Or Ericka acting like she didn't care whether or not she was my girl, but then getting pissed when she found out I had a baby by somebody else.

That accident that I had in high school scarred up a lot more than my face. It took away a lot of my confidence as a young boy trying to find his way as a man. I never got a real understanding of women because I spent most of my teenage years afraid of them. With my face all fucked up, I couldn't compete with those other cats that the girls at school went for, and I was always afraid of getting shot down. Even the fact that I was an athlete wasn't enough to guarantee me no luck with the girls. I guess I kind of just latched on to whoever would be willing to take me on. And the fact that most of them were fine as all outdoors was a plus. I know that's crazy, but all kids want to be accepted. And every young cat wants to have a fine woman on his arm so he can look big to the rest of the fellas. That's just how it is. I didn't make the rules.

But now that I think about it, Toni and me didn't even really have nothing in common. I doubt if she really even knew me after all those years of dating. Hell, I damn sure didn't know her. I didn't know that she had a problem with sex. Hell, I couldn't even get her to tell me why she wouldn't do it with me.

And I guess after all this time, I've come to realize that I've been afraid to put myself out there for any woman that I've ever been with because I was always afraid that she wouldn't be able to love me unconditionally. And now that I finally found a woman that would, I couldn't trust her judgment enough to let her. I ran her off into the arms of another brother. And even though Desmond was married, he at least had her friendship. The way it looked right now, it didn't look like she wasn't interested in having anything else to do with me, friend or otherwise.

Chapter 30

In My Element

It hurt like hell to watch Maurice walk out of my life that last time. Part of me wanted him to stay and grovel until I broke down and gave him one last chance. That part of the routine had been in place for so long, that deep down inside, I was all set to take him back. That's what I had always done. I truly believe that many couples stay together not because of love or money. Kids don't even keep most of them together. It's fear of stepping outside the box and doing something different with their lives. People get so caught up in what's familiar and what's comfortable that sometimes we never even get a chance to experience new and different things. And being at death's door puts life in a new perspective.

I had to say goodbye to Maurice so that I could say hello to all the new experiences that were waiting to enter my life. I still didn't know whether or not I would have full use of my legs or whether I would even get to live life normally like I did before, but those were issues that I just couldn't allow myself to worry about at that moment. My main concern was trying to jumpstart the remaining part of my life after being at a complete standstill for most of it. It was a scary thought. But it was also pretty exciting.

For the most part, the rest of my friends and family were supportive. They thought that I was crazy to up and leave my support system, but they seemed to trust my desire to start over and live a different type of life. And nobody ever told me that they didn't think that I should go. Instead, they all pitched in and did everything they could to make my dream a reality. Even Tomika seemed to be relieved that we were moving. She didn't really make a big fuss about leaving her school and her friends. I think she was just excited about the prospect of having her Mommy home from the hospital.

After spending the rest of the summer confined to a bed, I was just glad to be able to be outside in the fresh air. And it was not just any air, but crisp, ocean air.

After two months in the hospital and another two in rehab, Desmond drove Tomika and me to Virginia to see our new home. As soon as we pulled into the driveway, I was instantly in love. It was a large beach stye twin home with dark Cape Cod style shaker siding, and double two-car garages on the ground level and two additional levels of living space. A large porch extended the front of the house on the main living area of the second-floor balconies overlooked the front of the house, as well as offered gorgeous views of the Chesapeake Bay in the back.

An elevator took us from the garage to the main floor of my house. The large windows throughout the house allowed for spectacular natural light. Desmond had redone the hardwood floors and had painted the living area a soft sandalwood color that would nicely compliment my earth tone furniture and decorations. The kitchen was a sunny yellow with colorful, festive Mexican tile backsplash and a stained-glass sink. The living area was open and spacious, and there were two large bedrooms on the main floor, both with ensuites, and a half bath. There was also a huge office that directly faced the ocean with a desk turned in the direction that I could sit in and enjoy the view while I worked. Part of the deck was closed in as a sunroom with a staircase that led up to a crow's nest on the top floor. A path out the back led over the sand dunes to the beach. And there were two bedrooms and two bathrooms upstairs, along with a bonus room. The house was completely handicap accessible. Not only did I have an elevator, but the entryways had been widened and even some of the countertops had been lowered to accommodate a wheelchair. Desmond had thought of everything.

"I see you left no stone unturned," I joked with Desmond. He smiled.

"I tried not to. And the beauty of it is that this can all be changed back whenever you're ready. I can take that chair railing off the stairs. I can even move the cabinets back to their normal height," he laughed.

"No, I wouldn't make you go through all that. But seriously, Des, this is the most beautiful place I've ever seen. I can't believe that we're actually going to live here."

"Yeah," Tomika chimed in. "I even got enough space in my room to practice my kicks for Tae Kwon Do."

"Oh, that reminds me," said Desmond. "There's a spot open in Wesley's class for Tomika, so she can keep up with her martial arts."

He bowed to Tomika and then assumed the left fighting stance. Tomika reciprocated and they proceeded to chop and kick at each other like they were Maven and Chun Lee.

I laughed and shook my head at them.

"Y'all are not gonna be sparring up in here. Make me round house both of you back out the door."

"Mommy, you can't kick in that wheelchair," Tomika giggled.

"Yeah, but I can run over you with it," I joked with her, maneuvering the chair toward her.

She screamed playfully and ran toward the back door.

"Don't go far," I called behind her.

"I won't!"

Next, we took a tour of Desmond's townhouse right next door. His was almost the same as ours, and also accessible. It was decorated in a typical male bachelor pad fashion, but it was neat and orderly and actually had many contemporary additions to the décor to make the place interesting. It didn't even need a woman's touch. He had done a good job decorating all by himself.

Next, we went downtown to take a tour of Desmond's office and my new place of employment. Desmond belonged to a group of black investors that got together and bought almost a whole block in Portsmouth's downtown area and put black-owned businesses in the buildings.

Desmond was one of the founding members of the project and had quickly established himself as the best in the building renovation business. Because both he and Sonia graduated from Hampton University and she had strong ties in commercial real estate, together they had acquired several old houses and buildings downtown that Desmond had been remodeling and leasing them for a nice profit. The house that was now our home had been sold to him at a steal and he and his team turned it into a beautiful twin home.

It did my heart good to see black people being able to make those kind of power moves. And I was hungry to learn as much as I could about the business. I gave up the opportunity to go to college when I finished high school. But as I listened to Desmond talk about how he got his renovation projects and city permits, I felt tingly on the inside because it appeared that I was finally in my element.

Some of the businesses in our immediate area included a Starbucks, restaurants and bars, a bookstore, lounge, as well as an old-fashioned butcher, bakery and fruit stand. It was clear that the idea to rebuild the block was successful from watching the mass of people of all different shades and backgrounds hustling in and out of the shops, sitting outside in front of the restaurants enjoying the food in the sunshine.

It felt good that our people were supporting such a major part of the city's downtown economy. And I felt honored to be a part of it. By the end of the day, I was ecstatic about my decision to make a fresh start in a place where new beginnings appeared to be flourishing. I was going to be just fine.

Chapter 31

No More Climbing Stairs

Not surprisingly, Maurice honored my request for him not to come around anymore during my healing process. But this time, I didn't feel as though it was really his conscious decision to stay away. Deep down, I never doubted whether or not Maurice really loved me. The problem was that he wasn't capable of loving me the way that I wanted and deserved to be loved.

And even with these realizations, it still discouraged me that I was not yet able to completely move on. There were times when I would pick the phone up to call him and realize what I was doing and sadly put the phone back down. We had been a couple, but just like the rest of my circle, I still considered him to be a friend, as well. Not just a friend, he was part of my family. And a small part of me regretted making the decision to cut him completely out of my life. Well, no need to dwell on the past. That was part of my problem. I had given the past way too much of my energy. And it was time to focus my energy on my present and future.

My girls were so helpful to me during my transition. Renee took me to my therapy appointments in her minivan because it was easier to maneuver in and out with my wheelchair and everything. And Renee and Toy came over to lend a hand wherever they could. They were sad to see me go, and they only agreed to let me move because I was moving to the beach. They all agreed that it was a perk having me move there. They looked at it as being able to take a free vacation.

Even Dr. Curtis was extremely supportive of my decision to move. She agreed to keep me on as a paid employee and even paid to have my computer rigged with the software to do her dictation and her past due accounts from home until Desmond got his office up and running.

My family and friends were a big help during the moving process. Desmond even hired movers to come and pack up all my things and transport them to the new house. But in that wheelchair, I still couldn't help but feel useless. I had been working extra hard in physical therapy, but the feeling didn't seem to be coming back into my legs fast enough. I wasn't feeling like I was playing an active role in changing my life. Watching everyone else buzzing around me moving things around in my house made me feel like a bystander in someone else's transformation. I knew that the feelings I felt were the enemy trying to convince me that I had made the wrong decision. So, instead of making them real by giving them a voice, I prayed and asked the Lord for strength and healing and patience. And then I ordered everyone around like a drill sergeant, making sure that I was able to hold on to as much control over my transition as possible.

My therapy team was wonderful. The feeling in my lower body finally started to come back and before long, I was able to walk with a walker from one side of the room to the other. I had an occupational therapist that helped me learn how to maneuver around the house in my chair to cook, clean, and take care of Tomika. And eventually, I would even gain enough strength to support myself on the countertops in the kitchen to cook.

As usual, Tomika proved to be the most versatile little girl ever created. She fell in love with her school and everyone in it on the very first day. She became instant friends with the neighbor children and her social calendar filled up quickly. Between Tae Kwon Do, her new Girl Scout troop, and daily excursions at the beach with her friends, I found myself at home twiddling my thumbs a lot.

A couple of days after the moving company set down the last of my stuff, and I absentmindedly assumed the task of sifting through the never-ending boxes that were the last ten years of my life. The movers had been nice enough to place all the boxes in the rooms for which they were marked. The kitchen boxes were placed in the kitchen; the boxes marked bedroom were placed in the bedroom, and so on.

Even still, I quickly became overwhelmed because most of the stuff required placement somewhere in the house that I couldn't reach without help, and I had more than grown tired of having someone else to help me with it. And although I appreciated everyone's help, I couldn't help but feel a sense of resentment for even having to ask for help at all.

I was beginning to question whether or not I had made a wise decision by moving. Maybe this wasn't such a good idea after all. Sensing my frustration, Desmond, my hero, jumped right in to rescue me, as usual. He began to unpack stuff, just like he didn't have his own stuff to unpack next door. We were in my office/den, and he had opened one of the many boxes of books and began to place them on the built-in book-cases.

"Okay, Ericka, which way do you want me to organize these books on these shelves? Do you want fiction on its own shelf and non-fiction by itself, or all of them together in alphabetical order, or does it matter?" he inquired.

"Um, put all the novels on the lowest shelf so that I can reach them. But don't put anything in the hutch yet, because I think I'm going to use that for all my work-related stuff," I responded, thoughtfully. "Then again, don't worry about those books right now because I need to go through them all. I need to get rid of some of this mess."

Where did all this crap come from? Those four huge boxes of nothing but books were making me nauseous.

Sighing heavily, I added, "I'm never going to get all this shit unpacked."

Without hesitation, Desmond scooted the box of books in front of where my wheelchair was parked, then straightened up to face me. He looked at me like he was waiting for me to say something else.

Puzzled, I asked him, "What are you doing?"

"Waiting for you to tell me which books you want me to put on the shelf."

"I told you I needed to go through that stuff."

"I heard you," Desmond said with a slight smirk. "So, start digging."

"D., with all these books I got in here, that could take days. You got your own stuff to do at your own house. I don't want to keep you over here doing all my dirty work. I can manage. Really,"

Desmond squatted down in front of my chair until we were eye to eye.

"You don't get it, do you? Do you really think I coaxed you three and a half hours away from all your family and friends, whom you could depend on for support just to leave you in the middle of all these boxes for you to fend for yourself? Ericka, what do you think I am, a sadist? Maybe you didn't hear me at the hospital. I'M GOING TO HELP YOU! Okay? I know you're used to being Miss Independent, but right now you need me. And I'm not going anywhere, anytime soon, so get used to it."

His attempt at being firm slowly gave way to a wide grin. He gently touched my face.

"Buck up, missy. I don't mind. Really, I don't. If I did, I wouldn't be here."

"But I can never pay you back for all this, De."

"I'm not looking for you to repay me, Ericka. And besides, you've given me more than enough already. While I was taking care of Sonia, it was you who got me through some of the roughest days of my life. You were the one who encouraged me to keep going when I wanted to give up. Hearing you talk about your dreams of having a beach house and owning your own business encouraged me to keep looking for light at the end of the tunnel. And now, I'm here to carry you just like you carried me."

"But how was I able to do all that? I never even knew that Sonia was sick. Well, I did, but I didn't know she was your wife, or that you even had a sick wife. How could I have possibly been so supportive? And besides, all I did was complain about Maurice."

He chuckled.

"Yeah, you did do a lot of that. But you never gave up hope that things would get better between you two and in your life in general. Your zest for life is contagious. You love to ride motorcycles, for goodness sakes. You're the only woman I know that owns a crotch rocket."

I couldn't help but laugh.

I don't just have any old crotch rocket; I mentally corrected him. I had a Kawasaki Ninja top of the line chromed out crotch rocket with red candy paint.

"Well, doesn't look like I'll be riding that too much for a while."

"See, that attitude is priceless. Other people in your situation wouldn't be so daring as to suggest that they might even have a chance to get back on it. But I hear it in your voice that you have every intention of riding that damned bike again. Your can-do spirit is what I love about you. You don't even want me to help you go through these doggone books even though it will probably take you till next year to sift through all this junk by yourself."

I was glad to hear that the vibes that I was sending out were positive because at that moment I wasn't feeling all that optimistic.

"I never thought about myself as being an inspiration to anyone, especially you. In fact, with all that you had going on; I'm surprised that my bitching didn't finish sucking the life right out of you. When I really get going, I can be somewhat of a whiner," I admitted, emitting a faint laugh.

"That's true," he joked. "But the difference between you and other whiners is that most whiners whine standing still. But you whine in the midst of actively searching for a way out. Just like now. You're complaining about how much work you have to do here and all the while puttering around in this house trying to do everything by yourself. Except that now, you're basically whining for no reason because you actually have more help than you could ever know what to do with."

I laughed harder. He was right and I was embarrassed to have been acting so ungrateful.

"Sorry. I'm a lousy patient, huh? It's just so scary having to get around in a wheelchair. I see people in them all the time, but I guess I never thought about how restricting it could be. I've never even so much as sprained my ankle. It's driving me nuts to be able to do anything hardly for myself. And it's demeaning to have to ask people to do small stuff like put books on the shelf when I've always been able to do everything for myself."

My mood instantly turned somber again and suddenly I didn't feel so jovial, anymore.

"That's why this therapy is so important, E. You've got to concentrate on getting your body back in shape so you can beat this. Instead of letting thoughts of what you can't do anymore sink you into being depressed, let it piss you off enough to work extra hard in physical therapy. The harder you work, the faster you'll progress."

"I tried that. I got mad and tried to go upstairs by myself

without using the chair lift last night. I got tired and fell back down when I got to about the fifth step."

A look of horror came over Desmond's face.

"You did what?"

"Calm down," I replied, nonchalantly. "I didn't hit my head, and I had left the wheelchair at the bottom of the stairs, so I was able to pull myself back into it."

"Dammit, Ericka! I meant for you to use that energy for therapy, not pull a stupid stunt like that when you're here by yourself. You could've really gotten hurt. What if you had hit your head and had to wait till morning for one of us to find you?"

I shook my head.

"I know. But I thought if I pushed myself hard enough, I could do it. And besides, a little bump on the head doesn't scare me nearly as much as not ever being able to get out of this damn chair."

Desmond leaned over and gave me a tight squeeze.

"Look, missy. I wish I could tell you that you were definitely going to get out of that wheelchair tomorrow and be able to take a stroll with Tomika and me down at the beach. I really do. But the truth is, none of us know what's going to happen. The best thing we can hope for is to improve your quality of life as much as possible so you can get your swagger back. And if nothing else, therapy will help you learn to do most stuff by yourself again. But you still have to stay positive, work hard, and take care of yourself in the meantime. So that means no more climbing stairs when I'm not here. You got it?"

I nodded.

"I'll call the therapist and make sure that it's okay for you to practice taking steps, on the ground, of course, with me between sessions. But you have to promise me that you won't do anything crazy like that again. Promise?"

I looked sideways at him but remained silent.

"Ericka?"

"Oh, all right," I huffed. "I promise."

"If I catch you doing anything like that again, I'm going to start tying your ass down in this chair before I leave here every evening."

I couldn't hold it in, anymore, and broke out in peals of laughter.

He threw a towel at me.

"Ooh, I just love a man who knows how to take charge," I cooed, playfully.

"Oh, you ain't seen how forceful I can be. Let me catch you going up those stairs again without using that chair lift and see what happens."

Chapter 32

Stop a Bullet Like 50 Cent

I eventually coerced Desmond into allowing me to come to the office and work twice a week so I could get a jump on what I would be doing and have a say in the decorations in the office. And I also wanted to meet the clients as they trickled in to get familiar with our new surroundings. Desmond was worried that I was doing too much too fast, but I assured him that I wouldn't overexert myself.

With all the fuss that he constantly made over me, I was surprised one morning when he called and requested that I be ready in an hour because he had a meeting with a very important client, and I should be there.

Finally, some action, I thought to myself. I was excited about the fact that he was finally treating me like a real employee. I was beginning to think that he just coaxed me to come out here so he could fuss over me like a mother hen.

After I had finally settled into Desmond's Suburban, I noticed that he was unusually quiet. I figured this must be some high-powered celebrity or someone who had millions of dollars wrapped up in a business renovation project.

"So, what's the urgency? Who're we meeting with today?" I asked, curious.

He smiled. That man's grin could still light a fire under my skirt.

"You'll see," he said, simply.

"Is it Missy Elliott?" I pressed. Missy Elliott was the logical choice since she was originally from Portsmouth.

He shook his head.

"No, but he's a former ball player. And I'm not saying anything else."

I turned to look out the window. It would be futile to keep probing Desmond for information. I had more than learned that he could be the most secretive man I knew. But I still couldn't help but wonder who this mystery client was. Whoever it was, I was glad that I had dressed to impress for the occasion. I wanted to make a good impression, and besides, he might be fine, single, or both.

A tall, handsome gentleman approached the vehicle as we pulled up to the curb. I would know that tall drink of water anywhere. It was Germane Jacobs. He'd had a great career in college ball at NC State before choosing to play basketball abroad instead of heading to the NBA like most players, preferring to expand his horizons beyond the US. Europe agreed with him, as he made many lucrative investments before returning to the states to become an image consultant to new pro athletes and becoming a life coach, of sorts, teaching them everything from public speaking to money management.

"What's up, Des," said Germane, warmly taking Desmond's hand.

"Ain't nothing to it, man," returned Desmond with a million-dollar smile.

"Germane Jacobs, I'd like you to meet my administrator and partner, Ericka Middleton. Ericka, this is NBA great, Germane Jacobs."

I smiled big.

"No need for introductions, Mr. Jacobs, I've followed your career since you played at NC State in the late eighties."

He smiled appreciatively.

"My friends call me Gee. And any woman that's a fan of basketball is a friend of mine."

I blushed. Wow. I was rubbing elbows with college basketball legends. Taking your life back had its advantages.

"So, Gee. What brings you to Hampton Roads? You own a business here, too?" I asked.

"Well, I'm actually from Chesapeake, originally. I serve on the board of directors who actually put the plan of obtaining the real estate into action. I don't have a business here, but I have some controlling shares in the venture."

Damn. Fine and business savvy.

He continued.

"But my fiancée is opening up a paint and body shop here. The grand opening is in a couple of months."

"Oh, cool. Congratulations. I just moved to the area. I'd like to meet her sometime."

Oh, well. There goes the notion of dating an NBA star.

He smiled.

"Good. 'Cause here she is, now."

I turned my head in the direction of his smile and screamed.

It was Toy.

She ran over and leaned down to hug me in the wheelchair.

Desmond was still grinning from ear to ear, and Germane seemed to be confused by the whole scene.

"Oh, my God, Toy? When did you get engaged, heifer? I didn't even know you had a boyfriend!"

She laughed.

"And you prissy bitches thought I played ball every day because I was trying to be a man."

She gave Germane a warm embrace and an affectionate

peck on the lips. It was so weird; I had never seen Toy behave that way toward a man before.

Still obviously puzzled, Gee asked, "You two know each other?"

"Yeah, baby," she chuckled, "this is my best friend, Ericka. You know, the one who can stop a bullet like 50 Cent?"

I playfully gave Toy the finger.

Gee looked at Desmond who was thoroughly enjoying the scene.

"Man, you were in on this, too?"

Desmond held up both hands.

"Guilty as charged, man. Toy and I ran into each other a couple of weeks ago at Starbucks. That's when she told me about her shop and the engagement. But she swore me to secrecy because she wanted to surprise Ericka."

Germane smiled.

"Wow, it's a small, small world. Well, that's alright. Man, we gonna have to double date once y'all get through with our house. But you know, business before pleasure."

Desmond and I smiled nervously at each other.

"We're not a couple," we said in unison.

"Oh, for real?" asked Germane, surprised. "My bad. Could've fooled me."

"Umm, baby, don't you and Desmond have some things to go over about the house?" asked Toy, taking the heat off Desmond and me for a moment.

"Oh, right," Gee said, thoughtfully. "Well, it was nice to meet you, Sis."

"Welcome to the family," I said, shaking his hand, again.

"I'm taking E. to lunch while you guys talk business," Toy said.

I looked at Desmond, hesitantly.

"Technically, I'm supposed to be working. Don't you need me in this meeting?"

Desmond smiled.

"Nope. This was my sole purpose for bringing you here. You two go on and have a good time. I'm sure Toy has lots to tell you."

What a surprise it was for me to find out that she was going to be living so close to me; especially when I had just moved away to a town where I thought I wouldn't know anyone but Desmond and Tomika. But I was even more surprised to find out that Toy had a boyfriend. She was not a lesbian, and she was not bisexual. She was indeed all heterosexual woman and had actually made a pretty decent catch for a woman who acted like a stud.

"Girl, how the hell you manage to pull this off?" I gushed once Toy and I were Desmond and Germaine left us alone to talk. "And how you just gonna keep a secret like this from us? Hell, from me?"

Toy shook her head, smiling, and suddenly I saw her in a completely new light. She still had that same tomboy swag. Yet, something in her face was different. She was glowing. Her hair was actually done and not in a ponytail. Her outfit was cute and looked well thought out. And bitch, do you have on foundation?

"I was gonna tell you when the time was right. But y'all heifers got so much drama, you don't give me a chance. You were in a coma remember, Rip Van Winkle? And besides, I didn't want to jinx it, in case it didn't turn out to be nothing."

"That's true," I laughed. "I guess I have been the center of attention for the last few months. Thanks for sticking by me. How did you two meet, anyway? And when?"

"Don't be mad," Toy said, covering her mouth to suppress a giggle. "Remember that summer league I played in against his team, and I went to block his shot?"

Summer League at St. Augustine's College gym is the place to be if you want to see professional basketball players on all levels in action. Many greats like Vince Carter, Jerry

Stackhouse, and Tracy McGrady have been spotted playing at summer league. We go there all the time hoping to catch a glimpse of some of the ball players that we watch on television.

Toy is one of the few women that plays side by side with them every summer. That game, she had been guarding Germane during a tournament game and it got heated. She blocked his shot as he went up to dunk during a crucial play. Toy is only about five-foot-nine, but she has a mean vertical. It was amazing! The crowd went bananas over six-foot-eight Germane's shot being blocked by a woman, even though she ended up on the floor under him when they both crash landed back to earth. He was horrified that he may have seriously injured her. And impressed that a woman had been able to stop him from making the basket. Unbeknownst to me, he asked her out to dinner after beating her team in the game that night.

"Bitch, that was two years ago!" I yelled at her. "Have you seriously been keeping a whole relationship from us for two whole years?"

"I'm sorry," Toy pleaded. "I told you. I didn't want to jinx it. I mean, look at you and Maurice. No offense, but you had enough on your plate dealing with him and his foolery. I just didn't think it would be fair to add to the mix, whether it was good or bad."

I considered what she said for a moment and then shrugged.

"Thanks, I guess."

"And one more thing, Ericka."

"What, heifer?"

"Don't tell Natalie and Toy, yet. I want it to be a surprise to them, too."

I rolled my eyes before reluctantly agreeing and giving my friend a tight congratulatory embrace.

Chapter 33

The Only Old Maid in the Group

After a few of more weeks of preparation, the time finally came for the grand opening of Toy's auto body shop. It was called simply and appropriately, 'Toy Car Repair.' Her opening coincided with a special event put on by the people who made the whole downtown development project possible. The committee put on a huge block party, closing the streets surrounding the businesses they created for a whole host of events. Among them were live music and entertainment for the kids, an open house with samples and swag from each business, and a heath fair sponsored by the primary care practice that had set up shop.

Toy got together with Maurice and put together a car show as part of her grand opening. They both offered discount goods and services to a select number of customers in exchange for their participation in the car show and celebration. Reese supplied the tire rims and Toy gave them a custom paint job at a deep discount to display their vehicles so that all the people who attended the festival could see examples of her work.

The festival was an overwhelming success. My parents came to town, as well as Natalie, Renee, Tarik and all the kids. It was awkward seeing Maurice for the first time in a few months. I wasn't sure what to expect since we didn't part on the best of terms. It was awkward for everyone else, too. Not only would my immediate family have a chance to witness our first post-break up meeting, but a group of Reese's friends and colleagues were there, too, because they had cars entered the car show.

I forced a smile upon finally seeing him and we gave each other a stiff embrace. Luckily, we were separated most of the day. After the welcome to Toy's grand opening, I joined my family and friends in the rest of the festivities of the block party, while Toy, Maurice, and crew stayed behind to prepare for the car and stereo judging.

After the festivities, we all retired back to my house to continue our celebration. Everyone loved my place and the decorations I chose to make it cozier. And after they saw our view of the water, everyone agreed that our moving to the beach was the best move that Toy and I ever made. We laughed and chatted excitedly, glad to finally all be back together. And anxious to catch up on each other's lives. Toy finally revealed the news of her engagement to Natalie and Renee and of course, we both got cursed out for keeping it a secret.

"Y'all are the most secretive heifers I've ever seen in my life. Before we move on, anybody got anything else they want to confess?" Natalie asked.

Renee had been unusually quiet ever since we started talking wedding plans. We all noticed, but we had been so busy gushing over the wedding, nobody took the time to ask. Toy looked at her.

"Renee, your mouth has been unusually quiet tonight. You got to be hiding something."

Renee rolled her eyes at Toy.

"What you mean? Y'all been so busy talking a mile a

minute that I ain't had a chance to say nothing. Then you gon' accuse me of being quiet. All of y'all make me sick."

"Well, damn, excuse me for being excited about snagging a ball player," said Toy, playfully displaying sarcasm.

Then she slapped Natalie and I high fives.

"Okay?" shouted Nat and me in unison.

Natalie cleared her throat in an exaggerated motion and held up her hand. It was then that we noticed she was wearing an engagement ring.

I narrowed my eyes at the diamond sparkling on her hand.

"I know that ain't what I think it is," I said.

Toy playfully punched her in the arm.

"Bitch, no you didn't just accuse us of keeping secrets and you been walking around here all day sporting a rock and ain't said a word."

Natalie laughed.

"Well, my fiancée ain't rolling big enough to put a disco ball on my hand like yours. I guess you just didn't notice."

We all took turns hugging Natalie.

"Girl, about time Tarik stopped being so damn scary. Y'all been together almost ten years," Toy said.

"It wasn't just Tarik," Natalie told her. "Girl, I wasn't ready to get married. Savion will be fourteen in a couple of months. I'm set in my ways. Why you think we never moved in together? And besides, four more years and Savion is grown. I'm about to get my life back in a major way. Hell, I was thinking about moving to Jamaica after he goes to college. I'm like Ericka. There's too much life out here that I haven't experienced yet."

She took my hand.

"Girl, you are my hero. The way you just up and moved like that away from everybody, including your man? Got me to thinking about whether or not I was missing something by tying myself permanently to Tarik."

"But you obviously decided to say 'yes.' What made you change your mind?" Renee wanted to know.

"Well, both Savion and Tarik's daughter are about the same age. And neither of us really wants anymore kids. So, we agreed that it would be more fun to have new experiences together as a unit. And besides, we're not rushing to have a wedding. I'm not trying to compete with Toy's Starr Jones extravaganza. I'm okay with getting our reformed lesbian here over the broom before we even start talking about planning my wedding."

Toy looked sideways at Nat.

"Natalie, don't get your head busted in here, okay?"

We all laughed. Toy would be married a long time before she would be able to live down her extreme tomboyish mannerisms with us.

"Well, damn," I said, shaking my head, "I'ma be the only old maid in the group. Y'all jigs ain't gonna use me as a cover up when you get bored with your husbands and start cheating with other men, now!"

"Girl, please. if I ain't had an urge to cheat on Tarik in all this time, you know I ain't going nowhere," Natalie said, dryly.

"Yeah," followed Toy, "and you know I ain't trying to be with no other men. I'm gay, remember?"

We all roared with laughter.

"Well, that makes me feel a lot better," I said, sarcastically. "Even 'Butch' here managed to find her a husband. I'm the only one here with no man," I whined, plaintively.

Renee spoke up.

"Well, not necessarily, Ericka," she said, slowly.

We all stopped joking and looked at her.

"What you mean, Renee," Toy asked her, suspiciously.

Renee looked down at the table.

"Terrell's gone."

I stared at her.

"What do you mean, 'gone?'"

She looked at me; tears threatened to fall from her eyes. But she wouldn't let them.

"He walked out on me about a week ago. Said I was smothering him. He needed space."

We all surrounded her in a group hug. Terrell and those kids were her world. I couldn't imagine what she was going through.

"It's gonna be okay, baby. Maybe once he's gone for a little while, he'll realize that he misses you and come home," Toy said soothingly. It was odd hearing Toy speak to Renee like that because they were almost always sniping at one another.

"Yeah, Renee," added Natalie, "just keep praying and make sure you keep the lines of communication open. There had to have been a breakdown somewhere. He didn't just up and leave on the spur of the moment."

"I'll tell you where the breakdown was," Toy spoke up. "Renee, I'm sorry, baby, but there's too much communication going on your part and not enough on his. I told you a long time ago, you were going to run that man away with all your bossy nagging."

"I know. I think I blew it this time, y'all," she said, quietly.

"Not necessarily. You just need to tell him that you realize where you went wrong and ask him to come home so you can work on it. That's your husband, girl. And if you want him, you gonna have to fight for him," I added.

Toy looked at me.

"Not bad coming from the only woman in the house with no man."

I smirked and gave her the finger.

Then Toy took Renee by the shoulders and looked her in the eye.

"Now, you listen to me," she said sternly. "When you get Terrell back home this time, remember this. Whenever you get the urge to argue with him, instead of using your mouth to talk him to death, use it wisely and give the man some head. It's the best way to keep peace in your house."

We all howled in laughter. Even Renee couldn't control the urge to laugh.

After Toy lightened the mood again, Natalie suggested that we take a ride back downtown the next day to look in the bridal boutique around the corner from our office. Toy pretended to be exasperated over the fact that we had almost taken over her wedding as we laughed and giggled and made plans to get her hitched. But I know that she was truly glad to have her best friends in the world there to help her. Besides, had we let Toy do all the planning, she would have just had us meet her in Dillon, South Carolina, where everybody I knew that couldn't afford to or didn't have time to plan a wedding because they were pregnant, got married. Neither was the case for her, but Toy didn't have a clue about planning a wedding, and actually seemed appalled at the fact that she had to wear a dress. She needed us now, more than ever. Good thing they hadn't settled on a date, yet. We bombarded her with all of our ideas while all the fellas went to Desmond's house and had drinks and played dominoes. Later, they came back over to my house to eat and to play a hot game of Taboo.

After a while, somebody remembered that we were at the beach, so everyone kind of abandoned the game to go outside and explore the area. Maurice cornered me on the back deck after mostly everyone else had gone to the beach.

"You need any help with anything?" he asked.

"Nah, I think I'm straight. But thanks," I replied.

"You got a nice little setup, here," he remarked.

"Thanks. We like it here a lot."

"Looks like the beach is agreeing with you. You're looking good," he said, nervously.

"Thanks," I said, looking at my feet. "So are you."

"So . . . you a'ight?"

"Yeah. I'm good, actually. What about you?"

"I'm straight. I see you just about put that wheelchair down for good. That therapy is really helping you," he said.

"Yeah, I'm hoping to get rid of this cane by Christmas."

"It'd be good if you could walk down the aisle at Toy's wedding without it."

"Yeah," I said, looking out at the waves crashing against the sand.

We stood there in uncomfortable silence on the deck watching the rest of the crew frolicking in the water.

I noticed that Reese had gradually inched close enough to me to touch my hand, as I propped against the railing of the deck. I stood there pretending not to be uncomfortable.

Reese took my hand and turned my body to face him.

"I miss you," he said.

"Don't do this," I said.

"I'm not trying to mess your head up, E. Middle. But you need to know that I still love you no matter what. You said that you didn't want me around, so I stayed away. But when Toy called me and asked me to do that car show with her, I couldn't say no. I had to see you. And I need to let you know that my offer still stands. If you need me for anything, I want you to call me, okay? I don't care what it is."

He took my chin in his hand.

"You heard me?"

I nodded my head, actually pulling off that brave front that I had pretended to have. But I was still a little weak when it came to Reese. And I still kind of missed him, too. Before I could respond, Tomika came bounding up the back stairs.

"Unca Reese, can you help me look for seashells?"

The spell was broken. That was close. He looked at Tomika.

"Yeah, baby girl. You ready to go, now?"

She nodded, enthusiastically, and then turned to me.

"Mommy, you coming?"

I smiled at her.

"You go on with Uncle Reese, baby. I'll be there in a few minutes."

I watched them as they crossed the street together, hand in hand, feeling sad about the decision I made to let go of Maurice, but happy about everything that letting him go allowed me to grab hold to.

Chapter 34

Home Again

After the day's festivities, we had to have an old-fashioned slumber party. All the guys stayed over at Desmond's townhouse and all the women stayed with me. We laughed and giggled and actually stayed up later than the kids, reminiscing about high school and boyfriends from back in the day, drinking wine, smoking a new cannabis strain, courtesy of Germaine, and eating junk food. The next day, the guys cooked breakfast and then us girls heading out to the bridal boutique while the fellows took the kids fishing.

We had a marvelous afternoon and by the time everyone left, I had mixed feelings about seeing them go. I truly missed having my girls at my disposal and although I had Toy, I missed being able to go to Renee's and eat when I didn't feel like cooking or Natalie's spontaneous trips to go wine tasting or to ride go-carts or play Putt-Putt golf. But at the same time, I was ready to let them go because I was so anxious to get back to my new life that I had found in Hampton Roads.

I was doing things for the first time in my life that I never even dreamed that I would be interested in back home. I had wrapped so much of my energy in developing a relationship with Maurice; he had become my only interest. I didn't have a clue about what I really liked to do, anymore, until I moved away. The only thing I really enjoyed was riding motorcycles, and I wasn't sure if I'd ever be able to do that again. In the short time I had been at my new home, I had actually developed a social calendar. For the first time, I belonged to a book club, which was really exciting because I've always loved to read. And I was hosting this month's meeting at my house. I had also been to a couple of spoken word events at the WHRO public radio station in Norfolk and performed. They even played my performance on a radio broadcast. I took Tomika to the Children's Museum in Portsmouth and to Nauticus in downtown Norfolk.

However, there was one event in my life that quickly approaching that I hadn't been looking forward to. And that was the trial of Kane, the guy who shot me. The DA had been hounding me for months about testifying, which I didn't see the point, since I never actually saw him pull the gun. But because I had witnessed the whole dice game thing, I think they wanted to find some testimony that would eventually lead them to a case against Maurice. And I had a problem with the court using the victim to damn someone else besides the one who committed the crime against them.

Besides that, I knew him from around the way when we were kids. He grew up in my neighborhood and was good friends with my high school sweetheart until they suddenly began to hate each other. There was never any love lost for him on my part. He was always bad news, and I couldn't stand his ass. I would've been glad to snitch, but not at the expense of someone I cared about.

Thankfully, my prayers were answered. I'd heard that the guy Kane was shooting at mysteriously came forward and turned himself in and told the whole story. Even though he had warrants out for his arrest for a string of armed robbery and kidnapping charges. And it was also my understanding that there were no deals to be had on either of their parts, so he was going down either way.

Not only was I getting involved in a lot of new, fun things, my job with Desmond's restoration company, Home Again was working out great, as well. I was more than just an administrative assistant; I was more like the director of operations and what I said went. Desmond relied on me for everything in the office and whenever anyone had a problem or question, he always told them that they had to run it by the 'boss lady.' And I loved being the boss lady. He compensated me well, and he allowed me to basically come and go as I saw fit leaving me time to be more involved at Tomika's school. Desmond turned out to be the best boss and friend I ever had. The attraction between us remained but had been compartmentalized to make room for both of us to heal. But we were closer than ever, spending evenings together eating dinner, watching movies, or playing with Tomika. It was a non-traditional family dynamic. But it worked for us.

My life was definitely on an upswing, but it was not without its share of setbacks. Not only was I not interested in attending that trial, but my rehabilitation was also not going as quickly as I had hoped. Although the doctors describe my case as remarkable, I was discouraged about not being able to do more. Don't get me wrong. I was grateful for being out of that wheelchair, finally. But I still couldn't help but feel resentful about having to walk with a cane. The fact that someone handicapped me trying to harm someone else is something that I struggle with. I hated not being able to walk at a normal pace, anymore and having to use one of those mobile carts in Wal-Mart or the grocery store. I hated not being able to ride my motorcycle. I hated not being able to jog on the beach. And most of all, I hated not being able to keep up with my nine-year old like I used to. The one upside to having Tomika at a young age was having enough energy to run and play along with her. But after I got out of the hospital, I noticed her slowing down so not to get too far ahead of me. She's such a thoughtful child. She makes such pains now to not leave her mom behind. And each time, I feel a pang of guilt that she's made herself responsible for me, as if I'm her kid.

I thought that if I got active and kept my mind occupied that I wouldn't have these types of feelings. But my attempts to be active constantly reminded me of my new limitations. Desmond suggested that I take the hospital's advice and go through a counseling program for survivors of violent crimes. I politely took the information, but never thought about calling the number because, in my opinion, counseling ain't for black folks. But Desmond reminded me that I moved for a new start and that not only did new beginnings come from adopting new hobbies, but also adopting new ways of thinking. So, I promised him that I would consider therapy.

Overall, I was very pleased with the decision I made to relocate. I couldn't deny my residual feelings for Maurice but since I finally went out and got a life, for once my emotions were forced to take a back seat. Even with the demons I dealt with surrounding my injuries, there were too many other positives in my life that I no longer had the time to be miserable and dwell on my failed relationship. I missed Maurice, yet I no longer felt the need to have him validate me with his affection. And I was proud of the way I handled my solo encounter with him, even if Tomika did come and help me out a little bit. But I couldn't shake the fact that he looked so handsome, and he smelled so good when he hugged me at the car show.

I chuckled in spite of myself as I lay in bed that night while reflecting on the best weekend I'd had in a long time. I fell into a deep, blissful sleep.

I must have overslept because the sun was mercilessly blinding me in spite of my not having got up to pull the curtains. I drug myself out of bed to get breakfast started. Tomika had probably strewn cereal from the kitchen to the den in front of the television, where she knew she wasn't supposed to have food. Before I could round the corner good, I noticed that my refrigerator was left open again. I had been through this before, but this time I was ready. 'What's he looking for in there, this time?' I thought to myself. We had been here so many times before, to act surprised would be insulting.

"Alright, refrigerator raider, I don't have any whipped cream or chocolate syrup for you this time. So, you can come out, now." I said, dryly.

As I approached the fridge, I froze in my tracks and stood with my mouth wide open.

"What? Who were you expecting, Desmond?" Maurice asked slyly, sporting a towel and a wide grin.

I jerked up in my bed in a confused state of panic. Now that was definitely new. In the six years that I had been with Maurice I had never had a dream about him; especially an erotic dream. Why the hell did I dream that after all this time? Not only was I confused, but I was also completely turned on. I thought once again about taking a cold shower. Instead, I laughed heartily out loud and rolled over to go back to sleep, as I dismissed the notion. It was then that I realized that although I may have taken a temporary leave of absence from the job of dating, it was perfectly okay for my eyes and my imagination to remain actively employed.

(THE END??)

Keep reading for a
sneak peek at Book 2

Thank you for reading *When Ericka Woke Up!* An author's journey wouldn't be possible without the support of readers like you. If you enjoyed the book, please consider leaving a review—your feedback helps others discover the story.

Don't forget to follow me on social media for updates on new releases, upcoming appearances, and special events. I'd love to stay connected!

IG: @evoutlaw.writer
Facebook: https://facebook.com/evoutlaw/
YouTube: https://youtube.com/@ev_outlaw.writer
Website: https://evelynoutlaw.com

Book Club Questions

When Ericka Woke Up *Questions for Discussion*

1. Was there any one character in the story that you were drawn to more than the other characters in the book? Why?

2. Do you think that Ericka's previous relationships with her murdered childhood sweetheart and Tomika's father played a role in the way she approached her relationship with Maurice? Explain.

3. After reading Ericka's take on Maurice, did your opinion of him change after reading his side of the story? Why or why not?

4. Was Desmond's explanation of why he kept the details of his marriage from Ericka plausible? Explain. And was his offer to help her start over at the beach believable? Why or why not?

5. How would you have solved the issue with Maurice if you were Ericka?

6. *(For the guys)* Can you relate to Maurice's reasoning surrounding his actions or lack thereof in his relationship with Ericka? Explain. Do you feel as though he should get a pass for how he chose to move throughout the relationship?

7. Was there anything in the story you felt the writer failed to explain to your satisfaction? Explain.

8. What was your favorite part of the book? Share a couple of your favorite passages from the story.

9. What was the theme of this novel, in your opinion?

10. Would this novel make a good movie? If so, who could you see playing the main characters of the story?

Fixing a Broken Toy

Ericka and Toy have each emerged from a painful past, taking brave steps toward healing through therapy. When Toy encourages Ericka to join her in counseling with the same therapist, it seems like a positive move—until their histories begin to collide in unexpected and dangerous ways.

As buried secrets resurface, threatening to unravel the progress they've made, the therapist must help them confront the truth: they're bound by a shared trauma, one that could destroy the fragile lives they've fought so hard to rebuild.

Chapter 1

A Hot Morning Mess

The urgent blare of my alarm aroused me from a dead sleep. "UGH," I groaned plaintively, reaching for my phone on the nightstand to shut off the infernal siren. Relieved by the silence, I fell back onto my pillow and let out a self-pitying sigh. I turned my head towards the neighboring side of the bed to see my fiancée, Germaine sporting a huge grin, watching my every move. I returned him a faint smile of my own, a little self-conscious at being ogled despite looking a hot morning mess.

"What?" I asked him before turning away from his gaze, my face hot from the embarrassment of having so much attention lavished on me when I wasn't at my best. Not that my best was all that great. And besides that, having him leer at me that way made me slightly uncomfortable.

Germaine turned my face towards him again. "I can't look at you?" He continued to examine me, lovingly and expectantly, with those beautiful hazel eyes.

Damn, he's fine. How in the world did you manage to pull this off? I asked myself.

"Yeah," I said to him, shyly forcing myself to return his gaze. "But why now? I'm just waking up, I got a bonnet on my head, and my breath probably stinks, too." I raised my hand to my mouth.

He laughed. "Girl, even Beyoncé ain't fine first thing in the morning."

I cocked my head to the side.

"How you know?"

He pursed his lips, giving me the side eye.

"Man, listen. The only person who has Michael Jordan money besides Michael Jordan is Jay-Z. The NBA wasn't even paying me enough to date an extra in one of her videos. So, you can get that image out of your mind. But I'm saying. Beyoncé ain't got nothing on you on her best day. Who cares what you look like first thing in the morning? You always look good to me." He reached up and pulled my bonnet off my head and began running his fingers through my hair. "And besides, my breath stinks, too. See?"

And in one swift motion, he rolled over and grabbed me toward him and began showering me with kisses. I screamed in laughter and protest.

"Stop! Stop!" I yelled at him, almost out of breath. "Quit it, Germaine! You're gonna make me late."

He let off the tickling, but he remained in place.

"How do you be late as the owner?" he asked.

"I still have work to do."

He lightly stroked my shoulder with the tip of his index finger.

"Yeah, but you got good people, babe. That place practically runs itself. What is it that demands your attention so urgently there that you got to be up at six a.m. when you got this fine hunk of gingerbread man laying here beside you?"

He stretched out the length of his body under the sheets, making a sweeping motion with his hand, as if he was presenting a prize to the audience on the Price is Right.

He was right. Nothing was so important that I had to get up at O-dark-thirty and rush to work like I had to punch a clock. And he did look amazing. He was virtually an Adonis with freckles with a perfectly chiseled body like the statue of David. His dirty blonde hair cut low with bushy eyebrows and luxurious eyelashes to match. His clean-shaven face sported ginger speckles on his face and nose. He even had a few dots on his lips. He was a gorgeous, polka dotted sight to behold and I was in love with every square inch of him.

I leaned into his firm body and wrapped my arms around his neck, planting a wet juicy kiss on his pouty lips, no longer caring about my morning breath or his. His eyes closed and he enveloped me as if he were attempting to step inside my very soul. And I relaxed under him, releasing most of my inhibitions and fears. He was better to me than any man could ever be and yet, I was still unable to let my guard down completely with him. After all this time, I had to steel myself so he wouldn't notice me repelling from a simple touch. I knew I had to get myself together before I ran him away.

My phone rang, interrupting my thoughts. Germaine continued to stroke and caress my body, landing light butter-fly kisses on my neck and making his way down my mid-section, refusing to acknowledge the nagging ringing of my cell phone. I tried to follow his lead. Whatever it is will just have to wait. This is more important. Besides, this was actually kind of nice. The ringing finally stopped, and I smiled to myself, relieved that this time I was able to ease back into the groove with Germaine.

I was just started to feel his breath just below my navel when the ringing started again, snatching me completely out of my zone. My eyes shot open, annoyed. Germaine, however, remained unfazed, nosing around my lady parts like a curious puppy exploring new surroundings. I turned my head towards my nuisance, debating on whether to answer it just to stop that interminable ringing. Finally, I relented. Still flat on my back, I reached over and snatched the phone from the nightstand and looked at it. I rolled my eyes and exhaled sharply.

"Mm-mm," Germaine protested. I could feel him shaking his head back and forth with his face buried between my legs. His low deep voice reverberated through my entire body.

"I've got to," I whined. "If I don't, she'll just keep calling."

He stopped momentarily to come up for air. "Turn it off."

"Babe, she's my mother."

"So? She should have thought about that before."

I sucked my teeth and aggressively swiped the screen to accept the call. I barely got 'hello' from my lips before she shouted, "What the hell takes you so long to get to the damn phone? I been calling and calling you!" She was talking so loud, I know Germaine could hear her as if she was on speaker phone. Suddenly, I was transformed from a sexy, independent businessperson into a fearful, self-conscious and invalidated teenager.

"I . . . I was in the shower," I lied.

I glanced down into Germaine's now disappointed face. He shook his head and rose from the bed, watching me be berated by my mother via telephone.

"I got a mammogram on Thursday. And I need to go to the grocery store too."

I sighed inwardly. "What time is your appointment?"

"Two o'clock! I told you that last week when you were down here." Damn, Germaine and I were supposed to go to the drag strip that evening. I was never going to make it back in time.

"But Mother, I told you that you needed to make your appointments in the late mornings, no later than eleven, so I don't get caught in all that traffic trying to make it back home in the evenings."

"Well, you should've thought about that before you took your ass all the way down to the coast to live! You just wanted to go down there to try to live like white folks. Trying to be somebody. You still ain't shit."

I cut her off before she could finish.

"Okay, Mother. I'll see you on Thursday."

"And you better have your ass here on time!"

I looked over at Germaine, who had been watching me flounder. He looked as though he pitied me. I lowered my eyes, unable to continue to face him. By the time I looked up again, he had left the room without another word, closing the bathroom door behind him.

Want more? Subscribe to our newsletter for exclusive story-related content delivered straight to your inbox.

https://evelynoutlaw.com

About the Author

Ev Outlaw embarked on her writing journey in 2008 with the release of her debut novel under her maiden name, Evelyn K. Lemar. After taking a break to focus on her career and new marriage, she returned to the literary world, rebranding her original book as the first in a series using her married name.

As an enthusiastic empty-nester, Ev enjoys life with her deejay husband, Trey. When they're not having frequent jam sessions at their home in near Raleigh, North Carolina, you can usually find them on the road in their RV, where Ev indulges in reading, coloring, or building Lego models.

To contact Ev about book discussions or be notified of new releases, visit her online at EvelynOulaw.com.